Whoever you are, I want you

The expression in his hooded eyes mesmerized her—stern, speculative, but inviting an answer that need never be spoken aloud. She went to stand beside him, looking down into his upturned face.

Stephen gave France the glass and, without taking his eyes from hers, gripped the front of her right thigh, squeezed gently, then stroked the length from knee to groin.

"What shall we drink to?" she asked, every cell quivering, her skin retaining the sensation of his touch.

He turned to the fire. "How about...now?" He brought his gaze back to hers. "Let's drink to this moment."

Beneath his words France felt a brittle intelligence that made her hesitate. "Perfect." She smiled brightly and touched her glass to his. "To now."

ABOUT THE AUTHOR

Alicia Brandon is a pseudonym for two writers,
Stella Cameron and Linda Rice. Before turning
to writing romances full-time three years ago,
Stella edited medical texts. Linda worked in
public relations before the birth of her child,
then continued to write articles. Though Stella
has written several Superromances on her own,
this is the first one they have penned together.
Both women live with their respective husbands
and children in the state of Washington.

Love Beyond Question
ALICIA BRANDON

Harlequin Books

TORONTO • NEW YORK • LONDON
AMSTERDAM • PARIS • SYDNEY • HAMBURG
STOCKHOLM • ATHENS • TOKYO • MILAN

Published October 1985

First printing August 1985

ISBN 0-373-16121-2

Printed in Canada

Chapter One

"Don't you even wonder what he did?"

"Rachel!"

"Well—look at him. He's gorgeous. I can't see him ripping off little old ladies, or shoplifting, or..."

A warning glare from France Marriotte's hazel eyes stopped her assistant's next suggestion. "Did you start those wreaths? Tomorrow's Thanksgiving and I don't have to tell you what that means. On Friday we could get the first rush of Christmas eager beavers."

"Not if today's anything to go by," Rachel replied. "The place has been dead. I'll get to them after lunch." Her elbows rested on the counter by the cash register as she stared dreamily through the back window of George's Landscape Nursery. "You've got to admit he's fantastic, though. Probably the best-looking man in Tulsa, and he has to be a con. What a waste."

France pointed to a pile of evergreen boughs trimmed from the first delivery of Christmas trees. "The wreaths."

"Yes, *ma'am*." Rachel Kemp tossed carefully styled blond hair and grinned as she ducked around France. "He's probably sex-starved, too, shut away....All right, all right." She knelt, grabbed a branch and some wire and started winding them together.

A wheezing noise signaled that the ancient coffee-pot had finished perking. France filled a cracked blue mug and stood by the window. She braced an elbow on the other forearm as she sipped the hot liquid. Steam rose through cold air, misting the glass and blurring her vision of the man outside.

What *had* Stephen Foley done? France was twenty-nine, divorced four years, and cautious with her feelings and imagination. She didn't have teenaged Rachel's naive enthusiasm for intrigue, even when it took the form of six feet plus of muscular, devastatingly handsome male. But in the three days Foley had been employed at the nursery on work-release from prison, she hadn't stopped noticing him—or wondering about him.

The information sheet she'd been given stated only his name, the fact that he was thirty-four, and the time he would be dropped off in the morning and picked up in the evening—the same type of data she'd received on two previous workers from a minimum security facility on the outskirts of Tulsa. A counselor, intending to encourage, had reassured her at an orientation meeting that anyone she hired would pose no threat. The employment program was intended to accelerate the rehabilitation process for men nearing the end of their sentences. She hadn't wanted to know more then, but now...

"It's starting to snow. Looks like we could get a lot more." France took a deep breath and squeaked a knuckle in circles on the window to make a porthole. "Toby likes him," she said absently. "That has to mean something."

Toby—Fifty-seven Varieties, as Rachel called him— was France's rangy black mutt. The dog had appeared at the nursery a year before, half starved but feisty, and had allowed France to adopt him. She smiled inwardly at the memory and watched the dog trotting at Foley's heels between rows of trees and shrubs.

"I thought you weren't interested," Rachel muttered.

France looked over her shoulder at the girl, who sat back on her heels among the greenery and cocked an eyebrow at her employer.

"I'm not. And it would be easier on your delectable knees if you worked at the table. I'm going to see if the poor man wants some coffee." Without waiting for a reply, France walked outside, still carrying her own mug.

Snowflakes peppered her eyelashes and short auburn curls. She blinked and moved slowly past a heap of cut evergreen trees. The scent of pitch, carried on snapping air, made her nostrils flare appreciatively. Oklahoma had always been her home and she loved its contrasts: spring's wild thunderstorms; the long, breathless summers and fickle winters; the subtly changing landscapes.

Cold struck upward from the hard earth and she stamped her feet. Tomorrow she must remember to wear heavier socks.

Stephen Foley lifted two trees and started for the growing stack by the back fence. Toby loped ahead, his nose lifted like an aristocratic hunting dog.

"Break time." France didn't feel as bright as she hoped she sounded. "How about some hot coffee?"

Stephen hesitated, shoulder muscles flexing slightly beneath a red plaid jacket. "Thanks, but I'd better get this done."

France wanted him to look at her. "Mr. Foley. It can wait. A man deserves a rest now and then." An impulse almost made her touch him. "Doesn't he?" she added quietly.

In a single long stride he reached the fence, leaned the trees into the pile and faced her. "I guess he does. Coffee sounds great."

Unconsciously, she handed him her own mug. In the same instant they both noticed the traces of lipstick that clung to the rim, and France flushed. "I'm sorry. I wasn't thinking. I'll get you another cup."

She held out her hand but he ignored it, taking a slow sip of coffee instead. Gentle, indigo eyes met hers, darkened and held. "I'd rather have this one. Thanks."

The effect he had on her was unnerving. He was a very tall man, slender, taut, but not as thin as his facial features might have suggested. Dark brown hair, lightly sprinkled with gray, was tousled in front where he repeatedly brushed at it. His face was angular, his mouth wide and mobile, and the quality of those blue, blue eyes disturbed France in a way she knew should send her running. Instead, she sat on a wrought-iron bench and studied the toes of her rubber boots.

"How long have you owned this place?" His low voice was soft with a hint of Oklahoma drawl less pronounced than her own—husky, sexy.... France felt a tug in the pit of her stomach.

She waited until he slumped down beside her and stretched out his long legs. "I don't. My father does." France indicated the carved wooden sign over the shop door. "George." I'm only his manager.

"Is he ill?"

"No, just bored with being a shopkeeper. He concentrates on landscape design."

"Have I seen him?"

"I don't think so. He almost never comes here. Thinks I'll assume he's checking up on me. Most of his work's done on paper. He has a crew that picks up what he needs from the nursery. Remember the two men who came for bark this morning?"

Foley nodded. He leaned his forearms on his thighs and rolled the mug between both palms. He appeared to have forgotten it was hers. "Your father's an artist." It was a flat statement and his tone was distant.

She picked at a twig caught in the wristband of her cerise parka. "Mmm. Most people don't realize that."

"But you don't mind being a shopkeeper?"

France bristled slightly. "You make that sound like an indictment." Hot blood rushed to her cheeks. *Indictment...of all the stupid comments.* But he didn't seem to notice. "I wasn't being critical. I've never spent much time around plants before, but I can see how they might grow on you."

Her laugh brought his head around. "What's so funny?"

"Plants growing on you." She covered her mouth with one hand and saw answering amusement flicker over his features. "My brother does that. Makes awful, supposedly accidental puns and looks ingenuous afterward."

"Sounds like my kind of guy," he remarked. "Older brother?"

"Twin."

The lucid eyes touched her lips before he glanced at the sky. "Snow's getting heavier." He stood up and set the cup on the bench. "Thanks for the coffee."

France watched him walk away. Was it the approach of Christmas that was making her lonely and vulnerable? This was no different from any of her years since Larry had left. What was it about this particular man that aroused those familiar sweet, sad feelings?

Maybe Paul and her father were right. It was time for her to stop being a hermit. Her first traumatic ventures into the singles world after the divorce had sent her into social hiding, but surely not every unmarried man in the world would expect her to jump into his bed an hour after they met. France hunched her shoulders. The loneliness would pass again. A strong woman shouldn't need a man in tow to feel whole. Hard work was the answer.

Tidy, wooden-sided beds of plants, mostly dormant now, stretched across the nursery yard. She liked her work. Being close to the earth and growing things filled her with a sense of peace...at least it had until Stephen Foley stepped from a dark green prison van one morning and strolled into the shop. *Darn it*. There he was again, popping into her mind whenever she wasn't wary.

France picked up the empty mug and balanced it on her knee. Tiny flakes of snow settled quickly on its cooled rim, and she flicked at them with one hand. The fresh, white ground covering was rapidly building, and Foley's boots made a crunching sound with each step. He hefted another tree onto his shoulder and moved toward the fence, his breath forming clouds of vapor. France watched him but he didn't appear to notice.

"You can come into the office later...if you need to warm up." France shivered and pulled to her feet. Her voice had echoed back at her a little too loudly, as if magnified by the surrounding silence. He glanced at her when he turned and she raised the mug. "There's more coffee, too, if you want it. It's lousy, but at least it's hot." She'd never invited a release-worker inside before, but there had never been one at the nursery when it was this cold.

"Okay." He nodded. "Appreciate it."

She started for the office, knowing without a doubt that he followed her with his eyes. Rather than ruffling her, the idea excited her, added a definite spring to her step. But she controlled an urge to check behind her until she reached the office. And by then he was already sorting through another pile of trees.

The weathered door squeaked when she nudged it open. It took several seconds for her eyes to adjust to the dim light.

"How's this, France?"

She lifted her head and picked out her assistant in the shadows near the ceiling. "Rachel! That's dangerous. You need a ladder."

Balanced on top of an old wooden file cabinet, the young woman leaned gingerly forward, trying to hitch a completed wreath onto a nail in the wall.

"Don't worry, I won't fall. In my last life I was a cat burglar. Ho, ho. Speaking of which, what did you find out about *him*? How long's he in for? "Does he have a girl friend?" Rachel scrambled down. "Is he as sexy close up as—"

"For heaven's sake, how should I know?" France interrupted. "You've been just as close to him as I have." She felt exasperated and tried to ignore the arch look the younger woman gave her. Rachel was no fool. She knew France had stayed out far longer than was necessary simply to offer the man coffee.

"I only thought—"

"Sometimes thinking can get you in trouble. It's coming up the Christmas season, remember? Holiday spirit? How many people are likely to take time to talk with Mr. Foley—at the prison or anywhere else? Not many, I'll bet." France didn't know why she felt she had to defend her actions to Rachel. Perhaps because her *real* motives were hazy. "The ladder's in the storage shed. Please get it. I don't want you attempting to hang another wreath until you do. And take your coat. It really feels like the North Pole out there.''

''Yes, Mom.'' Rachel grinned. She shrugged into her jacket and headed out the door, slamming it behind her.

France rubbed numb hands together. Suddenly it felt good to be alone. She laid her own wet parka across the back of a chair and removed her boots. The warmth of the small room made the evergreen scent even stronger. She picked up a fir branch and sniffed it before starting to tie a swag.

Concentrate. She wanted, desperately, to block out the intrusive thoughts, but each time a patch of red moved beyond the window, France's gaze caught it. The man never seemed to tire. Occasionally he glanced toward the office, and although she knew he couldn't see through the glass, his calm expression still unsettled her. *What had he done?* The nagging question plagued her while she continued to twist the greens together, trimming them with pinecones and ribbons.

Finally Rachel returned with the ladder, and the two women worked until lunch.

''We can't make any more wreaths until we get a fresh supply of wire.'' France tossed the empty spool into the wastebasket. ''Why don't you pick up some more at the wholesaler's during lunch? It won't hurt if you're a little late getting back. And while you're at it, look for one of those long poles with a hook on the end. We shouldn't need a ladder to get these things up and down.''

''Sure.'' Rachel stretched her neck. ''But are you sure you don't mind being here...alone?''

''I'm not alone.''

''That's what I mean.''

France tapped a sock-clad toe. "I know what you mean, Rachel. You worry too much. Everything will be fine."

After Rachel left, France pulled her own brown bag from the desk drawer. Foley always brought a simple black metal lunch box from the prison, and now she could see him sitting on an upturned wooden planter to eat.

She moved closer to the steamy window, wondering if she should ask him inside. He had to be half frozen in that thin fabric jacket. Toby shifted impatiently at his feet, snapping up proffered scraps of food. Foley tipped his head and laughed, then ruffled the dog's floppy ears. The rangy animal danced around him, trusting, begging. Even at a distance, France could see the delight, the tenderness in Foley's eyes.

Toby liked him. A warmth spread outward from somewhere deep within France, and she leaned her temple briefly against the wooden window frame. She believed from the moment of Stephen Foley's arrival, when he'd surprised her by shaking hands, that he was a thoughtful, gentle man. But the unfounded conviction puzzled her. He was a prisoner, a man with another life— a past she knew nothing about. He should fit the mold she'd set for him before they met. But he didn't.

Foley dropped a final bit of food onto the snow for Toby and turned to the window. Had he felt her watching him? France smiled and raised her hand in a wave. Without thinking, she went to the door.

"The invitation still stands. Come inside and get warm."

"Are you sure?"

"I wouldn't ask if I wasn't. All I need is a case of pneumonia on my hands." She probably shouldn't be alone with him in the shop. But why not? He didn't frighten her.

"Thanks, then. Sounds good." He came toward her and knocked his boots against the step to loosen the cakes of snow. The cold had reddened his cheeks and nose.

"You should have come in sooner." France closed the door behind him. The wooden floor creaked beneath the man's weight, and France noticed the way his head nearly touched a low ceiling beam.

A wild scuffling at the door grabbed their attention. Toby shot through his flap at the bottom, sneezing and waggling his limber body from side to side.

Foley went down on his knees. "Sorry fella. Did we forget you out there?" The dog shook free a shower of melted snowflakes and Stephen laughed, covering his eyes with a forearm.

"I think you've made a friend, Mr. Foley. And Toby doesn't like many people."

He stood up once more, too close. "He's a smart critter."

France took a step backward, colliding with the desk. "Coffeepot's on the counter. Help yourself." She slid into her chair and moved a stack of papers from one side of the desk to the other, then back again.

"This feels good. Sometimes you don't know how cold you are until you start to get warm." Instead of filling a mug, he cradled his hands a scant inch from the percolator.

And sometimes you feel too warm for comfort. France's cheeks glowed, and she kept her head down until the silence became too much for her. The only noise came from Toby trying to get comfortable in his basket.

"You take as long as you need. I think I'll just put a few more nails in the wall for displays." Normally deft, her fingers refused to cooperate. The hammer slipped from her grasp, not falling all the way to the floor, but ending up with the head resting between finger and thumb.

Foley cleared his throat. "Can I do that for you?"

"No. No, thank you. I'm used to this sort of thing."

Two nails went in smoothly. France smiled over her shoulder and completely missed the next one. She was using a close examination of her unscathed hand to hide yet another blush when she felt the hammer being taken away.

"Did you hurt yourself?"

France shook her head. "Missed—everything."

"Let me work at it," he said, not looking at her. "I'll thaw out more easily with something to do."

France stood beside him for a moment, watching him scan the wall to see the distance he needed to leave between nails. Then he pounded one in methodically.

"Thank you," she said. "I should be getting on with the paperwork anyway. Any excuse and I leave it."

He *was* kind—and so much more. Not an ordinary man in any sense of the word. But *who* was he? She didn't notice he'd paused until she realized they were staring into each other's eyes. Breathtaking eyes that did something odd to her heart. Her bright smile felt unnatural. This was senseless.

France swung her chair around to reach the file cabinet, and the pounding resumed.

"Well, ma'am, I think that's about as many as this wall will take. Let me know if you need anything else like this done. I'd better get back outside."

The long, fine-boned hand that set the hammer on the edge of her desk was chapped, the knuckles blistered.

France hid a wince. She wanted to hold his hand between her own, to smooth the injured skin.

"Right," she heard herself say. Then he was gone, and all the warmth seemed to leave with him.

Rotten timing, as usual. Or was it something else? Maybe Stephen Foley's unattainability made him more attractive than if she'd met him at a party, or if he'd been one of her brother's nice, safe friends.

Rachel, returning with her usual whirlwind effect, stopped France's musing. The rest of the afternoon slipped by until it was almost time to go home and clean up. That evening France was to help her sister-in-law, Joanna, make the pies for tomorrow's Thanksgiving dinner.

A familiar rumbling in the nursery yard sent her first to the window, then, slowly, outside. Without a backward glance, Stephen Foley climbed into the green van and was driven away.

"France, put your coat on. It's like the North Pole out there, remember?"

"Right" she shouted with a laugh that didn't sound right. Her eyes stung. Must be the cold.

"You sick, Stephen?"

"No, Chip. Just not hungry. Never was much for breakfast."

"Come on, I know better. Want me to ask Jonesy to have the doc take a look at you?"

Stephen rolled onto his side in the narrow cot and smiled at his roommate. "I think you've missed your calling, buddy. You should have been somebody's mother. Thanks for the concern, but I'm fine. And if you don't get to the dining hall, there won't be any food left to worry about."

Chip turned away, limping slightly on an artificial leg. "Old war wound," the man laughingly called it. The amputation, he'd once confided, was the result of playing motorcycle chicken with two fellow Hell's Angels when Chip had been twenty. Stephen flipped on his back again. Hard to imagine balding, middle-aged Chip as a greasy-haired kid swathed in black leather.

One more week. Lord. He covered his eyes and found his hands shaking. Today was Saturday, the fifth of December. In seven days he'd be out of this place and starting to pick up his life. His gut contracted. Freedom was what he wanted, all he'd waited for during the longest, most destructive year he ever hoped to spend. Why the hell did he feel like crying?

France.

He reached under the bed and pulled out the sketch pad. He was good with a pencil, but portraits would never be his strong suit. Nevertheless, he'd captured her gamine features, the hesitant way her lovely eyes lighted, as if she half expected rebuff.

How long had he known her now—if you could call their tentative encounters knowing each other. He set the pad on this thighs. It was only thirteen days since he first walked into the nursery, yet he was more aware of her than of any woman he'd ever met.

No point thinking about it, friend. She's been good to you because she wouldn't know how to be anything else. You don't mean a thing to her.

So why had she turned up late the day after Thanksgiving and pushed a pair of gloves at him? Said they were old—used to belong to her father. Stephen hadn't been fooled. They were brand-new and she was late because she'd stopped off somewhere to buy them. *You're making too much of it, Foley.*

His blistered fingers had healed. Stephen stretched his hands wide, turning them to look at each side. Even the nails looked civilized again.

Every day she had found an excuse to join him when he ate lunch. She brought a brown bag and there was always something she couldn't eat—usually a second sandwich or an extra doughnut. Then there'd be that uncertain smile as she offered him the food. He'd have eaten the bag itself if she'd asked him.

Once she claimed she had left something in her truck and came back with two hamburgers, one a normal size. the other huge. "Guess my eyes were bigger than my stomach," she'd said, giving him the larger one. He shut his eyes and saw her face. She was a poor liar, and from the shape of her, he doubted if she ever ate two of anything.

Should he tell her he was being released? No, she'd smile. France would be glad to know he was about to be free, but would feel nothing more. And it was a good thing. She was too special to be tainted by what his future was likely to become.

Just as well he wouldn't be at the nursery much longer. When he was gone, some other man would get the benefit of her unselfish kindness.

He swung to slam both fists against the wall.

Chapter Two

Her hands fascinated him. Slender fingers, the nails short but well-shaped—filled with soil now. Stephen watched France pulling leggy plants from unsold hanging baskets in the greenhouse. She moved deftly, swiftly, slicing cuttings below stem joints, plunging each tip into rooting compound, then burying it in flats of sand.

Tomorrow. He was getting out tomorrow. How would she react if he told her? Better stick to the decision he'd made and say nothing. It would be harder on him but more fair to her. Find some excuse to come back afterward when there'd be no chance for her to cover her surprise. Then her true feelings should be easy to read.

"Will they live?" Anything to make conversation—to hear her voice.

She peered over her shoulder and grinned. "You should be an expert at all this by now. The motto is Death or Success. With plants you can be sure of one or the other eventually. But I think most of these will make it."

"Would you like me to do some? You probably have plenty of work inside." Minutes seemed to stand alone—each one a step closer to his new beginning—and their parting.

"Yes—and no. Yes, I'd like you to help. That's why I suggested we work in the greenhouse this morning—so I could show you how to do this."

Relax. His hunch had paid off. She would rather be out here, grubbing in the dirt, than anywhere else. "What did the 'no' mean?"

"It was a half fib really. I do have loads to catch up on in the office, but I don't want to. Here, you try."

His hesitation was deliberate. She didn't need to be bored with stories of how his grandmother had shown him how to do this when he was a boy. "This way?" He started slashing stems while she studied his technique.

After the third ruined effort—each one neatly severed on the wrong side of the shortest joint—he looked up, smiled affably and had to smother a laugh. Her beautiful features were puckered in consternation, one grimy hand buried in those marvelous, gleaming curls.

When she caught his eye, she deliberately softened her expression. "You're good with the shears, but maybe I ought to show you just one or two more before I turn you loose."

Sensitive. Always so careful not to hurt his ego—even though he was a stranger, and a con, to boot. "Thanks," he muttered. "I'd appreciate it."

Instead of handing her the tool, he opened the blades, holding them ready by a drooping stalk. She only paused an instant before closing her fingers over his and guiding them to the right spot. He waited again. Slowly she squeezed until metal squished through sap.

One of France's fingertips caught between two of his and he kept it there. Her head was at his shoulder, the arm stretched along his. He could smell her, fresh and clean, and feel her breath warm on his neck. What would she do if he kissed her? His insides fell away, leaving throbbing heat in his loins. *Fool. She's a contented, desirable woman. You're the last man she's going to want.*

"I can do it now. If I have any questions I'll come and find you." The moment had passed and Stephen moved purposefully away. He heard her boots squeaking a path to the greenhouse exit but made no attempt to turn around. The sooner he was out of this, the better. Being close to her every day, gradually feeling interest turn to liking, then... He'd been without a woman too long. Any female would look good at this point.

After the door slammed, he straightened and rubbed the back of one hand over his eyes. He was deluding himself. In his mind, he could visualize every inch of her, and he knew with a wrenching certainty that he always would.

Back to the rotten cuttings. The impossibility of ever having France Marriotte was just one more of the little disappointments life had decided to bring him.

Snow was falling again when France emerged from the greenhouse and she flapped her arms across her body. Another load of Christmas trees had been dropped off while she was working on the cuttings. Tomorrow would be the second Saturday of the month and probably one of the busiest days of the year in the nursery business. The thought held little joy. Stephen didn't work on Saturdays and Sundays, and the weekends had become drab times of waiting for Monday mornings.

She went to find Rachel, hoping the girl had checked the invoice from the tree-farm people. On her way into the office, France noticed the absence of Stephen's lunch box. He always set it on top of a pile of fertilizer sacks by the door. Great. That would give her a perfect excuse to get him something really good from a nearby restaurant again—he'd begun to look thinner lately.

By the time France went outside to tell Stephen she'd be gone for a while, he was already sorting the new trees into piles by size. Why couldn't she take him with her? There was probably something against it in the instructions she'd been given, but who remembered every little rule? Of course, there was always the chance he wouldn't want to go to a restaurant with her. He came past, dragging a single tall tree, and France made a snap decision.

"That's the one!" She leaped from the step. "It's perfect."

He paused and stared at her quizzically. "What?"

"My tree. I always pick one out early before all the best ones are gone," she lied. It was a family joke that France waited until Christmas Eve and took the saddest specimen left because she felt sorry for it. "Would you mind putting it in the back of my pickup?"

"Sure."

France waited for a moment as he started for her ancient Chevy half-ton, then jogged back inside the shop. "Rachel, I found the ideal tree for my condo. I'm going to have Mr. Foley help me get it into the stand. Can you hold down the fort for a while?" She grabbed her purse from beneath the counter and fumbled in a side pocket for her keys. "Okay?"

Rachel's silence persisted until France looked directly at her. "Is something wrong?"

"You're going to your place, alone, with a convict?" The girl's pale blue eyes rounded.

"That's right, Rachel. If I didn't think the man was perfectly safe he wouldn't be working here at all. They assured me there was nothing to worry about, and he's been with us long enough to prove it. Even my dad thinks this hiring system we've gotten into is a good idea."

"He wouldn't think it was a good idea for you to take him home."

France emitted an exasperated sigh. "I'm going to get him to put my tree in its stand, that's all. And you go too far sometimes, young lady." The gloves she pulled on had holes in every finger on the right hand. She should have gotten a pair for herself when she bought Stephen's. "Remind me to buy new gloves next week.

"When they call from the supply house, lock up and go for the order. Take the other truck." She worried about a rip in one glove. "You might as well go on home with the stuff afterward. We won't need it till tomorrow. There's not going to be much business in this weather anyway. Too cold. You can catch up on the soaps. I'll probably work on the books when I get back."

"But..."

"No buts, Rachel. Enjoy. See you in the morning." France went out and closed the door firmly.

Stephen had already put the tree into the bed of her rusting brown truck. He was holding one end of a stick while Toby dragged at the other, his head snapping from side to side.

Gravel scrunched beneath her feet. "Would you like to drive?"

Stephen released the stick and straightened. "Drive?"

"The truck. It's an experience no one should miss."

"Where are we going?"

She held the keys toward him, but he made no move to take them. "I can't manage by myself. You don't mind getting the tree into the stand and inside my condo for me, do you?"

"You want me to drive you home and put up your Christmas tree?" He took the keys slowly from her outstretched hand.

France nodded. "Please."

"Are you sure that's a good idea?"

"Why wouldn't it be?" She avoided looking at his face, knowing the question she would see there and unsure of her own reaction. Her hand shook slightly as she opened the passenger door. Stephen moved behind her, touching her elbow as she climbed up. He slammed the door and stood for a moment looking at her through the open window. The expression in his eyes changed subtly, like a cloud bank shading an early-evening sky, then he tossed the keys into the air, caught them and walked around to get in.

Toby jumped against the vehicle and whined, his tail wagging. "No, boy." France shook her head and he collapsed in a doleful heap. "You can't come this time, old mutt. Pretend to be a guard dog for a while."

The engine sputtered, ground and finally turned over. "Where to?" Stephen asked, checking over his shoulder to back up.

"Maple Ridge. I'll show you the route."

"I know it."

One more tiny scrap of information. He wasn't a stranger to the area, yet she had never seen him there. If she had, she would have remembered.

France's Tudor-style condo was a ten-minute drive from the nursery. Neither of them spoke, but she felt tense waves of silent uncertainty pass between them. He must be wondering why she would take a man she didn't know to her home, a man whom she had every reason to treat with caution. Her own thoughts ran on identical lines, but she didn't have the answer. She only knew that she wasn't afraid of Stephen Foley.

Once she glanced cautiously sideways at him. He inclined his head as if he sensed her appraisal, but kept his eyes on the road, his profile sharply defined against a gray-white background. France wanted to ask where he lived, what he did, when he would be free.

Stephen turned the vehicle off the main highway onto narrow, tree-lined streets. "You'll have to give me directions from here."

France heard her own distant voice say, "Second left," then, "This is it," as they made a sharp turn onto Laurel Lane.

"Mine's number four. The one with the weather vane." There were only eight units in the condominium complex, each with a small patch of snow-covered grass in front and a driveway screened from its neighbor by a tall boxwood hedge.

They parked and Stephen pulled the noble fir from the bed of the truck. "I'll need a saw to make a fresh cut," he said, not looking at France.

She found both saw and tree stand in the carport and returned, blowing dust from the stand. "Here you are." She handed him the tool and held the trunk steady. "It hasn't been used in years. Hope it's not too blunt." In several broad swipes, he removed the end and stood the tree upright. "Obviously an expert."

France hated the forced cheerfulness in her words, and Stephen's noncommittal "Hmm" did nothing to lessen her discomfort.

Out of habit France tugged off her boots on the porch, but she was surprised when he followed suit. She unlocked the front door and led him past the kitchen and dining room to the living room.

The area in front of a bay window was raised and carpeted. "Just a minute while I move these." She grabbed an armful of cushions from the ledge and threw them on a love seat. "Put it here, please."

When he didn't respond, France turned to look at him. He had set down the tree and was studying the room. She followed his gaze as he tried to assess it. It was a striking blend of warm earth tones thrown into sharp relief against champagne and ivory, the furnishings modern but comfortable. A single primitive sculpture dominated a corner by the fireplace, its lines and color echoed in a terra-cotta-on-black wall hanging. Stephen seemed to have forgotten her. "Lovely," he said softly.

France bathed in a rush of pleasure at his obvious approval. "Thank you. Paul helped me choose the furniture and my dad was the color consultant when I wasn't sure of my instincts. But I'm solely responsible for the taste in artwork."

Stephen's attention focused on her intently. "Who's Paul?"

His tone puzzled France. "My brother."

A muscle in his jaw twitched, then his lips parted slightly and he expelled a slow audible breath.

Immediately she wondered if she should have pretended Paul was a boyfriend, someone who might show up at any minute. She didn't really have any idea what kind of man she was alone with.

"This is the perfect spot." He passed her and positioned the tree, turned it several times, then stood back. "Does that look like the best side?"

France relaxed. "Yup. Great. Couldn't have done better myself." She curled her toes into the rug, anticipating another awkward silence. "Well...you didn't bring your lunch today. I'm going to fix you something."

"No." He cut her off sharply. "I'm sorry. It's just that I don't want you to go to any trouble." The gesture he made with his left hand was awkward, apologetic.

"It isn't any trouble," France insisted. "I haven't had anything myself. Sit down, I won't be long. Play something on the stereo if you want. And light the fire, please—it's chilly in here." Before he could answer, she swung out of the room, humming under her breath.

In the kitchen, she put on the kettle and opened the refrigerator to study its sparse contents. The only thing France hated more than cooking was grocery shopping. She often allowed her supplies to dwindle to nothing but a jar of peanut butter and the curling ends of a loaf of bread. Frequent visits to a nearby French restaurant saved her from starvation. One of Paul's favorite quips was "Develop an allergy to crepes, kid, or you're going to ruin that svelte bod."

She took off the parka and threw it over the back of a chair. Her navy sweater sagged at the hem. It had been Paul's and was several sizes too large. France ineffectually hitched at the hem, then gave up. She wasn't trying to impress anyone.

Pita bread filled with canned shrimp and cream cheese was as close to "haute cuisine" as she was going to come. But the package of cheese was too hard to mix with the shrimp. Still humming, she tried to decide how long it would take to soften in the microwave. She pressed the buttons and went back to the refrigerator to rummage in the crisper for the alfalfa sprouts she remembered buying.

Light strains of music drifted from the other room. Stephen had evidently decided to take her up on the suggestion that he put something on the stereo. Thoughtfully France closed the refrigerator and leaned on the door. Was it loneliness that made her reckless? And she knew she *was* being reckless. This man wasn't even with her because he wanted to be, yet she felt ridiculously, almost tearfully, glad that he was there.

The microwave buzzed and she checked the cheese, but it was still too solid. She set the timer again and stopped, finger poised in midair over the start button. What was the record? It sounded vaguely classical. France punched the button and turned around. She didn't remember having any albums like that.

Inexplicably her heart seemed to skid, then speed up. An invisible magnet drew her into the hall and along to the living-room doorway.

In the corner of the room stood a baby grand piano, a legacy from her mother, who died when France and Paul were fourteen. France rarely played, and when she did it was inevitably jazz, thumped out with more enthusiasm than talent.

Stephen's back was to her, his head bent as he made rapid runs across the keys. The collar of the plaid jacket separated thick hair at his nape. He leaned into the music, swaying with it.

France inched carefully into the room until she could see the side of his face. He had lit the fire, and its flickering light shadowed his features. His eyes were tightly closed. The cuffs of the jacket and of the rough gray workshirt beneath fell away from strong wrists. Across the backs of his broad hands a fine sprinkling of dark hairs showed up against skin that seemed faintly tanned. She noticed again just how sensitive his long fingers appeared.

A cushion began to slide from the pile on the love-seat beside France. The muted patch of umber in the fabric caught the edge of her vision and she bent swiftly to retrieve the cushion. As she straightened, the music stopped abruptly in the middle of a bar.

"Please don't stop," France said, hugging the cushion to her breast. "You play so beautifully."

Stephen remained still for an endless moment before gently closing the cover over the keyboard. "You're obviously not an expert."

His terse comeback should have stung, but she felt his confusion. "No, I'm not. But I've heard enough good music to be able to recognize it." She went to stand beside him. He was probably embarrassed by his impulse to play.

When he didn't reply, France began to feel as if a hand were tightening around her larynx. She didn't have to go back to strangers and a sterile cell at the end of the day. He was hurting and alone—more alone than she had ever been. Her empathy reached out to him wordlessly before she touched his shoulder. "Stephen?" she whispered.

The force with which he shrugged away shocked her. In one powerful, almost violent motion, he slid from the piano bench and stood staring down at her. At a mere five feet five, France felt dwarfed by Stephen's height, and she struggled not to flinch under his penetrating gaze. His mouth was a tight line, the muscles in his jaw rigid.

Her stomach flopped over like a beached fish. "I'm sorry if I startled you," she mumbled.

A long sigh was followed by visible relaxing of his tensed muscles. He closed his eyes momentarily and rubbed a hand across his brow. "Forgive me. I..." His neck jerked convulsively as he swallowed.

Stephen took a step toward her and France dropped the cushion, retreating instinctively until her hands rested behind her on the closed piano.

"Please," he said. "Don't look like that. I wouldn't do anything to hurt you."

His words mirrored the fear that must be on her face. France shook her head and tried to smile. "It's all right.

You were into the music. I understand. I'm going to go back and finish..." She stopped, noticing a trace of blood above his eyebrows. "You're bleeding. What have you done to your forehead?"

He touched his brow and France saw more blood on his palm.

Forgetting his previous reaction to her, she took his hand and turned it over. "It's coming from this cut." She pulled a tissue from her jeans pocket and dabbed at a small puncture wound.

Gently he lifted her hand. "I thought I felt something." He released her at once and pressed the tissue onto the cut. "It's nothing. I must have caught it on this." The point of a tack showed through his jacket pocket. She remembered that he'd been securing loose fence slats earlier in the day.

France could feel his closeness, the warmth that seemed to emanate from him. Breathing became more difficult. A pulse beat visibly in the side of his neck, and he was looking not at his hand but directly into her eyes.

She eased sideways. "I...oh, good grief. I forgot the cream cheese. It's probably a puddle in the microwave by now." Wanting to stay, but knowing she mustn't, she edged around his unmoving form. "There's a bathroom off my bedroom. Why don't you wash up. I..."

The puckish grin that formed deep dimples beside his mouth flustered her more. She was chattering like an awkward schoolgirl.

Stephen cleared his throat. "Thanks. Point the way." He continued to smile.

France walked briskly into the hall and threw open her bedroom door with enough force to slam it back against the wall. She jumped and went inside without meeting Stephen's eyes. Thank God she'd made the bed. "Let me know if you need anything.'' She lifted her head and marched out past him.

Stephen moved to the center of the room. It was like her, he thought, soft and feminine. The decor had the same flair as the living room. He took off his jacket and removed the bent tack from the pocket. A wastepaper basket stood beside her walnut dresser. He tossed the tack into it and laid the jacket on the bed.

His hand had stopped bleeding, but he felt filthy. Pine needles had lodged under his collar and a layer of gritty dirt adhered to the hair on his neck and arms. Slowly he unbuttoned his shirt and slid it off.

Her scent was in the room. She smelled of wildflowers, clean, like wind over a prairie in spring. Her bedroom was in deep blues and greens, the walls papered in muted stripes with an overlay of sweeping Oriental grasses. The bedspread and drapes were striped also, and his feet sank into the deep pile of a navy rug.

He draped his shirt on top of the jacket and headed for the open bathroom door. As he skirted the bed, he stopped to pick up a photograph from a low wicker table. France was smiling up at a blond young man whose arm was draped possessively around her shoulders. Her brother? Stephen didn't think so, and the sudden constriction in his chest disturbed him.

He studied the picture more closely. She didn't look much different, a little younger perhaps. and the huge, green-brown eyes had an expression of uncomplicated trust that was missing now. He set the photo back in its place. The mature France Marriotte was even more beautiful than the girl in the picture. Her creamy skin and oval features were the same, her mouth as invitingly full and sexy, but now there was a seductive promise of total woman about that slender body that could easily drive a man crazy. Stephen could already attest to that.

In her bathroom, surrounded by more reminders of female mystery, he turned the cold water on full. He washed away the streak of blood, then dashed his face and neck, allowing the moisture to run in rivulets over his naked shoulders and chest.

With arms held rigid he braced his weight against the sink and ran his eyes over the things she used: lotion, toothbrush, an assortment of little jars and tubes. Tonight, his last in prison, she would be clearer in his mind than ever—the sound of her laugh and the husky way she hummed, the curve of her mouth when she smiled, her pale, smooth skin.... He didn't know if he could stand it again. Night after night, since he had first seen this woman, he'd broken out in a cold sweat just thinking about her. "Masochistic fool," he muttered. Why in hell hadn't he refused to come here with her? He could have.

Slowly he lifted a squat bottle of perfume from a shelf beside the mirror and removed the stopper. Immediately the familiar scent became stronger. Stephen slid the stopper back and replaced the bottle. He squeezed his eyes shut and rubbed his wet face. She couldn't know what being so close to her was doing to him. If she could read his mind, she'd probably run, unless... "Fool," he murmured again.

When he dropped his hand, he looked past his own mirrored image into the haunted gaze of France Marriotte.

Chapter Three

"I...excuse me. Did I put a clean towel in there? I was in such a hurry this morning."

He stared back at her in the mirror, his blue eyes almost navy, and impossible to read. Moisture created a sheen on the tense, watchful lines of his face, his neck, his well-muscled shoulders and chest, where dark, curling hair arrowed starkly downward to a flat, rigid belly.

Stephen hunched his shoulders and leaned against the edge of the sink. "Thanks." His attention flickered to the towel clasped in her hand. "I didn't think to check."

She would only have to take a step to be able to reach up and run her hands over his rippling back and down his spine to the tapered waist.

The taut arc of awareness that had formed between them tightened, almost vibrated along France's nerves. Her flesh started to turn cold, then suddenly she was on fire.

A drop of water fell from his hair to the base of his neck and began to course between his shoulder blades. Impulsively, France blotted at it with the towel. She laid one hand on hard muscle at his side and continued rubbing, slowly carefully, until he dropped his head forward and expelled an uneven sigh.

For what seemed like an hour she waited, still touching his skin, until he straightened and faced her. "Thanks again." He raised one brow. "Thanks."

France started, uncomprehending. "You're welcome."

"The towel?"

"What?"

"Please. Could I have the towel?"

She felt dull crimson flood her face. "Oh...yes. I'm sorry." Stephen had taken one end of the towel but France still clutched the other.

"Do you have any idea how beautiful your eyes are?" He spoke softly, each word with distinct emphasis.

"Am I supposed to answer that?" She began to feel as if she'd been submerged in an ocean too long.

"Nope." With one long, square-tipped finger he made tiny circles on the back of her hand. "I guess I was using the question as a way to tell you. I haven't had much practice talking to lovely ladies recently."

The air was definitely becoming thinner. "You mean your normally smooth repartee is rusty?" Why was it that all she felt was intense excitement and sexual awareness? What had happened to caution?

He touched her face hesitantly, outlined cheekbone and jaw in a jerky. fleeting motion. "I mean this is the first time I've been alone—really alone—with a woman in a long time. And I'm not sure I'll be able to handle it if you keep looking at me like that. Besides, smooth repartee was never my strong point."

France ran her tongue over her lips. "You should be used to women staring at you."

Stephen studied her mouth. "Ms. Marriotte, you are a very sexy lady. If I didn't know better, I'd say you were giving me the come-on. That, mixed with my fantasy, is a dangerous combination."

He was going to kiss her. France stumbled backward, finally uncurling her cramped fingers from the towel. "Lunch is ready—in the living room." She spun away on wobbly legs and walked rapidly from the room.

She'd put the food on a glass-topped table in front of the couch. Firelight bounced off shiny surfaces and reflected in the bowls of two wineglasses already half filled with rosé. The decision against coffee had been unconscious. But as France surveyed the room and the carefully arranged table, she knew Stephen could interpret the wine as one more element in a plan to seduce him. She crossed her arms and shivered slightly. Was that what she wanted? To make love with this man?

She felt him behind her. "Looks wonderful." As he passed, he ruffled the curls at her nape. His shirt hung open and he draped his jacket over the arm of the couch before he dropped to his knees in front of the fire. Stretching sideways, he picked up both wineglasses. "Join me?" He held one toward her.

Whoever you are, Stephen Foley, I want you. The expression in his hooded eyes mesmerized her—stern, speculative, but inviting an answer that need never be spoken aloud. She went to stand beside him, looking down into his upturned face.

He gave her the glass and, without taking his eyes from hers, gripped the front of her right thigh, squeezed gently, then stroked the length from knee to groin.

When his hand closed over her hip she sat down abruptly, breaking the contact. "What shall we drink to?" Every cell quivered. Her skin retained the sensation of his touch.

He turned to the fire. "How about...now?" He brought his gaze back to hers. "Let's drink to this moment."

Beneath his sensitivity France felt a glitter and brittle intelligence that made her hesitate. He would always have the right answer. "Perfect." She smiled brightly and touched her glass to his. "To now."

Crystal clinked on crystal. France sipped, watching Stephen over the rim of her glass as he took a long swallow and frowned in concentration.

"Don't you like it?"

The crease between his brows remained. "It's fine. Everything's fine. That's the problem."

France put down her wine and hugged her knees. "What do you mean?"

"I don't understand all this." His sweeping gesture encompassed the whole room and France. "Being here with you, feeling safe and relaxed. Why do you make me feel safe?"

"I don't know."

"Maybe it's that incredible, calm face of yours—those great soulful eyes."

I want you to make love to me, Stephen. Not because of my calm face, or because I have soulful eyes, but because you find me beautiful and desirable. Suddenly she felt ashamed, as if he could see inside her head and read the wanton message. Hot blood rushed to her cheeks.

"Good Lord, you're blushing. It makes you look like a sweet, embarrassed kid."

"I'm no kid, Stephen."

"No, France, you're not. Shouldn't we get back to the nursery? Rachel will be expecting you."

He'd never used her first name before. On his lips, it sounded like a caress.

"I gave Rachel the rest of the day off. And this is where I want us to be." She should have been shocked at her own words, but she wasn't. "I know what I'm doing."

"Yes, I think you do. But I don't know why. You don't know anything about me—or very little. And what you do should be enough to send you scrambling for cover."

"Do you see me going anywhere?"

Stephen set his glass beside hers and took a crumb of bread from a plate. He rolled it into a doughy ball. "France?"

Her head snapped up at his urgent tone but she said nothing.

"Are you telling me that you want us to make love, that you want to have sex with a total stranger who is also a convict?"

Her limbs turned to rubber. "I wouldn't have put it that bluntly. And you're not a stranger—at least, you don't feel like one anymore."

"I'm sorry." Stephen tossed the bread into the fire and reached for her hand. "I've got no right to speak to you like that."

France tightened her grip within his. "All I know is that you and I have been watching each other ever since we met. I know I haven't been imagining it." She stared down at his wrist. "There's an attraction between us. More than that. I may be the only woman you've gotten close to lately, and that could be the reason you've followed every step I've taken. But I don't think so. And if it is, so what? I'm a big girl." Empty words. She felt small—and vulnerable.

Slipping a firm hand behind her neck, he pulled her close until his breath warmed her lips. "This conversation—" he brushed her mouth lightly with his own "—is beginning to sound like something out of a movie. The only thing that jars the plot is you. You don't fit."

He released her and sat back on his heels. France had never wanted any man's kiss as much as she wanted his now.

Stephen began to close the top button of his shirt.

"Please don't." France stilled his hand and ran her fingers beneath the rough cotton to caress the tantalizing male flesh. She combed his soft chest hair with her fingers and rubbed a flat nipple with her thumb before she knelt to place a kiss on his tensing flesh.

"Oh, darlin'...I don't think you ought to do that."

France closed her eyes and gripped his waist. She inhaled the clean scent of him and blew softly on his skin as she kissed a path to his navel.

His groan was almost pleading. "France." One trembling hand cupped the back of her head, holding her face to his belly.

"Do you really want me to stop?" Her own body pulsed with longing but she forced herself to straighten and look into his eyes. "Do you, Stephen?"

"This is bizarre, wonderfully bizarre. I wish I didn't have the nagging feeling you're sorry for me. Doing your bit for the troops, or whatever."

France recoiled, half turning away as if he had slapped her. "I...I'm sorry if I've embarrassed you. I never meant to make you uncomfortable. Let's forget this...."

"Hey, hey. Hold on." He massaged her hunched shoulder and leaned close. "I'm the one who's sorry. I just can't believe you feel the same way I do. It's too much...sweet lady."

His lips met hers, firm, slightly parted. Carefully, with a controlling effort France sensed, he ran his tongue along the contours of her mouth, then drew back.

Unable to wait for him to return to her, France clasped his shoulders, pushed aside the shirt, and stretched upward to seek his kiss again. Desperation underscored desire. Why did she know without question that she'd never be the same after today? His mouth, slanting over hers, blocked out everything but the feel of him and the demand that ached in her loins.

"Stephen?" With a persistent nuzzling motion he had pushed her head back and pressed his mouth to her throat. France buried her fingers in his hair. "Stephen, look at me. I want to see your face."

His breathing was labored. When he lifted his face the blue eyes were brilliant. He tried to kiss her.

"Wait."

"Darlin', I don't know if I can."

France kissed his eyes shut and his hands found her breasts unerringly through layers of fabric. An immediate dart of arousal shot deep inside her. "This is what I want, Stephen—to make love with you. That's all I was going to say."

"And I want you." He pulled the sweater over her head and let it fall. "But I'm afraid."

She helped him unbutton her faded pink shirt. "Afraid? I don't know what you mean." Their fingers fumbled together and Stephen pulled her into his arms, surrounding her in a tight embrace.

His shaky laugh moved her hair. "I don't want to hurt you, and it's been a long time. Right now, I'm hanging on with everything I've got. You understand what I'm saying?"

"Yes," France whispered against his shoulder. "It's okay."

"It won't be. It's going to be all over in about ten seconds. And for you, that's not going to be okay." His grip became a vise.

"It'll be all right. We'll make it perfect." France gritted her teeth, wondering if she had been mysteriously transformed into someone else.

This time she made no effort to help him undress her. She remained passive while he managed the rest of the buttons and slid off her shirt. It caught at her wrists, and she smiled as he struggled to loosen the cuffs from the wrong side.

The shirt was finally tossed aside and he spanned her waist to lift her upright. "I think I'm finally getting to see the real France Marriotte. This is something." He stroked her ribs through a wispy flesh-toned teddy.

For once she was glad she had an incurable weakness for expensive, sexy underwear. Stephen traced the skin beside a narrow satin shoulder strap, followed it to softly rounded flesh where transparent lace barely hid her nipples.

"You're so lovely." He cupped her breasts and gently pushed them together. Through the lace his tongue found a nipple, worked it to a harder crest.

France's legs started to crumple but he wrapped one arm around her hips and held her. "Oh...Stephen..." He had surrounded her breast beneath the teddy baring it to the magic of his lips.

Stephen unsnapped her jeans. His movements were increasingly hurried, his breathing rapid. When he lowered her to the rug in front of him, France noticed the pulse in his neck, throbbing as fast as her own.

In a lithe motion, he stood. Fascinated, shocked at what he could do to her just by his physical nearness, France shivered and rubbed her arms. Explosive sensations wound into her womb as he took off the rest of his clothes.

A beautiful, male body, France thought. Perfect. She studied him almost languidly, taking in the way his upper torso blended into slender hips, the long, well-muscled legs sprinkled with dark hair. Good legs—strong, touchable. She was taking inventory and they both knew it. His need for her was something neither could ignore and the evidence caused France to burn all the way to her toes.

For what seemed like an eternity he stood naked before her, as if giving her one last chance to change her mind. The idea drove her to her feet. As the teddy slithered to the floor, she pressed her body to his, feeling their skin bond wherever they touched.

His hips jutted against her, his urgency hard on her belly.

"Forgive me," he muttered, and lifted her. She wound her legs around him, pressing her body closer to his as he entered her. France thrust against him once and felt a wild shudder course through his length. "Oh, my God..." The tortured words hissed against her ear. "I didn't want that...."

"Shh. Shh." France locked her arms behind his head and kissed him fiercely.

Slowly she lowered her feet to the floor, keeping her mouth on his, and they sank together onto the soft rug.

Instincts she didn't know she possessed kept her hands moving, massaging, teasing, until she felt Stephen respond to her ministrations.

"You're irresistible." He laughed into her hair, his breath tickling her ear. "Totally irresistible."

"Stephen?" She shifted until she could see his face. "Tell me what you're thinking."

His hair was damp; his lashes were spiky and his lips so close. "That I want to make love to you again and again...and make this moment last forever." He kissed her, unable to know how her heart was expanding to fill her entire chest, how her joy was mingling with apprehension.

He kissed her eyes closed, and she was glad to give herself over to the darkness and purely physical sensations. She responded to the insistence of his lips and hands, moaning low in her throat, arching against the grip that held her fast. He buried his face between her breasts, and then his tongue traveled in relentless exploration.

His chin was slightly rough on her tender skin. France blindly tried to hold him but his movements were quick, fleeting. Stephen played her body like a finely tuned instrument, expertly brought it to a point where it waited only for his signal to start the rush of music that would lead to a final, obliterating crescendo.

"What do you want, France?" He spoke against her belly.

At first she didn't understand. "Mmm? I...oh, Stephen."

The moist, burning trail pressed downward to the pulsing softness between her thighs. *Is this me?* Another second and his insistent tongue sent a throbbing spear of heat through her core and the question didn't matter anymore. The fire spread inside, driving a muffled cry past her lips, and she ground her fingertips into the bunched muscles at his shoulders.

"France? Yes?" He raised himself over her, stared down into her eyes. His gaze didn't flicker in response to her wordless nod but became sightless as his body joined one with hers.

Stephen's pace, slow at first, carefully controlled, increased until her breath jarred in her throat. It wasn't possible to give too much, to want too much. Every tiny particle of France opened to receive him, seared at the gliding stimulation that was velvet and iron. Her flesh begged and received, gave and felt him accept, and a fragment of her mind acknowledged that she would never be free of this moment, or of this man.

"Now, Stephen. Now." Her own voice sounded distant and strange, and ended in a sob.

"My sweet darlin'." He came down on her for an instant, then arched away, supporting his weight on his forearms. His lips were parted, teeth clamped together as he reached into her.

France vaguely felt the rug burn her skin as they slid sideways, and then the air around her exploded into a million fragments of light and rushing sound. The force of their climax dragged out two cries that became one with the total abandonment of reason.

Stephen pulled her into his arms with tenderness, holding her, pressing her face against his neck. France lifted her mouth to the prickling roughness of his jaw, then balled her fists on his chest and burrowed close, like a small animal seeking safety.

"I love your name." He sounded drowsy, and his body was warm and damp, heavy from their passion. "France—soft, silky." He nuzzled the top of her head and seemed to doze.

What if she could never have him again? France's mind suddenly spun in circles like widening ripples on a rain-spattered pool. *You said you were a big girl. You never asked for more than his toast offered—now. And he never offered anything else. How could he?*

The dying fire crackled, still warm at her back. Stephen's grasp tightened and he shifted. His muscles flexed. "What's that perfume you wear?"

His unexpected lucidity, the suddenness of the question, startled her. "I can never remember the name. Something French."

"It smells like wildflowers." He growled and nipped playfully at her chin. "In the future wildflowers are going to mean instant arousal...which could prove embarrassing in some situations."

She wasn't ready for the future. "As long as you're with me, it'll be just fine."

Did she imagine that he tensed for an instant? Probably. It was the first time either of them had suggested this might not be their only encounter. She wouldn't allow herself to think about it.

Stephen turned her, pinned her on her back. His fingers, laced with hers above her head, stopped her wandering thoughts. He straddled her and stared down into her eyes with a seriousness that jolted. "Is your brother blond?"

"What?" She tried to move but he held her fast.

"I wondered if Paul looks like you."

"And you chose this moment to ask?" She swallowed and found she couldn't look away. "We have the same coloring."

"Who's the guy in the picture—the one on the table in your bedroom?"

Unfamiliar tears prickled beneath her eyelids. "You don't have any right to question me. I haven't asked you anything." She saw his teeth sink into his lower lip. The grip on her hands slackened. "But since you're interested, that 'guy' used to be my husband. Until he decided marrying me had been a whim...his words, not mine. We were divorced four years ago."

"But you still keep his photo in easy reach?" An acerbity had entered his voice.

"Yes, damn it. Just like I keep a picture of my mother on the wall by my dresser. One died and the other is dead to me, but I loved them both. I'm not the kind of woman who can love and then forget, regardless of the impression I've made on you today." Hot tears squeezed free; she couldn't contain them. With all her strength she wrenched away and sat up, coming into contact with Stephen's unyielding chest.

He pulled her to him and held on tight until she stopped struggling. "Stop it. Please, stop it. I'm sorry. I know apologizing isn't enough but...how can I explain a feeling I don't understand?" He stroked her shoulders and back, pushed his fingers into her hair. "I guess this had been a bit more than either of us was prepared to handle."

A bit more? France sniffed and rubbed at her nose. "Would you mind holding me for a while? I haven't done much crying lately. Makes me feel silly."

"There's nothing silly about you." He studied her. "A red nose suits you. Puts color in that pale little face." He covered his head, pretending to ward off France's threatening fist, then swept her into his arms and carried her to the bedroom.

Away from the fire the air was cool. Stephen lifted the covers, deposited France beneath them and climbed in beside her. "Go to sleep, France." He molded her against his length. "We'll have to go back soon."

Even as he held her she felt him drawing away. "Not yet." What had made her think she could separate sex from emotional involvement? She'd never been able to before.

Stephen drew her face into the hollow of his shoulder and rested his chin on top of her head. His breathing seemed tight, and he made irregular patterns across her shoulder blades with the tips of his fingers. With his other hand he smoothed her body from breast to thigh. A flash of longing swept through France; she arched her head back, seeking his lips.

As he stared at her mouth, his dark lashes lowered to cast shadows beneath his eyes. His kiss had the fleeting quality of a butterfly's timid caress. Then he untangled their limbs and got out of bed.

"Rest, while I take a shower."

She clenched her fingers to stop herself from holding him back. The cold that slowly wormed into the place he left empty had nothing to do with temperature.

Smile, she ordered herself. *When he comes back, smile at him. Let him know it's all right.*

France got up, wound the quilt about her and trailed into the living room. Quickly, she gathered their clothes and, as a last thought, picked up the plate of pita bread. She wasn't hungry, but Stephen must be. *Stephen.* His name echoed through the hidden crevasses of her brain. She could still feel him inside her. The quilt was heavy and France wrapped it more tightly, supported its weight over one arm. A sudden rushing glow engulfed her and she knew she would never regret what had happened.

Back in the bedroom she selected a multicolored silk blouse and dark gray woolen slacks from the closet. When she tried to analyze why it seemed important to wear something different, she realized it was more than the desire to please Stephen; she wasn't the same woman who'd dressed that morning.

But France didn't put on the pale blue camisole and panties she'd taken from a drawer. Instead, she flung Stephen's rough plaid jacket around her shoulders, put her arms into the sleeves. His clean scent, mixed with pine and earth, surrounded her.

The clock on her bedside table said three. She felt as if they'd left the nursery days ago. France walked to the window and parted the drapes an inch. It had stopped snowing. Beyond the trees of a neighboring estate, two red brick chimneys pointed identical fingers at a gradually clearing sky.

She sighed. It didn't matter why he'd been put in prison...or did it? How long would it be before he was free? Did she dare ask him? She tipped back her head. No, she couldn't ask. If he wanted to tell her, he would.

Stephen's hands, caressing her hips under the jacket, broke her confused reverie. She hadn't heard him approach.

He wrapped his arms around her. "I thought you were sleeping. Why didn't you join me?"

"We both know the answer to that."

His hands found her breasts, surrounded them, gently teased her hardening nipples. In a single motion, he removed the jacket and pulled her back against his damp nakedness. "Would it have been such a bad idea?"

Her desire for him was as fresh and raw as it had been when he'd first touched her. She felt the throb of his answering arousal but, at the same time, a flicker of reason struggled to life. "It's late." She faced him, placing her hands on his chest. "Let's eat while we dress, to save time." Why didn't she feel as calm as she sounded? She wanted to kiss the skin she touched.

"You're right." Strands of gray at his temples glistened from the shower. Although he wasn't smiling, the lines fanning from the corners of his eyes seemed deeper. "We'd better hurry."

They dressed without speaking, but their eyes met a dozen times. France knew Stephen saw every move she made, registered each item of clothing she wore. And for her, he was an image branded on her soul. The plate of food remained uneaten on the dresser.

When they finally stood by the door, Stephen said, "You look wonderful." He glanced around. "Where's your coat?"

"Forgot it." France went swiftly into her bedroom and grabbed the blue fox jacket her father had given her for her birthday.

As she reached Stephen, he took the coat and held it while she slipped her arms into satin-lined sleeves. "Lucky lady. You're stunning in that. But you're equally stunning in anything...or nothing. Especially nothing. France..."

"What?" she said. The stress in his tone had been different from anything she'd heard there before. "What is it?"

"Never mind." His hands lingered at her neck, his thumbs barely touching pale skin beneath her chin. An odd, pained expression crossed his features for an instant before he placed a hand at her waist and guided her outside.

By the time they reached George's, a thin ray of sun split the gloom, although dusk was rapidly sucking away the day. When Stephen drove into the yard, the strange light stretched through the slats in the fence, sweeping fuzzy lines across the snow.

France opened the door and hopped down before Stephen could reach her. "Toby's glad to see us. Aren't you, boy?" She crouched to stroke the wiggling dog while Stephen came to stand beside her.

"What would you like me to do?" he asked. The neutrality in his voice sounded strained. "Shall I finish the trees?"

"No," she said, too loudly. "No. They'll be coming for you soon." With this mention of the part of his life they'd been avoiding, a thick curtain seemed to fall between them.

Stephen dropped down beside her, resting one knee on the ground, and ruffled Toby's ears. "You're special, France." He kept his attention on the dog. "Maybe..."

Whatever he had intended to say was lost in the sound of an engine. The van swung through the gates and parked behind the Chevy. France tried to shut out the noise of a heavy door opening, the footsteps on the snow-covered gravel.

"Good-bye," Stephen whispered.

"'Bye," France muttered hoarsely, wanting to add "See you Monday," but conscious of the other man who had joined them.

"Okay, Foley?" Although the prison employee wore no uniform, authority emanated from his beefy form.

He had power over Stephen. The thought turned France's stomach. She watched Stephen walk to the van with Toby close behind.

"Ms. Marriotte?"

France saw Stephen give Toby a last pat before he ducked and slid inside the vehicle. He slammed the door and rested his arm along the rim of the open window. She couldn't understand the expression in his eyes.

"Was everything satisfactory, Ms. Marriotte?"

France started and felt her cheeks redden. "Yes, thank you. Fine."

The man handed her a sheet of paper. "Good. This is the information you'll need on the new man. He'll be dropped off at the usual time Monday morning."

Chapter Four

"A new man? I don't understand." France's mind turned black for a fractured second as a hidden shiver tore through her.

"Don't worry, ma'am, we won't leave you high and dry. There shouldn't be any problems with the new worker. If there are, we want to know."

The paper crumpled between her fingers like fragile parchment. "I don't care about that." She looked at the wrinkled wad in her hand. "I mean, I'm sure the person you've selected will be fine, but..."

She glanced quickly at Stephen, knowing that he'd heard the conversation. Her heart dropped at the sight of him, and she fought painfully against the desire to throw open the door and pull him to her.

Stephen. He needed her now; every inch of her felt it. How could she not, after they'd shared each other so intimately. Even now she could feel the remnants of their passion still warm and moist inside her.

Stephen leaned back, his broad shoulders forced defeatedly against the seat as if someone had punched the air from his lungs. He wouldn't look at her, but stared at the dash, his face set in an expressionless mask.

"Is anything wrong, ma'am?" The driver's cool gaze shot from Stephen to France, a thin veil of suspicion crossing his meaty features. "If you don't like the man they've picked out for you, there's plenty more to choose from."

Why can't Stephen stay? She wanted to scream at this man but knew she didn't dare. Stephen *was* a prisoner. He'd been convicted of a crime, and she had no right to fight the system. "I know, I know." Frustration tinged her words. "But why the switch? Training takes time."

The driver glanced at Stephen, then shrugged his thick shoulders. "Don't know for sure, ma'am. I only follow orders."

"I see."

Stephen raised his head, pulling France's gaze to his with an icy intensity. Shock clawed her stomach at the strange, steely remoteness in his eyes. She didn't have to see it. She could sense the invisible barrier he had raised between them. It felt cold and final like the closing slam of a barred cell door.

"Right, then." The driver motioned for Stephen to roll up the window.

Stephen continued to stare at her through the smudgy glass. The uncomfortable dryness in France's throat snaked down her body, turning her legs to sawdust.

She had to let go. The unwelcome certainty jangled in her mind. He was a convict and he was going back to prison. There could be no place for them in each other's lives. Stephen Foley had cast the dice long before, and she knew that she would never see him again. Toby rubbed affectionately against her leg, but France, lost in her own frustrated thoughts, was oblivious.

The driver made a swift U-turn in the nursery parking lot before easing the van back onto the street. France stood motionless on the packed snow until Stephen's face was a pale blur. Her pulse throbbed in her throat. Even at three hundred yards, she knew he continued to watch her.

He was gone. Hot tears pushed from her eyes. She tipped her chin and sniffed, fighting to control a sudden surge of anger. She hated the prison and she hated Stephen for doing whatever he'd done that kept him there. Never had she felt so empty, so helpless.

A snowflake settled on France's nose. She swiped at it, then headed slowly for the office, with Toby at her heels. Fresh snow outlined the spiky branches of dormant trees and shrubs, making them stand out softly in the bleak, gray dusk. She kicked sullenly at a mound of ice and jammed both hands into her pockets. The hateful sheet of paper crinkled into a ball beneath one clenched fist. France didn't care whose name was on it. After Stephen Foley, it didn't matter.

She unlocked the office door and pushed it open. The sweet, pungent scent of fresh-cut fir and pine filled the room. Ordinarily, she loved the smell. It had always reminded her of happy Christmases, filled with warmth and family love. Now it reminded her of Stephen.

The telephone rang briskly beneath a pile of invoices on the desk, jarring the silence like shattering glass. France lurched around, then reached for it, her heart thudding in her ears. "Hello?" The tightly strung sound of her own voice disgusted her. Stephen's face flashed across her mind, but it was foolish to think it would be him. He'd just left. Besides, he couldn't call. "No, this isn't the Plaza Theater. You've got the wrong number."

She stared at the receiver. Would it do any good to call the prison, request that Stephen be reassigned to the nursery? What questions would they ask her, and how would she answer? "If you need assistance...," An operator's voice, taped and dissonant, reminded her to hang up.

"Sorry." Lord, she thought. Now she was talking to recordings. She had to relax. Slowly France replaced the receiver, then pulled the rumpled form from her pocket and smoothed it flat. Somewhere on it she knew she would find a phone number. The decision to call ignited a ray of hope.

She punched in the digits, then waited for a connection. A draft across the office floor chilled her legs and she perched on the edge of the desk, one arm wrapped around herself for warmth.

"Hello? Is this the work-release office? Good. This is France Marriotte...from George's Nursery. Yes, I'm pleased with the man you've been sending." She moistened her lips. "No, nothing's wrong. It's just that—"

The man on the other end of the line asked her to wait. He sounded tired.

France hated to be interrupted. "Listen, I was just told I was getting a new man on Monday. There was nothing wrong with the old one. It was working so well. Wait. Don't put me on hold."

Damn. France started to pace. Minutes passed. "What? Stephen Foley's going to be paroled?" Disbelieving, she repeated the words. "That's wonderful. Yes, of course I'll be happy to give him a good reference." She ran the fingers of one hand through her thick curls. "Right. You'll send the papers I need."

Stephen had been paroled. She shouldn't feel stunned but she did. "No, send the new man. I'm sure he'll work out fine. Good-bye."

The receiver slipped loosely from her grasp. Stephen's actions didn't make sense. He must have known he was being released, yet he hadn't told her. France's mouth twisted. The reason was painfully simple. He didn't want her to know. And why should he? To Stephen Foley, their satisfying interlude had been merely a pleasant diversion.

The revelation still hurt, even though she half expected it. She lifted her head and focused on the pile of Christmas trees still heaped outside the window, their stocky branches merging into the dusk. Had she so totally misjudged him?

A long, ragged sigh heaved her chest. What else could she expect? After all, she'd practically seduced the man. Now she had to be mature enough to handle the consequences.

"What in the... ? France, are you all right? Have you been robbed?"

The words ricocheted through the shadowy office. Startled, France spun to face the door. "Paul." She sagged against the edge of the desk.

France's twin brother flipped on the fluorescent strip. "It's freezing outside, the door's wide open, it's dark in here. What's the matter?" He glowered at Toby, curled peacefully in his basket under the counter. "I suppose that mutt helped put the loot in the bag."

The light hurt her eyes, and she squinted at him. "Everything's fine. And don't pick on my dog."

"Where's Rachel?" He shut the door behind him, then glanced around, his face filled with concern.

"I sent her home early." France drew in a long breath.

Paul frowned. "Why are you all dressed up?"

"I'm—I'm going out later." The words tumbled from her lips. "Look, would you give me a second to settle down? I've just had the wits scared out of me. I didn't even hear your car."

"Sorry. Must have been because of the snow in the parking lot." He crossed the small room, then reached behind her and pulled out the desk drawer holding the cash box. "Should I call the police?"

France pressed her fingers into the fabric of his trench coat. "Paul, you're not listening to me. I haven't been robbed. Relax."

He raised his head and hazel eyes that could have been her own, stared back at her. "What's going on, then? You don't make a habit of sitting in the dark before closing time, freezing to death. I know better."

He probably did, France thought. She and her brother, like many twins, usually possessed an uncanny understanding of each other. Most times it was fun, but now the possibility disturbed her.

Nervously, she picked up an outdated seed catalog and thumbed through worn pages. "You worry too much. We're not kids anymore, Paul. I'm wrapping it up a bit early tonight because of the weather and I simply forgot to close the door." She fought to push her lonely frustration deeper, knowing that her brother would never understand about Stephen. How could he be expected to when France herself was totally bewildered?

"A pretty thin excuse." He puffed out a breath and watched it dissipate in white vapor. "Look at that, will you? Pure ice."

"You exaggerate." His obvious concern touched her. She plopped down casually in a rickety swivel chair and pushed another in Paul's direction with the toe of one boot. "Make yourself comfortable. At least there's no snow on it." She smirked.

A slow grin curved his mouth as he dropped into the seat. He was a handsome man, several inches taller than

France, and leanly athletic. Although they didn't look too much alike, people always knew they were family.

The chair squeaked as he leaned back, the harsh light glinting on his thick auburn hair. "Very funny." He pushed up the collar of his coat. "Lord, it's arctic in here. But since it appears that you're okay, I'll tell you what I drove out here for, then head home. I know Joanna's got supper on the table."

"This had better be good," France retorted. "I wasn't expecting you until tomorrow." Although he was a busy man, Paul usually managed to drop by the nursery on Saturday mornings. He'd helped their father, as had France, throughout their teen years.

"I know. We had an early deadline this afternoon so for once I was able to leave on time. Just thought I'd drop by to say hello."

Paul was city editor of the *Tulsa Review*, an evening daily newspaper. He loved the work. Reporting and editing were in his blood.

"I'll bet. Something's on your mind, isn't it?" France stretched out her legs, crossing them at the ankles. "And I have a feeling I'm going to regret asking you what it is."

"I brought you this. Hot off the presses." He pulled a folded newspaper from his pocket and tossed it onto France's lap.

"Just what I need. You know I don't have time to read newspapers."

He shook his head. "One of these days, you're going to wake up and decide to become informed."

"I glance through the sports section almost every day."

"That's pathetic, France. The world doesn't revolve around football."

"Maybe it should." She snuggled into her fur collar and grinned at him.

"I want you to come to a party." He raised one hand. "Don't say no until you hear me out."

"It's not another newspaper gathering, is it? I swore at the last one that I'd never go to another."

"You're jumping to conclusions again. You need to get out, meet new people. France, I worry about you."

Meet new people. If only you knew. "It *is* a company party, isn't it?" She raised her brows in questioning reproach.

"He nodded. "Mmm. But it's New Year's Eve. Almost a month away, and I know you haven't made any other plans. Come on. Say you'll go with Joanna and me. You'll have a good time."

She peered at him, long and hard. "Why do you always make saying no so damned difficult?" She hesitated, exasperated, yet loving him for his persistence. "All right. But no all-night festivities. I need to be in prime condition to watch the Cotton Bowl."

"Don't worry." Paul pulled himself from the chair, then planted a kiss on the top of France's head. "Why don't you pack it in for the night? I'll hang around until you're safely in the pickup."

"Going home doesn't sound like too bad an idea." France stood up and reached for a pile of invoices. A sick wave rolled through her when she realized the work-release paper lay on top. The image of a tall, handsome man, sensitive and sexy, flashed into her mind. Where was Stephen now? What was he doing?

"You're frowning. You'll be a wrinkled old bag in no time if you keep this up." He yanked the papers from her fingers. "You work too hard. Leave 'em here. They'll wait until morning." He tossed them into the wire basket on her desk.

Stephen's image faded slightly, but not the unbidden excitement tingling along her nerves. "You win." She reached for her purse, patted Toby, then waited as Paul pulled the door shut behind them.

"Don't forget this." He handed her the newspaper.

"When will you give up?" With a chuckle she tucked the paper under her arm. As an afterthought, she scraped the fresh snow away from Toby's dog-flap near the bottom of the door.

Paul leaned against his Datsun station wagon as France bumped out of the lighted nursery parking lot in the pickup. She peeked at him in the rearview mirror and saw his hand raised in a wave. Her insides warmed with affection. Paul cared about her deeply. It was just as well that he didn't know his sister had changed.

Her long fingers clenched the steering wheel. A few hours earlier, she'd violated her own standards by making love with a stranger, a devastating man, mysterious and slightly wild. He'd teased her soul, strummed chords beyond her most dangerous imaginings. Though he'd moved beyond her grasp, he'd unleashed a bounty of rioting feelings.

For the first time in years, her condo seemed dismal and lonely. France left her coat on and turned up the thermostat. Everywhere she looked, reminders of Stephen shot at her—the black hole of the fireplace, the scraps of uneaten lunch on the coffee table. Even her fragrant Christmas tree darkened the alcove where Stephen had placed it, its naked branches echoing her own emptiness.

She closed her eyes to shut it all out but only heard again the haunting strains of the music he had played and the way he'd whispered, "Darlin'."

Every muscle pulled taut. She needed to take a hot bath. It would help her unwind, try to forget.

Even the bedroom seemed suddenly wrong. The bed linen, mussed from lovemaking, held the imprint of two bodies. Was it her imagination or did the clean, earthy scent of Stephen still linger?

Quickly, France yanked off the blankets and sheets. She felt driven to purge all evidence of his presence and in jerky, determined movements, crammed the linen into her laundry hamper.

She dropped onto the bare mattress and stared at the telephone on the nightstand. Damn it all. She rolled onto her stomach and pounded the bed with a tight fist. It did no good to hope. He would never call.

Mechanically she stood up and stripped off her coat, blouse, slacks and underwear. Pulling a fluffy pile robe from the closet, she headed for the bathroom to fill the tub. She couldn't allow herself to picture Stephen's image in the mirror, or remember that he had been the last to use the shower. Quickly she twisted on the hot water and felt its ovenlike steam reach out to her. How wonderful the soothing heat felt. It eased and relaxed her as she slid into the water. She would make herself forget.

Then France saw it—a tiny drawing propped against a bottle of perfume next to the sink.

"What in the world is that?" She hoisted herself from the rub, rivulets of water dripping down her body.

Reaching for the scrap of paper, she held it gingerly between wet fingers. Stephen Foley was an enigmatic, perceptive man. He hadn't been able to walk out of her life without leaving a message.

A pencil sketch of a lovable, boyish figure smiled at her. Was it possible that parts of him looked a bit like Stephen? The little humorous man sat in front of a fireplace not unlike hers, his head ringed with a row of hearts. She chuckled. Its simplicity reminded her of a childish valentine.

A glance at the bold initials, "S.F." scrawled into the corner confirmed what France already knew. Stephen had drawn the picture, then placed it where he knew she would find it. It was his way of telling her that he would be back.

A swell of happiness surged in her. The drawing was small, the message obscure, but she clung with joy to the hope it gave her. Only when she twirled around in the small room did she realize she was standing in a wide puddle of water.

Grabbing a thick towel, she hugged it to her. laughter welling inside. The mess on the floor didn't matter. Stephen was coming back to her.

She prayed he wouldn't wait too long.

HOURS STRETCHED into endless days. Each knock at the door, each ring of the phone sent a blaze of excitement zinging through her. But Stephen didn't drop by, nor did he call. France's euphoria slowly changed to despair, and finally to sullen apathy.

Her work became a blessed elixir. The hordes of customers that flocked into the nursery made her lose track of the number of trees and wreaths she and Rachel had sold.

Snow continued to fall intermittently, providing a breathtaking backdrop for the Christmas season. France decorated her tree and played holiday music on the stereo. But nothing seemed to cheer her. She felt like a ghost, a vacant image. Stephen had stolen a vital part of her.

No one guessed the turmoil that existed behind her calm expression. She went through all the appropriate motions, purchasing gifts for her family and wrapping them. Paul overflowed with a festive spirit, and he and Joanna made plans for the annual family gathering at George Richards' house the night before Christmas.

On Christmas Eve, France inched the pickup onto her father's driveway and parked it behind Paul's station wagon. The fluffy Douglas fir she'd selected from the nursery shimmered with lights in the center of the picture window.

Paul threw open the door before she even had a chance to climb the steps to the wide porch.

"France, Merry Christmas. Here, give me those. I'll put them under the tree." In a swift move, he took the packages she carried, then handed her a steaming drink. "Hot buttered rum. Dad's special brew."

In the living room George Richards tossed a log on the fire, then stood to greet his daughter. "There you are, honey. I'm glad you're here, with the roads so bad and all." His face was red from the heat.

"Dad. I've got chains in the back of the truck and several bags of sand for ballast. Don't worry. I'm prepared for anything."

He pulled her into a hearty embrace, his gaze dark and warm. "Knowing my daughter, I believe you probably are. Merry Christmas."

"Merry Christmas. Where's Joanna?" France glanced around the room for her sister-in-law.

"In the kitchen, I think, working on the appetizers. Maybe I better check on her," Paul said mischievously.

"Just leave some food for the rest of us," France teased. When he left the room, she sat down on the sofa next to her father.

George Richards had settled his large frame comfortably, balancing a drink on one knee. A pang of regret sobered France at his thinning dark hair. She noticed that more gray streaked through it, and the lines on his weathered skin appeared deeper. She loved her father, and it saddened her to see him starting to age more rapidly.

He took a long sip from the glass. "How are you, honey?"

France concentrated on the brightly wrapped gifts under the tree for a second before answering, "Fine, as usual."

"No you aren't," he said.

The flat statement caught her off guard, and she shifted uncomfortably. "Of course I am. I don't know what you mean, Dad." France took too big a swallow from her steaming drink, forcing her to clear her throat.

"You're working too hard at the nursery." He gave her knee a squeeze. "And you don't laugh enough, not like you used to."

France tensed inwardly. Her despondency the past few weeks had taken its toll, and she apparently hadn't disguised it as well as she thought.

Paul and Joanna, laden with two trays of hors d'oeuvres, pushed through the swinging kitchen doors. France breathed a silent sigh of relief at the interruption.

"Put those plates right here, on the coffee table. I'm starving." France knew she spoke a shade too stridently.

Joanna slid her platter onto the table, then stretched to give France a hug. "Sorry. I haven't been ignoring you, but I had some nachos under the broiler."

"With Paul in the kitchen helping you, I'm surprised you have any left." France liked her sister-in-law. Joanna, petite and blond, had a vivacious, open personality. She and Paul hoped to have children, and France thought again what a good mother her brother's wife would make.

"It feels wonderful to get out of that office for a few days." Paul draped himself carelessly across an arm-chair and popped an egg roll into his mouth. "Holidays do strange things to reporters. They seem to think it's okay to ignore deadlines and harass editors. A few even forget to come back to the office."

"Don't pay any attention to him." Joanna stood be-hind the chair and wrapped her arms lovingly around her husband's neck. "It makes him feel better to complain. We've heard all this before, darling."

"No, you haven't. Not this. I even had a run-in with the managing editor the other day." Paul rubbed the backs of Joanna's hands absently. "Several years ago, the paper had a young man on the staff—a real go-getter, I'm told. It was before they hired me, so I never got the chance to meet him. Anyway, the fellow went syndicated and eventually left the paper. He really made it big, but apparently ran into some bad luck along the way and had to spend a year in jail. Tough break for him, but now that he's out and back in the area, the newspaper wants to hire him back at about four times what they pay anyone else in his field."

Paul shook his head in disbelief. "He'll be working with the editorial page people, not with me, so I'm probably out of line in complaining. But I don't care. As far as I'm concerned, it's bad publicity for the paper."

"It's not your problem, sweetheart, and there's noth-ing you can do about it." Joanna stuffed another egg roll into his mouth. "It's Christmas Eve. Be quiet and enjoy your family."

"Wait a minute," France bristled. "I don't think you should berate this guy just because he's had a run-in with the law. You don't know what the circumstances were. He's trying to pull his life back together. At least you can give him credit for that." The harshness in her voice surprised her, but the mere mention of prisons sent France's mind spinning in a whirlpool with Stephen Foley at its center. She felt compelled to defend this other man. "We've had really good luck at the nursery with the men from the work-release program, you know."

Paul's brows raised in surprise. "Sorry, Sis. I didn't realize you felt so strongly about the subject."

"She's got a point, though." Their father rubbed his chin. "Every fellow they've ever sent us has been a hard worker."

"All right, point taken." Paul raised his palms in defeat. "I won't say another word."

France stood suddenly, pretending to inspect the stack of Christmas music tapes piled next to the stereo. Talking about jail and prisoners did nothing for her holiday spirit. She didn't want to be reminded of the man who'd captured her heart, then twisted it. Although she had almost abolished Stephen Foley from her conscious thoughts, he was still deeply entrenched in the recesses of her soul.

None of her family could have realized the dull longing that simmered in France as she smiled her way through the evening. She ate too much food, sang carols while Paul played his battered guitar, and opened presents with a forced delight that threatened to choke her.

Midnight passed before she finally dragged herself from a warm spot in front of the fireplace. Paul and Joanna decided to leave, too, and the three tramped down the ice-crusted steps to the driveway.

"Don't forget about the party New Year's Eve." Paul brushed at the inch of fresh snow that had accumulated on France's windshield.

"I've planned my entire life around it." She couldn't keep the light sarcasm from her voice.

"It's going to be at the publisher's house. You've been there before. Perhaps you'd rather meet Joanna and me there. Then you'll have your own transportation, if the going gets too rough." He smiled down at her.

"That's the best idea you've had in a long time."

France hoisted herself into the cab of the pickup, then backed it carefully down the slippery driveway. A slight smile flickered about her mouth for several blocks. Despite her reservations, she was actually looking forward to the party. Lord knows, she needed a change. Perhaps she would meet someone new and exciting. The unlikely possibility amused her.

COLD MOONLIGHT SHIMMERED down on the blocks of parked cars when France pulled up in front of Paul's publisher's home New Year's Eve. A nipping wind shivered bare branches, and thousands of stars, pinpricks of light, glowed in the clear winter sky.

She pulled her black velvet jacket more closely around her and breathed in a grateful sigh that no one had seen her arrive. Climbing out of a pickup gracefully wasn't easy to do in heels and a dressy velvet skirt.

A cacophony of reveling voices leaked from the other side of the closed front door, making her wonder if anyone would even hear the doorbell.

But the door swung open almost immediately. "Come in, come in." A man she didn't recognize grabbed her arm, directing her inside. He took her purse and jacket to a bedroom.

"France, over here." Paul gestured to her from across the room. Joanna stood beside him.

"See, I made it." France smiled at them, then scanned the crowd. Several faces seemed familiar, but most were strangers.

"I'm glad. You sure look nice." Her brother beamed with pride.

"Thanks." Almost unconsciously, she smoothed the rich folds of her skirt against her legs. Everyone else in the room glittered in party attire, and she was glad she'd chosen the beaded white camisole to complete her outfit.

"What do you want to drink? I'll get it for you."

"Champagne, of course. It's New Year's Eve."

Paul disappeared quickly into the noisy crowd.

France recognized an older woman from the features department at the *Review* who wove her way toward them. She grabbed Joanna's hand. "Isn't this a marvelous party?" She smiled at France. "France, isn't it? Yes, I remember you, dear. You're Paul Richards' sister. How nice to see you again." The woman leaned toward Joanna. "Have you seen him?"

"Who?" Joanna arched her brows.

"The new man. That hot syndicated cartoonist the paper just signed on. He may be an ex-con, but he's *so* sexy. And what a coup for the paper. With his talent and, ahem, reputation, he could have worked anywhere." The woman craned her neck. "He's over there. See him?"

France casually glanced in the direction the woman indicated. A group of people pressed around someone, but she glimpsed no more than a shoulder in navy corduroy. "All I see is a crowd—mostly of women."

"He's in the middle. They won't leave him alone, but I can't blame them. He's *so* darned attractive."

"None of those women are too shabby, either." Joanna narrowed her eyes. "Does anyone know what he did?"

"That's the *really* fascinating part." The older woman's eyes flashed. "He got sent up for attempted rape. You'd think a man as sexy-looking as he is wouldn't have to resort to something as disgusting as that."

"Rape?" France repeated, wrinkling her nose.

The tall man moved, and she saw his broad back, the brown hair that curled over his pale shirt collar. A chilling wave of premonition pulled at her, nudging and tugging.

"My God in heaven!" Her breath stuck in her throat. "Stephen."

Chapter Five

Stephen Foley disentangled himself from the throng of admirers. Someone handed him a glass of champagne.

There was still time. France wanted to run, but her legs wouldn't move. She tried to ignore the wild pulse pounding in every vein.

His controlled gaze swept the room, coming to rest on her. Dark blue eyes flickered with recognition and a muscle beside his mouth jerked.

Tiny beads of moisture popped along her upper lip. For a suspended, crystalline second, time seemed to stop before shattering into a thousand crashing pieces.

How many times had she imagined running into him? Never, never had she thought it would be like this.

Joanna held France's forearm, leaning closer. "What did you say? There's so much noise in here."

Her sister-in-law's question barely scratched the surface of France's consciousness. *Attempted rape.* The words cracked in her head like gunshots, violent and hard. A feeling of nausea swelled in her, sending a shiver down her spine.

Partygoers milled around Stephen, pressing him against the wall. France nervously traced the edge of her jacket with a thumb and an index finger as the men and women around him seemed to blur, then fade away. She saw no one—no one but Stephen. And there was absolutely no doubt that he saw her.

"No," her voice whispered between clenched teeth. *Attempted rape.* Again the words burned across her mind, seeming to solidify in a single, searing pain. She pressed her fingers against her temple, trying in vain to blot them out. Not Stephen Foley! Not the man whose image had occupied her thoughts almost endlessly for the past four weeks. He'd served time, yes. But not for that. Someone had to have made a mistake.

Her heart pounded louder and louder, like the warning beat of an Indian drum. Instinctively, her eyes flew open, zeroing in even more acutely on the tall man across the room.

Stephen edged toward her. His iron-dark gaze caught hers, and held. A hot streak ripped through her, and the drumbeat quickened. Moisture dampened her palms. She ran first one hand, then the other against the soft folds of her skirt, fighting the suffocating desire to run away.

"France, are you listening?" Joanna was staring at her.

"Of course. What did you say?" She tried to focus on the conversation.

"That's what *I* asked *you*. I thought you said something."

"Did I?" France smiled weakly. She hadn't spoken Stephen's name aloud. Or had she? The air in the room felt thick as she drew it through dry lips.

"Are you okay?" Concern laced Joanna's voice. "You look kind of pale. Maybe you need some fresh air."

"I'm fine. It's too hot in here, that's all." France drove back the wave of hysteria rising in her throat. Her sister-in-law had no idea what she needed. And she'd probably pass out if she did.

Despite what she'd just been told about Stephen Foley, France still longed to bury her face in the strength of his shoulder, to feel his breath warm against her face.

She shook as a familiar, tantalizing tingle rippled across her abdomen, then down her limbs. She knew what it felt like to mold every inch of her against the smooth firmness of him, skin to skin, muscle to muscle. She knew what it was to be filled with him, to soak in his power, his tenderness.

France's eyes misted at the thought of what they had already shared. He had touched her, opened her senses, made love to her. She needed this man. God, she still wanted him. Her silent admission startled and embarrassed her. A niggling inner voice sneered, *You should know better.*

Her blood continued to surge. She had to get away. "I...it's getting late, Joanna. Perhaps I should be leaving."

"You can't. You just got here. It's not even midnight."

"I know, but I'm tired. And I have to get up early in the morning." France hated to lie. "This kind of party isn't really my thing, anyway. You know that. Tell Paul I'm sorry, okay?" She tried hard to force the wobble from her voice. The air seemed to vibrate as Stephen pressed closer each second.

"Why don't you just go outside for a while? You'll feel better."

"I think he's looking at you." She'd forgotten about the features reporter. Now the older woman prodded France with an elbow. "He is. How exciting. He's coming this way."

"Nonsense." France swallowed and turned her back to Stephen. "There are at least fifty other people in this room. Why should he look at me?"

"You act as if you know him." Joanna's fingers pressed more firmly into France's arm. Her perceptive glance leapt from France to Stephen, then back again.

"That's crazy. How could I?"

"Where're you going, Sis? Here's your champagne." Paul pushed his way through several people and offered her a slim-stemmed crystal glass filled with bubbling liquid.

Suddenly France's chest felt like a lead sinker, heavy and unable to expand. She glanced almost simultaneously at her brother, at Joanna, at the woman reporter and at Stephen, mere yards away. His lips formed her name.

The walls seemed to press in on her, trapping and suffocating. What could she say to Stephen...now that she *knew*?

"I...I need to get out." She waved her hand at the champagne. "Sorry. I'm...sorry."

Her long fingers pressed the fabric of her jacket to her breast. She turned abruptly then pushed her way urgently to the door.

"France." Paul's voice followed her.

"Let her go." France heard Joanna interrupt him. "It's hot in here. She just needs some air."

With a disturbing sigh, France pulled the door shut behind her. The raucous sounds of the revelers faded as she stepped off the porch into a pure night world. Someone had cleared a narrow path through the snow on the sidewalk, and she followed it to a secluded spot at the back of the house.

France leaned her head against the side of the three-story brick home. Above her, brilliant stars blinked through a filigree of bare branches. She glanced around. Several shovels stood propped against the wall, and a broad expanse of snow spread out unmarred to the edge of a garden in front of her. Surely, no one could find her here. She needed time to think.

A slim band of pain ringed her forehead and she rubbed her knuckles along it, trying to smooth the ache away. Why? Why, in God's heaven, did Stephen rape... No, she corrected herself. He hadn't done it...he couldn't...or could he?

Hot tears welled in her eyes, and she tipped her head to the sky. Damn the stars! How dare they appear so peaceful when her insides were slowly, tormentingly being rent apart.

She sucked in her breath, relishing the way the cold night air bit like tiny daggers into her lungs. She deserved the pain for wanting him the way she did.

"France?"

Damn! The brick wall scraped into her back as she straightened. She could recognize that strong, low voice anywhere. Stephen had found her.

"Go away." She knew he wouldn't. And she also knew she couldn't trust herself with him, alone. Her heart constricted and she forced back the impulse to dash in the opposite direction across the snow. She wouldn't get far in her rotten, skimpy heels.

"It's cold out here." Light from the porch silhouetted his tall body against a snow-dusted hedge. It outlined the thick hair she longed to run her fingers through, and softly traced the straight lines of his shoulders and lean legs. Even though he stood at the far end of the house, she felt every female instinct within her tremble.

"Let me worry about that." Silently she cursed her voice for wavering. It mustn't give her away. Not now, when she had to be strong.

"We need to talk." Ice crunched as he moved toward her.

"Do we?" France pressed her back and the palms of her hands into the ragged brick, and watched him. She felt like a trapped animal. Cool moonlight reflected on the hard angles of his cheekbones. It glistened across the hidden depths of his eyes, then cast his shadow far over the snow. She'd forgotten just how handsome he was.

He stood before her, blocking out the light from the porch. "You know we do."

"I think I've heard enough already. Don't you?" The controlled steadiness of her voice amazed her. She wished she felt as sure as she sounded.

He winced almost imperceptibly and she cringed inside, despising herself for causing it. She heard Stephen let out a slow breath and felt the knot in her throat tighten. She didn't want to look at him. The moon made crazy patterns on the tangled branches of an enormous oak tree, and she strained to focus on them.

"All I know is that you haven't heard anything from me." He lowered his voice. "Look." His fingers closed around her wrist, and she felt her back stiffen. "Look at me."

"All right." She faced him, meeting his stare in the near-darkness. "Are you satisfied?" France tried to yank her arm free, but his grip tightened. Almost painfully, his fingers pulled at the soft fabric of her sleeve. Even in the dim light France glimpsed the determined set of his jaw. It startled her and her gaze dropped.

"I'm sorry." He released her.

A tremor radiated up from her toes. It wasn't caused by the cold but by the nearness of this man for whom her every cell clamored. She crossed her arms tightly, controlling a shiver. "You wanted to talk. I'm listening."

"Are you were running away from me?"

"I wanted some fresh air."

Stephen ran the back of one hand down her arm. "You're shivering." Silently he shrugged out of his jacket. He wrapped it carefully around her shoulders, then slowly traced its collar and lapels. "Perhaps this'll help. Since you insist on staying out here...." His voice faded.

The hypnotic pressure of his fingers brought memory after titillating memory careening back. Impulsively she lowered her cheek and rubbed it against the rough fabric. The movement stilled his hands, scant inches from the sensitive skin at the hollow of her throat. She sensed his inherent tenderness. It tugged at her, threatened to pull her into him.

"Now *you'll* freeze."

"I won't." His eyes lowered as he concentrated on her lips, her rounded chin.

"You will." France frowned, then held her breath as his fingers traveled slowly down, then hovered mere inches from the swell of her breasts. Instinctively, their tips hardened, begging for his touch.

"Maybe I don't care," he whispered. His thumbs rubbed back and forth along the fold at the material's edge.

"Stephen, please." She closed her eyes. She didn't want it, but the prickling fire smoldered, then flickered in the depths of her loins. Her nipples distended against the stimulating fabric of the camisole, and she heard his sharp intake of breath when her lips parted. Nothing, nothing had changed between them.

"France."

She opened her eyes, not daring to move. Their breath hung between them in frosty clouds. The moment seemed suspended. He bent his head, brought his lips so close to hers she could almost feel their firmness, taste their saltiness.

"No, damn it. No." The second split apart. He thrust his hands into his pants pockets, then stepped back, pushing himself against the wall beside her. "What the hell am I thinking about?" He glanced at her. "You know what you do to me, don't you?"

She felt crazy, short of breath. It was madness to even be here, alone with this man. But the very feel of his shoulder touching hers intoxicated her, stoked the fires. She pulled his jacket more closely around her, nestled into its thick folds. His body heat still filled them, and she savored his warmth, drawing it into her. The corduroy smelled of him, clean and excitingly male. "Tell me what I do to you, Stephen." What was she saying?

"I think you know the answer to that question. You're supposed to make me keep my distance."

"I didn't ask you to follow me out here."

"How could I do anything else?" He shrugged his shoulders. "I didn't expect to run into you tonight."

The flatness of his statement sobered her. "Seeing you was a bit of a surprise for me, too."

"I'm going to be doing drawings for the *Review* again. That's why I'm here. But I suppose you know that." He stabbed at a clump of ice with the toe of one shoe.

"Mmm. I heard in there. My brother's an editor on the city desk. That's why *I'm* here."

"Paul. Paul Richards is your brother?"

"Yes."

"Of course. It's obvious now. I can see the resemblance." He kicked hard at another frozen mound. "This isn't doing either of us any good. I'm going back inside, and you'd be smart to do the same thing. I should never have come out here after you. Return the jacket when you're through with it." He started to turn away.

"Wait, Stephen." France caught his arm. "I'm glad you're here—glad we're here. You were right. We need to talk.... We need more time to be alone, to...to find out how we feel."

"If anything, we've been alone too much already." Gently, he pulled his arm from her grasp. "Come on. We're both freezing. If you really want to talk, we can do it inside."

"There're too many people in there. Let's go somewhere else, someplace quiet."

"Wake up, France." Stephen's sharpness startled her. He'd never spoken to her like that before. "It's pointless. I was wrong when I thought we had anything to discuss. Think about it. What difference can it make, now that you know what I am—why I was in prison." He hesitated. "Let's just call it quits and say good-bye."

"I don't believe a word of what I heard in there." France stood in front of him, clutching the bulk of his jacket to her breasts. "You're innocent."

"Well, France Marriotte's probably the only person in the entire world who feels that way." A corner of his mouth turned up cynically.

"How do *you* feel?"

Her question hushed in the stillness, and she heard his rough intake of breath.

"That's my business—and I've had plenty of time this past year to give it lots of thought."

"Okay, okay." She sensed herself losing him. The thought terrified her. "I've got a better idea. Let's go dancing. We can unwind. I know a great club on East Fifty-first. You'll love it."

"Now I'm sure you're crazy!"

"Come on. Risk it. What do you have to lose?"

"Forget it, France. The only place I'm going is Denver Place."

"Denver Place?"

"Home."

Her laugh was hollow. "Are you serious? Is that where you really want to be? Or are you just afraid of being alone with me?"

"If you're going dancing, then go." He shot the words at her. "I don't want to join you. Is that so difficult to understand?" His eyes flashed back shards of moonlight.

"Fine. But I hope you know how stubborn you are, Stephen Foley." Sudden anger riled through her. "You're nothing but a stubborn fool." She dragged his jacket from her shoulders and threw it against his chest. "Here. You're going to need this to keep the cold out…if anything can."

Stephen watched France dash across the walk. There was still time to catch her, but what was the point? It would be wrong to take what he wanted so desperately and selfishly. For a few crazy moments after he first saw her in that awful crush it had seemed possible for them to be together again. *Dreamer.* Then he'd found her out here. And what he felt as soon as he got close was as much an overpowering sexual longing as…shoot. The distinctive grind of her Chevy truck engine scraped through the stillness. He headed for the house.

His life was going to be one long round of the kind of sick attention he'd gotten in there tonight. That, and the constant fear that one day another nut would accuse him of something else he hadn't done. He cared too much for France to subject her to that. Please, God, let him have the willpower to stay away from her.

"I'LL HAVE A MANHATTAN." France said vaguely. She scarcely heard the young barmaid's question. The girl smiled and set a cocktail napkin on the table. So young, France thought, then concentrated on tearing the napkin into narrow strips.

She felt old, but it didn't matter. Neither did the fact that the club reeked of cigarette smoke and stale beer. This wasn't where she'd planned to come when she asked Stephen to go dancing. She couldn't have endured being there alone, watching other couples—other lovers.

Her eyes smarted. Thank goodness there was more than one club on East Fifty-first.

The cool liquid of France's drink trickled down her parched throat. It soothed the dryness but not the seething hurt bubbling deeper inside. She'd done it again—let Stephen Foley go. Only this time she was the guilty one. She'd walked out on him like an angry little fool.

Guilty. She goaded herself sarcastically for her use of the word. How could she have been so reckless? She couldn't have done a better job of burning her bridges if someone had handed her a can of kerosene and a book of matches. The stupidity of her actions, her feelings of futility, forged a ball of pain in her abdomen.

She took another sip of her drink and squinted at the vivid neon lights bouncing off bottles behind the bar. They burned through the smoke in vibrant, snaky lines. A cheerless brilliance.

The table she'd chosen was in a dusky corner. She peered around her at the customers who filled almost every available inch of the tiny room. They all seemed engrossed in the familiar scene gyrating across a big television screen. Times Square. Laughing faces and a man who shouted into a microphone before the picture switched to couples dancing in a ballroom. A new year would soon begin. France leaned her elbows on the table and splayed her fingers across her face. No one would notice if she cried.

The table moved when someone bumped against it. She kept her head down.

"Aren't you even going to say you're glad I could make it?"

France started and dropped her hands into her lap. She clasped them together tightly to stop herself from touching him. *Stephen, Stephen*. If she looked directly at him, he'd know she'd been crying. "Hi. Glad you could make it," she said softly.

He slid into a chair beside her. Voices babbled senselessly around them while France felt herself closed off in a silent place...with Stephen. Finally she managed to meet his eyes.

"You okay?" He tipped his head a little and studied her face intently.

"Of course. You?"

"Fine." The corners of his mouth twitched. "Come on, darlin'. Let's dance."

Chapter Six

"To what?" France peered around the gloomy room. "Where?"

Stephen scooted back his chair. "Perverse—all women are perverse. But you'd win first prize if it came to a contest." While he spoke he rummaged in his pockets and sorted through a collection of change. "Don't move from that spot." He went to a jukebox tucked into a corner by the bar.

His long body bent over the lighted machine as he studied song titles. One hand rested on a lean hip beneath the flawlessly tailored jacket, the other was characteristically jammed into the front of his hair. A bubble of delight formed inside her and swelled. *Wonderful man, I don't think I give a damn what you're supposed to have done.* The magic he wielded over her hadn't dimmed.

Heavy bass chords hammered against the smoke-filled air; then the rhythm changed abruptly. Gently paced guitars accompanied a nasal lament about lost love and riding herd alone in the night. Stephen turned and raised his hands in exasperation. His brow was wrinkled as he led her to a tiny space in front of the rear door. France glanced at the green exit sign a second before she was drawn against the only body she wanted to touch.

"They'll lynch us," she said, laughing up at him. "People come here to watch the screen and drink, not dance. This racket's going to ruin Times Square and their big-band sound. What is this, anyway? I thought you had good taste."

He glowered at her in mock outrage. "*You* told me you wanted to go somewhere and dance. Now you blame me because there's nothing worth dancing to" A wry grin transformed his expression. "This is awful, though. The name of the piece sounded better than the others and, besides, I wanted an excuse to hold you."

France's stomach somersaulted. *You didn't need an excuse.* "I thought you weren't coming. What made you change your mind?"

"Those unbelievable, chameleon eyes of yours. They change color even in moonlight. When you stalked off, they were glittering green. Whether you knew it or not, you were flashing a challenge and gentlemen just can't resist that." As he swung her in a complete circle, she clutched his arms to keep her balance. Stephen steadied her and their thighs brushed. "This music's sounding better all the time."

His hands were warm at her waist, and France's skin prickled from his nearness. "How did you know where to find me?"

"I wish you hadn't asked that. Do you know how many clubs there are on East Fifty-first?"

"No," she muttered, concentrating on his vaguely luminous shirtfront.

Stephen threaded his fingers into her hair and forced her to meet his eyes. "Dozens. And I went into every one of them. I almost didn't bother with this dump because I was so sure you wouldn't come into a place like this alone. Do you like danger?"

"You're overreacting," she said, thinking that she was dancing with the most dangerous element to enter her life in a long time. "My brother and I came here once to watch the Cowboys play the Broncos. It's okay."

"Not for a beautiful woman alone...particularly not late on New Year's Eve when a lot of people are looking for someone to kiss at midnight."

France realized the music had stopped but couldn't remember when. They studied each other's expressions in silence, reading the shadows and highlights cast by shifting colored light.

Stephen frowned and dug into his pocket. "If we stand here like this much longer *we'll* be competing with Times Square. Why don't you help me choose the music this time? You probably know more about this kind of stuff than I do."

Slipping a hand through his arm, France pulled him back through the tangle of chairs. "I'll ignore your innuendos about my taste. I don't think I want to stay here anymore...unless you want a drink."

The Manhattan she'd ordered sat almost untouched on the table. Stephen picked it up, raising it to the light until the imprint of France's lower lip showed in a hazy, pink curve. Deliberately, he placed his mouth on the same spot and took a long swallow. "Somehow, I prefer sharing yours."

France's muscles tightened. A jolting sensation climbed rapidly up each vertebra. "Why do I get the feeling we've had this conversation before?"

"I'm not sure, but I get the same feeling. I don't know why you'd risk being with me after hearing what you did tonight. But you'll have to be the one to tell me to take a walk."

A tiny buzz started in France's brain and gradually became louder. "It's stuffy in here." She looked deep into his incredible blue eyes. "Would you take me home?"

"You want me to drive you home?

"Mmm. Please. But you don't have to put up the Christmas tree this time."

Stephen laughed. "We have two cars."

"Correction. You may have a car, but I haven't graduated from my elegant pickup. We could meet at my place...." Her voice trailed away. The thought of being separated from him again, even for a short while, made her feel panic-stricken.

"We'll go in the pickup. I can get a taxi back. But, France..." He cleared his throat while she waited. "Nothing. Let's go."

FRANCE'S SKIRT RUSTLED as Stephen settled her in the pickup. *Must be lined with some sort of satin stuff.* He closed his mind against the picture of slippery fabric brushing across her smooth legs. The door slammed closed and he stared at her in the darkness, seeing her eyes glint before she lowered her head.

"Here." She reached through the open window to give him the keys. When he threw them up and caught them again, she giggled—a soft, enticing sound—and he knew they were both thinking of the first time he had flipped her car keys into the air.

The engine clucked and shivered several times before it caught. Stephen grinned sideways at France. She smiled back and touched his hand, which curled more tightly around the steering wheel.

"Isn't it about time you got yourself a more reliable form of transportation?" He hoped his voice only sounded odd to him. Her cool fingers had left an imaginary imprint on the back of his hand.

"Bite your tongue." she drawled back, exaggerating her accent. "This is a *very* sensitive machine that has served me well. Plus which, I can't afford to throw money around on impressive *wheels*."

Stephen struggled for a slick comeback, but couldn't think of one. The silken black night crowded against the cab windows, more suffocating than inspiring. This was wrong—he was wrong to have given in and come after her. He had nothing to offer her but a share in the mess his life had become. Even at the party, with all those fawning people, the veiled disgust had been plain behind their animated expressions.

If things had been different...if it had never happened. If, if... He shook his head. Nothing would change. The time to stop this thing was now and he was the one to do it, before they went too far. And with France, it was almost impossible to hold back.

"How've you been?"

Stephen jumped and glanced at her. She was as uncomfortable as he. "Fine...lousy. How about you?"

Her head was pressed against the seat. Light from the dash outlined her throat, but her face was turned away from him. The faint greenish glow shone across her tousled curls. *Dammit, Foley. Make it quick and clean.*

"We're talking about nothing, Stephen." Still she didn't look at him. "But it'll be okay."

No, it won't, he thought. The last stretch of highway before Maple Ridge rolled by and he turned into the housing area. With a sudden thrust of speed, he drove into France's driveway.

Now. "France, wait a minute." He wanted to hold her but leaned farther away instead. "Forgive me. I'm going to see you inside and then walk back to the main road. I'll call a cab from a booth when I get there.''

''Why?'' The question was low but it split the frigid air.

A tightness in his chest began to make him feel light-headed. He had to get some air. ''Because that's the way I want it. We got carried away for a little while. New Year's Eve madness, maybe. Call it anything that makes you happy. But don't push this anymore.''

Without allowing her time to reply, he jumped down and went to open her door. She beat him to it. Almost shooting from the cab, she turned her foot against a frozen lump of slush and twisted her ankle.

France grabbed his sleeve. ''Blast it. Give me my keys.'' He could hear her breathing catch. ''You're so right, Stephen. We'll call it some sort of madness. I hope you enjoy your little stroll.''

She felt him hovering at her shoulder but didn't trust herself to look at him. He wouldn't even come in to call a cab. It was starting to drizzle, but he'd rather walk back to the main highway in the rain and melting snow than be alone with her. France struggled to control the muscles that quivered at the corners of her mouth as she went to unlock the door. It was already open and gave beneath her hand.

In the dim hallway, she flipped on the light and froze. ''Stephen!''

''What is it? My God, France, what's the matter?''

France felt him come in behind her and reached back blindly until she could grab the hem of his jacket. ''That noise. Someone's in here. Let me out.'' She tried to push through the narrow space between Stephen and the wall to reach the door. Two solid arms caught and held her fast.

A gentle rumble started as her head rested against his chest. "If that's being made by a human, we'd better call out the National Guard." His laughter rocked her and she clung to his lapels with both hands. "I think the cold's caught up with your kitchen pipes. Sounds like air rattling behind a blockage. Let's hope they aren't completely frozen. By the way, if you didn't leave your front door unlocked you wouldn't half expect to find unwelcome guests waiting for you."

"Don't preach at me, Stephen Foley. I usually *do* lock it. Anyone can make a mistake." She was shaking and hated herself for it. The one time she needed to be cool, the stupid pipes had to act up and ruin her effort.

"Okay, darlin', okay. Your heart's jumping so hard I can feel it. Just stay still a minute, then I'll help check things out."

Darlin'. That word... Softly intoned as only he could say it. Slow, winding, about to grab her willing soul. France obediently allowed him to hold her and wished the moment would last forever.

"Better?" Gently, he pushed her away. "Shall we take a look?"

France pressed her lips together and peered awkwardly up at him. "Thanks. I feel like an absolute fool." She grinned sheepishly. "I'm really not a scaredy-cat. Loud noise is about the only thing that scares me. I pick up anything that crawls and I probably wouldn't even notice a snake in my bed." Her breath caught in her throat before she clamped her teeth together. Nothing could have stopped the dull heat that rushed to her cheeks.

Stephen stared at her, one corner of his mouth twitching. "Don't try to put that one right. You sure have a way with words." The twitch became a lopsided grin. "Maybe

I'll use your phone while I'm here. I left my coat in the Porsche and I'm likely to be pretty soggy if I leg it very far. Anyway, I'd better make absolutely sure you won't go through another noise crisis. That was quite a performance you gave."

"I wasn't acting," she snapped, forgetting her embarrassment. He thought she'd used the pesky clanking sound—which seemed to have stopped now—to get him to stay. "If you think I pretended to be afraid just to get you in here, don't flatter yourself. Anyway, I'm more resourceful than that. I could have faked a twisted ankle or something."

The hall seemed to become smaller and Stephen filled all of it. His expression sobered. With exaggerated care, he slammed the door and leaned his left hand on the wall behind her head. Thoughtfully, he rested his chin on his chest. "You already tried the ankle. What did you have in mind for the 'something'?"

France felt the tension flow away, released on her own muffled snort. She landed a playful jab on Stephen's hard middle. "You're mean. Wait till I find your weakness," she said, laughing. "You can expect no mercy."

He caught her hand, straightened her fingers and trapped them against his chest. Their eyes met and France's grin ebbed. No trace of humor lit the intensity of his indigo gaze. "My weakness?" His heartbeat was strong and rapid, as fast as France's own.

The moment dissipated with Stephen's sharp withdrawal. "Pipe patrol." He had stalked purposefully into the kitchen before she could collect enough composure to follow him.

"The water runs and everything looks fine under here." Only his bent back and the soles of his shoes were visible between open cupboard doors beneath the sink. "Except your garbage needs emptying."

France's chin quivered. Traitorous prickling started behind her eyelids and she deliberately slowed her breathing. "You're crazy, Stephen." Why couldn't she hold this space in time—the teasing warmth that invaded sweetly and turned so quickly into pain? Even the pain was better than the emptiness she knew would follow when he walked back out of her life.

Stephen sat down abruptly on the floor, his wrists draped over his knees. "I think you hit it, France. Crazy. We both know we're dragging out the inevitable." He closed the cupboards, jabbing first one and then the other door with an index finger. "Where's the phone?"

He's right, France thought, *but it doesn't make it any easier.* "On the wall. I'll get the directory."

He pushed himself upright. "I make sure I keep the number of a cab company handy," he said stiffly.

Indignation flared in France until she saw the expression in his eyes. Hurting, just as she was, and just as confused. She wasn't imagining it—Stephen wanted her, too. "Yes," she whispered, and escaped across the hall to her bedroom.

The directory was under the phone on the bedside table. France's fingers felt numb as she removed the book. *Please, let there be a way for us to reach each other. Help me change this mess around. We could try being friends and move on from there.... Friends—who am I kidding?* She concentrated on the thud on the rug, then the click on polished boards beneath her shoes as she returned to the kitchen. Friends could become lovers—it didn't work the other way around.

"Here it is. Should be in the Yellow Pages," France said with a breathiness caused by the constriction in her throat.

Stephen was perched on the edge of the table, long legs stretched out, arms crossed over his broad chest. He chewed his bottom lip as he watched her.

France avoided meeting his eyes. "I'll look it up if you like." It seemed important to be doing something.

"Sorry I snarled at you." Stephen stood beside her and took the heavy book from her cold fingers. "Uptight, I guess."

While he riffled through pages and dialed a number, France pulled the overflowing garbage can from beneath the sink and hauled it through the door to the carport. She still wore the pea coat she'd put on in the truck, but damp air seemed to seep through the thick fabric to permeate her flesh and bones.

"Let me do that." Stephen seized the can, dumped its contents and steered France back into the kitchen. "Can't get the taxi company. Line's busy." He shoved the door into its jamb with an elbow.

She took off her coat and hung it on a wall peg. "How many did you try?"

He replaced the container. She couldn't see his face. "One. It's New Year's Eve, remember? I'd better start walking."

"You will not," she exploded. "Stephen?"

He rounded on her. "What?"

The challenge in his blue eyes turned her legs to jelly. "Take my truck back to the bar. It'll be easy for me to get it tomorrow."

Stephen shook his head and held out both palms. "I don't know what to do." His voice held an appeal. "I...damn it. I know I should leave. This isn't fair to you.

But I don't want to go. Tell me to get out, France. Please. Make it easier for both of us.''

She started toward him, but he transmitted a silent message that warned her to stop. "I won't do that." The words cracked thinly. "Can't we sit down and have the drink we didn't finish earlier? Is it impossible to talk sanely to each other?''

"Doesn't knowing what I was in jail for scare the hell out of you?" He twisted on his heel and stared at the ceiling. "Oh, darlin', it should.''

France fought her desire to go to him. "I'm not afraid of you.''

He shoved his jacket back to hook his thumbs through narrow belt loops. "Even after hearing what I am?''

"What are you, Stephen?''

His body jerked almost imperceptibly. "A man who was convicted of—''

"No!" France cut him off. "We don't have to talk about it. Not now.''

His eyes, when they met hers, glittered harshly. "What *should* we discuss—plants? My comic strip? Then what? You're lonely, so am I. It wouldn't be hard to help each other through the night, but what about tomorrow? Sooner or later you're going to start asking those questions." He held up a hand. "Don't say you won't.''

A defiant surge rushed through France. He was telling her how she felt, would feel in the future. "I can make my own decisions, thanks. Let me ask you something. What do you really think of me? No, wait—it's my turn. You can't pull all the shots here. Do you see me as a tramp who goes to bed with the closest warm body?" Her eyes felt strained wide open and her scalp tingled.

The brittle expression softened to a sheen that could have been moisture before he closed his eyes. "I think you're the most innocent, trusting woman I ever met. That first...the time we were together still seems like an impossible dream. Why it happened, I don't know, but I don't think either of us regrets it."

In about one second I'm going to make a fool of myself by begging you to make it happen again. France opened the dishwasher so hard the door bounced on its hinges. "We're going to have that drink. Then we'll try to get a taxi. The later it gets, the better chance we should have." She removed two clean glasses, willing him not to argue. "Is wine okay? Or would you rather have something else?"

"Do you have any scotch?"

France went to the pantry and produced a full bottle, which she flourished with a phony grin. "I'll join you. Maybe we can make a dent in this."

"You're on." Stephen took the whisky while France got ice; then he guided her into the living room.

While France held the glasses, he opened the bottle and poured a hefty shot into one and a thimbleful into the other.

France bit the inside of her cheek to control a grin. "Which of us is drying out?"

Stephen gave her the small measure. "The degree of effect alcohol has is directly related to body weight," he said seriously. "And from the look of that unopened bottle, you aren't used to it."

"I'm touched by your concern," France said. "Don't worry, I probably won't turn into a wild woman on this."

"Darn." A devilish smirk transformed his features. "Let's swap."

They touched glasses and raised them to their lips, each watching the other's face. "Happy New Year," France said quietly.

"Happy New Year." Stephen set his drink on the table and started to heap kindling and logs into the fireplace from the brass box on the hearth. He lit some paper beneath the pile and stood up. "I think we did this once before, too."

France sensed the fight he was waging. Why couldn't she say the things she wanted to tell him? Why wasn't she even sure what they were?

Stephen folded his arms on the mantel and stared at the flames licking the dark edges of the wood. Damp bark sputtered, then caught in a spray of flashing colors.

Very slowly, France approached him, her fingers clenched around her glass. When she got close she hesitated, then stood on tiptoe to brush the corner of his mouth with her own.

She felt a shudder pass the length of him before he looked at her. "It can't work. I want it to—believe me, France, I want it to. But everything's stacked against us, including a lot of things you'll never know about me."

Beads of sweat stood out on his temples and she wiped them with her palm. "All you talk about are the why nots, never the things we have going for us." Slipping an arm through his, she studied the fire's increasing glow. "Let it all go tonight. We need each other. That's enough for now. I'm only asking for a small piece of you—not a lifetime commitment." She laughed cynically as she slid her glass onto the mantel. "I went that route once before."

"The guy must have been a fool." Stephen straightened her hand along his forearm, outlining each finger. He bent to kiss them lightly and France's stomach flipped.

Carefully, she touched his hair where firelight created a burnished aureole. "Stephen, we have to forget the past." France laid her cheek on his shoulder and felt a fragile bubble of empathy enclose them. She couldn't allow him to slip away from her again.

In a desperate motion, he gathered her into his arms. "You *are* an innocent. We can decide to forget, but we can't erase facts." His jaw rested atop her head.

France hugged his waist beneath his jacket, rubbed her face against the smoothness of his shirt. She felt his heartbeat, smelled the winter's air and wood scent that seemed a part of him. She pressed her chin into the hollow of his shoulder. "If there was no past and you could do or be whatever you wanted right now, what would you choose?"

His mouth found her brow and she felt him smile.

"Hmmm. Well, genie. First I'd like to make love to you, all night, in that wonderful bed of yours." He covered her lips with his fingertips to stop her reply. "Not finished. Genies always grant three wishes. Then I'd like us to wake up together in the morning and shower together, and have breakfast together, and..."

"Hey, that's more than three. Then we watch the Cotton Bowl together."

Stephen's laugh was explosive. "What?"

"The Cotton Bowl. You haven't forgotten that, have you?"

"Uh, no. Of course not. I didn't realize you were a football fan."

"There's probably a lot you haven't realized about me," France replied archly. He became still and she looked up at him. He wasn't smiling anymore. "Kiss me, Stephen."

"My pleasure, ma'am." He nuzzled her hair aside and nipped her ear, then traced a line along her jaw and down to the hollow of her throat with the tip of his tongue. He surrounded her neck, tangling his fingers in her hair. His mouth and tongue teased her, meeting her cheeks, her closed eyelids, the bridge of her nose in fleeting brushes. When he touched her mouth, it was with his thumbs while he studied her eyes. Slowly, he bent to run his tongue along her bottom lip, across the smooth surface of her teeth. And all the time France massaged his taut body, pressed closer, longed to feel his skin on hers.

"France," he whispered against her lips.

"Mmm?" She met his tongue with her own, seeking the erotic textures inside his mouth.

Stephen's weight pushed against her and she almost stumbled. He caught her against him without losing her mouth. His kiss was deep, searching, rocking her head urgently back and forth as his breathing became louder. When he lifted his face it was flushed, his eyes like a reflection of a night sky. He dragged in a breath and held it.

France loosened his tie and pulled it from beneath his collar. Shakily, she started to undo his shirt buttons until he grasped both of her hands in one large fist.

"I want to take you to bed. Come with me, France— we'll close out the whole world. It's outside that door, but we don't have to let it in here."

"Oh, Stephen, we don't ever have to let it in." As he took her hand and led her to the bedroom, she knew she was right. Their lives lay ahead of them, fresh and clean. No more prison vans, and never any recriminations.

Stephen drew her into the room and closed the door. He blocked her path, slipping the velvet jacket from her shoulders. "I couldn't even feel you through this thing. But you were a knockout standing in the middle of that gabbling crowd tonight." He folded his jacket in half over the back of a small overstuffed chair. "You didn't belong. When I first saw you, there was a marathon second when I ate you up." He wound a heavy lock of her hair around one finger. "Your hair was like a beacon, as if it was drawing all the light in the room to it. And your eyes were huge. Then I saw your expression change and knew what that lady had told you about me. A hobnail boot in the gut couldn't have done any more damage. I've lived with the promise—and the threat—of seeing you again. I didn't know what I'd do if I didn't, yet I was terrified I would for the same reason. Does that sound insane?"

His cool fingers made tiny circles along her collarbone and came to rest at the base of her throat. Everywhere he touched, a prickling heat started and burned deep until her belly and thighs felt heavy with desire.

"How could it, when I've been through the same hell? But we're here now and the rest doesn't matter." She arched her head back, inviting his kiss, and Stephen reacted with a tenderness that suffused her in tingling warmth.

France moaned, answering her own building passion, and guided his hands to her breasts. Beneath the gauzy camisole she wore no bra, and she heard Stephen's sharp intake of breath as he found the unrestrained softness.

"God, what you do to me." He pressed one strong thigh between her legs. "You're incredible...beautiful."

The throb he started with the pressure of his leg darted into her loins. France wound her arms tightly around his neck and pressed herself against him. The fever that was overtaking her body was echoed in the hardness of his.

Resolutely, Stephen put several inches between them and hooked an arm under France's knees. He carried her to the foot of the bed and set her down gently. "We're going to slow this thing down, darlin'...."

She reached for him. "I don't want to..."

Two firm hands surrounded her upper arms and held on tight. "You will. Trust me. It'll be worth it."

Stephen took off his jacket and threw it on top of France's. Immediately the ice-blue shirt followed. She noticed his economy of movement, his lithe grace. Muscle rippled beneath smooth skin and then he was kneeling before her.

"Sit still and humor me." He smiled. A fuzzy sheen outlined his shoulders. Shadows lay in the hollows of his face and body and shifted constantly as he moved.

With maddening care, he kissed an exact outline around the square neckline of her camisole. "You smell as wonderful as I remembered. And I warned you what your perfume did to me." He placed another line of kisses from the tip of her left shoulder, down the outer edge of her strap to the vulnerable suggestion of swelling flesh. Nuzzling aside the fabric, his lips parted to taste her, and his sigh whispered across her skin.

"Stephen." France stroked his hair, fighting back the impulse to slide down beside him, draw him over her to make him give all that she wanted now.

"Take off the camisole."

A shudder coursed through him. When he lifted his head, he started to speak but brought his teeth together hard. The muscles in his jaw quivered. Tiny, fabric-covered buttons closed the front of her bodice. Stephen was an artist, a man with unerring dexterity, yet he fumbled with each small obstacle. Inch by inch, he opened the garment until it hung apart to reveal the deep cleavage between her full breasts.

Staring into her eyes, he gently placed his hands beneath the shimmery cloth until he could cup her breasts. France concentrated on the dull flush that darkened his impassioned features until the insistent pressure of his thumbs on her nipples made her tip her head back.

"You're in my blood, France," Stephen said, before his tongue replaced one teasing thumb. "Like a drug I want to stay addicted to." He ran a moist path to her other breast.

The unbearable weight of the flimsy camisole magically disappeared with his sweeping touch and she was crushed back against the mattress under Stephen's weight. The rough and smooth textures of him worked sorcery on her senses.

France curled her fingers into his bunched shoulder muscles, then flattened her palms and explored every inch she could reach. "You'll have to let me know if the reaction's favorable."

He kissed her briefly. "What?"

The pressure on her lips was immediately demanding and she struggled to take a breath. Stephen's hand was beneath her skirt, sliding upward over a smooth thigh. "Drug reaction," she murmured. "I hope it's a good one."

He laughed against her neck. "It will be."

France writhed, turning her head away. She forced a hand between their bodies until she could feel the pulsing rise of his desire. But heat, shooting to her core, stilled her attempt to free Stephen's belt, and she yielded to the purely physical ecstasy that broke over her in repeated swells.

"Stephen, Stephen..." She sobbed his name into his hair. "Come to me."

The rest of her clothes slithered noiselessly to the floor. Stephen shifted away. France's pulse quickened as he quickly stripped, then returned to cover her with his naked body, to wrap her in a firm embrace. He scooted them both up until their heads rested side by side on the pillows.

"Cold?" he asked, filling his hands with her hair.

"How could I be?" France arched into him and felt his tumid need. "Keep me warm, like this, Stephen." She urged him over her, opened her body to receive his, absorbed him into every secret, waiting place.

Stephen cried out, his words a jarred noise, muffled against the quilt. France couldn't make out what he said. But all that mattered was being joined with him, surging upward as one, the bonding of body and spirit. She wanted nothing more or less than to hold on to this capsule in time forever.

With the ultimate, engulfing force of their union, they shuddered as a single being and soared free of all boundaries. France felt tears well and slide across her temples. The joy inside expanded to drag a laugh from her throat before they lay breathlessly sated.

The warm dampness of their lovemaking had begun to cool on their skin when Stephen untangled their limbs enough to lift France and slide with her beneath the covers. She looked up into the eyes of a lover and suddenly her heart felt squeezed. With infinite tenderness, his visual caress covered her face as he swept tendrils of wet hair from her brow. A twisting doubt made her turn her head away for a second. Was she right about Stephen? She had to be. France rubbed his jaw, met his eyes and raised her head to give his lips a hard little kiss.

A shadow passed over his features. "All right, my sweet? Is anything wrong?"

He had sensed her slight withdrawal. Had she withdrawn? "Everything's wonderful." A small but sharp splinter of panic wriggled to life. Why now? A few minutes before... Oh, God. *You know he's innocent, France.*

If you didn't, you wouldn't be able to give yourself as you just did. You couldn't want him as you did—and will, again and again. He was watching her carefully. What was he thinking—that her physical appetite was spent and now she was asking herself those terrible questions?

Stephen kissed the end of her nose and she closed her eyes. "You make me feel safe," he said. "I told you that once before. I asked you why it was, but you never told me."

"I didn't know. Still don't."

"I think I do."

She felt cool air on her face as he moved. Looking up, she saw his upturned chin as he leaned on one elbow and supported his head.

"You've never questioned me. You believe in me without knowing or wondering why."

The squeezing sensation in her chest got tighter. "Yes," she breathed. "But that's because I'm right about you. You didn't do it, did you?"

A soon as the question passed her lips, nausea engulfed her. She did want him to deny his guilt. But his answer was to roll onto his back and lock his hands behind his neck.

France lay still. The only clock in the room was a small quartz alarm that made no noise, yet she heard seconds tick by. Although she felt icy, a film of sweat sprang onto her upper lip.

"Stephen, I didn't mean—"

"Yes, you did," he cut her off, swinging his feet to the floor in the same instant. His back was a curved shadow as he sat on the edge of the bed.

Her outstretched fingers met flesh that recoiled from the touch. "I'm sorry. I only wanted to hear you deny it.

Just once. I already know the answer, but I'd like you to tell me."

He was on his feet, staring down at her in the darkness, his eyes like glittering flashes. "If you're certain of my innocence, as you have so eloquently assured me, not once, but again and again, why did you have to ask?"

"I—" France's reply was cut off by the harsh sound of the doorbell. "Oh, God," she hissed before she could stop herself. Pressure inside her head threatened to burst it open.

Stephen switched on the bedside lamp and she shielded her eyes. "Who could that be? Are you expecting someone?"

"Turn off the light. Of course I'm not expecting anyone. Probably a New Year's Eve drunk. They'll go away." She would not look at him.

The insistent ringing came again and was repeated every few seconds until France met Stephen's gaze. She felt herself whiten. "We'll have to answer it."

"Stay there," he ordered, the lines of his face set hard. His pants were already around his knees. He jerked them all the way up and headed for the hall, still threading one end of his belt into its buckle.

France lay motionless until she heard an exclamation. The thud made by the front door when it slammed into the wall reverberated throughout the condo, and she leapt out of bed to grab a robe from the closet. She dragged it on and held it closed with both hands as she rushed from the bedroom.

"Stephen. What is it?" She turned the corner and almost collided with his back. "What is it?"

He stepped aside.

"Paul!"

Chapter Seven

"Is something wrong with Dad?" France choked on the question. "Joanna?" Paul's face was gray, only his eyes responded, shooting some emotion she couldn't read. "Answer me," she whispered hoarsely.

He ignored her, fixing his attention on Stephen, and then France translated the message in his features. *Oh, my God. He'll never understand.*

"Paul," she begged, "listen to me."

Stiff control became an explosive surge of energy as her brother lunged at Stephen, stopping short of the taller man, both fists clenched. "Listen to what, France?" He concentrated on Stephen, took in his naked chest, noted the belt still dangling undone. "Are you going to say something original like 'this isn't the way it looks'?"

Stephen slowly buckled his belt, keeping his awareness on Paul.

France stared, appalled at the sight of two men who meant so much to her facing each other in hatred. She couldn't choose between Stephen and her brother, not ever. "Let's go into the living room and sit down. We're all too upset to be rational."

"France." Paul rounded on her. "When someone at the party told me you'd been seen with Foley, I tried to convince myself they were wrong—or that you'd only had some polite conversation with the man. But you were gone, damn it, and then I discovered he'd left, too.'' He gripped her shoulders. "Do you know what you've done? You little fool—you've had sex with a convicted rapist!"

"Take your hands off her, Richards, or I'll take them off for you.'' Stephen spoke for the first time, and his voice was menacingly quiet. "And the sentence was for *attempted* rape. Not that it matters, but you're a newspaperman. I'm sure you want to keep your facts straight.''

Paul erupted. France felt rage boil from every pore as he piled into Stephen, driving a fist into his belly. Stephen's back thudded against the wall before he reacted, grasping Paul by the throat.

"Stop it,'' she screamed. "Please, stop it.''

Paul landed a blow on Stephen's jaw. France heard the crack of bone on bone as his head snapped back. As Stephen's knee found Paul's gut, both hands were descending on the exposed back of her brother's neck. She leapt forward, forcing her slight body between their two larger ones with all the strength she had.

The struggle stopped abruptly. Only the sound of heavy breathing punctuated the leaden silence before France started to cry. She tipped back her head, trying to stem the flow, and leaned against Stephen.

"Fix your robe,'' Paul rasped.

With shaking fingers, she wrapped it more tightly around her and cinched the belt. "Stephen and I met before,'' she started, then swallowed. "He didn't do what they said. Believe me, Paul. You've always trusted my judgment—now I really need your support.''

"Save it." Stephen eased himself away from her, rubbing his jaw. "Dear brother isn't going to buy it any more than anyone else would."

France took his hand but he pulled free. "Can we please talk about this?" she pleaded.

"Listen, Sis, I don't know how he managed to get around you, but he's no good. Take it from me." Paul slumped against the wall. "And although I hate to remind you, your choice of men hasn't exactly been outstanding. I don't like to mention—"

"Then don't," France shot back. "I want you out of here, Paul—now. Tomorrow we'll talk about it. Maybe, if I'm ready. Go home to Joanna."

"No, don't leave. *I'm* going." Stephen's voice cut into France, but before she could argue he strode toward the bedroom and she heard the door close.

"Go," she hissed, "before you wreck the rest of my life, Paul."

"What kind of line has he fed you? Are you so sex-starved you can't see past the end of your nose? I'm not leaving you here with him."

France raised a hand to slap her brother, but instead closed it in an impotent fist. "I want him. You can think what you like."

Footsteps behind her made her turn. Stephen was tucking in his shirt. His tie hung around his neck and the corduroy jacket was bunched beneath his arm. "Listen to him, France. He's right. You'll be safer with him."

"Foley, you son of a—. I'm going to finish you for this."

Through a mist of tears, France saw the distorted mask of Paul's face.

"What makes you think there's much left to finish?" Stephen's back was to them as he stood by the door and shrugged into his jacket.

"Before this you still had a job. You won't when I get to the managing editor."

Stephen swung to face Paul, and France cringed away from the fury she saw. "And what are you going to tell him, Paul? That he should fire me because your sister invited me into her bed?" He pulled open the door, letting in a blanket of cold, damp air. "See you around, Richards. At the office."

"Stephen," France cried.

He looked at her over his shoulder and his expression softened. "I'm sorry, darlin'."

Then he was gone, closing the door quietly behind him, leaving a void that spread and turned France's insides to frozen emptiness.

France's legs wouldn't hold her. Her knees buckled and she slid to sit on the hall floor, both arms wrapped around her shins. She wanted to cry but couldn't. With her head bent forward she rocked slowly.

"That bastard." Paul's voice came from a great distance. "France, France, I love you. I should have seen how lonely you were." He knelt beside her and wrapped her in his arms, held her head against his chest.

The well of misery and confusion gradually flooded her heart until, finally, the tears came. Her brother did love her, as much as she loved him, with a deep unshakable protectiveness. But the man her senses couldn't release had just walked out of her front door, again. No one could ever fill his place.

She sobbed, and Paul took over the rocking motion, moving their two bodies. "Don't. I can't bear it." His voice broke and she knew her strong brother was crying, too. If only she could make him understand what she felt for Stephen. "Come on. Sit in the kitchen and I'll make us both a hot drink. I need to call Joanna and tell her you're okay. She was frightened to death."

France let him hold her hand, as he had when they were children, and walk her to the kitchen. He scraped out a chair and settled her into it, wrapped the robe around her knees, then put on the kettle. His anxious gaze never left her as he called Joanna, plainly cutting short his wife's stream of questions.

"You're wrong about Stephen," France said at last when he'd hung up the phone. "He's a beautiful, sensitive human being."

Paul set two mugs of herb tea on the table and sank into a chair. France had never seen him look so tired.

"He worked for me," she continued. "We met at the nursery when he was on the release program. I know his sentence was a terrible mistake. What happened with you tonight will only reinforce his belief that no one's ever going to accept his innocence." She tried to block out the conversation Paul had interrupted when he rang the bell.

"France." Paul rubbed his eyes, then reached across the table to cover her cold hands. "Listen to me very carefully. You don't want to hear what I'm going to tell you, but you have to."

"You can't change my mind."

"I think I can." His grip tightened. "I know some of the details of Foley's crime. Not everything. I wasn't interested enough to stick around for it all, but what he did—"

"Was supposed to have done..."

"Just listen, France. Hear me out to the end. The guy was found guilty of assault with intent to rape. Do you know what that means?"

Numbly, she shook her head.

"It means he beat the woman up first. He physically attacked some woman who wouldn't give in to him. They said she was a mess. What helped convict Foley were the scratches she made on him trying to defend herself. No, don't shut this out."

France had attempted to pull her hands from his. She thought she was going to be sick. "I don't believe you," she whispered.

"Ask him. No, on second thought, don't. Don't ever speak to the man again. Just ask yourself this. Forgive me, but you didn't fight him, did you?"

Fresh tears slid down her cheeks. "I didn't want to."

Paul winced as if her words hurt him. "Okay." He drew in a long breath. "But if you'd said no, would he have taken the rejection gracefully, or would he have forced you, hit you, maybe? I guess we were lucky this time. Because, France, if he'd hurt you, I'd have killed him."

France stared in horror at her gentle brother, the rescuer who championed every cause. His face was the face of a stranger. "No. Oh, no, Paul, you're wrong. I was the one who brought him here. He didn't want to stay. Stephen tried harder than I did not to let anything happen between us. If there was an aggressor, it was me." She blushed and pressed her palms to her cheeks.

Paul stood up so forcefully he had to stop his chair from tipping backward. "I blame Larry Marriotte for this." He strode to the window and stared out into the night. "You never got over the guy. If you had, you'd have married again years ago. He made you think you weren't worth anything, and you believed it. I hate Larry for what he did to you. Foley's the smooth, sexy type who knows how to prey on an insecure female."

"Don't bring all that up." A dull pain hummed behind France's eyes. Why would Paul start on Larry now? "Larry and I got married too young. We both changed—he just did it sooner than I did. What happened to us has nothing to do with my feelings for Stephen, or his for me."

"The only thing that changed for that selfish bum was that he no longer needed someone to pay the bills. He was through with school. His uncle was dangling the carrot of a partnership under his nose and Larry didn't want a wife to cramp the social horizon he saw opening up for him. Dr. Lawrence Marriotte, brilliant young dental surgeon and eligible bachelor. You didn't fit in." He paused and she heard him suck in a breath. "You loved the guy. If he hadn't run off, you'd be all right. Stephen Foley wouldn't have had a chance to get his filthy hands on you."

France felt as if she were going mad. Paul had never said these things before. "Don't say any more," she begged quietly.

The sound of pottery shattering on tile startled her. "Damn. Look what I did." Paul dropped to his knees beside the smashed remnants of the schefflera plant that had stood on the windowsill. "Where's the dustpan or something?"

She went to his side and put a hand under his arm. "Get up," she urged. "Leave it. It'll give me something to do later."

"Oh, France." Paul stood up and held her, burying his face in her neck. "I feel so responsible. You didn't even want to go to the wretched party."

"Shh. Please don't do this. I already told you Stephen and I met before. We were bound to come together again eventually."

"No." He held her off, his fingers gripping her arms so hard they hurt. "Promise me, France."

"What?"

"Promise me you'll never see Foley again. There are other guys out there. You've never had any shortage of offers for dates."

France sighed and pushed him gently away. "And I've turned most of them down. If I was so sex-starved—as you suggested—why would I do that? Wait." She covered his mouth with her fingertips. "What Stephen and I found has nothing to do with you, or Larry, or what dates I have or haven't had. I wanted him and he wanted me. And as far as I'm concerned, that hasn't changed."

Paul still wore his coat and a woolen scarf draped haphazardly around his neck. He began to take them off. "Then I'm going to sleep on the couch."

"Don't be ridiculous. It's almost three in the morning. Joanna needs you."

"Joanna I'm not worried about."

France tugged the sleeves back up his arms and began to fasten buttons. "I'm twenty-nine years old. No one has to worry about me. Go home to your wife and let me deal with this my way."

He sat down on one kitchen chair and pulled out another for his feet. "I'm not going anywhere until you promise to stay away from that man."

Weariness made France's bones heavy. She longed to lie down, to sleep and forget the horror of the past hour. "Okay," she said. "I won't see him—at least for a while."

"Not good enough."

France started to simmer. "That's as good as it's going to get. I need time to think and I intend to take it. But what I decide is my business and I hope you'll stand by me whatever happens."

"I don't like it..." Paul began. Then he met France's unyielding glare. "All right. You said you wouldn't see him. I'll just have to make the best of that and hope you'll come to your senses. If he gives you any trouble, call me. Day or night. I only hope Dad doesn't get wind of this."

"There's no reason he should if we don't tell him." She watched him go reluctantly toward the door leading to the carport. "Please don't worry about me. And I love you."

Paul stood motionless for a moment, as if uncertain what to do. "I love you, too." He went out, and soon France heard his station wagon pulling out of the driveway.

She made it through an hour before calling directory assistance for Stephen's listing. There were three Foleys in the downtown area, but just one at Sixth and Denver, where Denver Place was located. With the worn-down stub of a pencil she wrote the number on the back of the envelope with her mortgage statement and propped it against the toaster.

He hadn't denied that he was guilty. France soaked a wad of paper toweling under the faucet and removed a few remaining particles of the soil Paul had spilled on the floor beneath the window.

Three cups of tea had grown cold while she stared at them. She tossed the last one down the sink and went into the living room for the scotch. Carrying both Stephen's glass and her own in one hand and the bottle under her arm, she trailed back to the kitchen and sat down.

Immediately she got up again and put the dirty glasses in the dishwasher. She took another clean glass and splashed in some amber liquid from the bottle. The whisky burned her throat and she coughed. "From the look of that unopened bottle, you aren't used to it," Stephen had said. Another gulp hit the same raw spot, but at least her veins felt a warmth that spread quickly to her muscles.

The phone seemed to beckon from the wall. She scooted a chair beneath it and carefully placed the bottle of scotch on the floor before picking up the mortgage envelope. Cradling the glass against her breast, she sat down and stared at the number.

Stephen had walked in the rain—how far? Had he managed to get a taxi? What would she say if she called him? How would he react?

Liquid sloshed as she set down the glass and twisted sideways to reach the receiver. Quickly she pressed the digits, listened to their discordant chime, then to popping static between distant rings. Four, five. He wasn't there—or he wasn't going to answer. *I don't know what to say to you.* Six. France started to hang up.

"Hello." He sounded breathless. After a few seconds he repeated, "Hello, France?"

She pressed the receiver tightly against her ear but couldn't say anything.

"Is that you?"

"How did you know?"

"I didn't. But I hoped it might be. I don't get too many calls at four in the morning."

"Did you get a cab?"

"Eventually."

"You sounded out of breath when you answered. Did you just get back?"

"No, I was in the shower."

"Oh." She closed her eyes against a mental image of water dashing over his lithe, muscular form.

"Are you okay, France? It got pretty rough. I'm sorry for the crack I made about you inviting me into your bed. I was lashing out."

France rested her head against the wall and rolled the cord between her fingers. "I know. We all got carried away. Don't blame Paul. He doesn't understand."

His sigh whistled down the line. "He really loves you. Must be nice to have a brother who cares so much."

"Sometimes it's a pain. Stephen?"

"Yes?"

"We talked for a long time after you left."

"I bet."

"He wanted me to promise not to see you again."

"And did you?"

"I told him you were innocent and that what you needed is trust."

"Thanks." His sarcasm was palpable, and France winced.

"I do trust you. If I thought I wasn't going to see you again, I don't think I could take it. I..." She sniffed and searched the pocket of her robe for a tissue.

"Don't, darlin'. It'll be all right."

All the tension inside started to ebb. It would be all right. Stephen said so. "Listen." She laughed as she spoke. "We're going to miss out on breakfast together. But there's still the Cotton Bowl. Will you come?" Paul hadn't exactly extracted a total promise from her.

"If you'd like that."

"I would." But she had to ask and it had better be now. "Are you going to try to prove your innocence? That's the one thing that'll shut up the gossips."

He didn't reply. France could hear him breathing.

"Stephen? What is it?"

"You said you believed in me." His voice was slow she had to strain to hear him.

"I do. That's why I think you should try to get the decision reversed."

"No, France. What you want is to hear my denial. The one thing you said you'd never need. If you need it, it won't matter a damn what I say. You won't believe me. Not in your heart. You and I just made sweet, beautiful love. At least it was for me. But you're all eaten up with guilt because there's still a possibility in your mind that I'm some kind of monster. I'm sorry, France. I said you'd be better off with your brother. Believe it. Listen to the man. Please stay away from me, because I'm no good to any woman. Touch filth and it rubs off."

Sobs jarred her throat. "No. I shouldn't have brought it up."

"Don't cry. I can't bear to hear you cry."

"I want to see you, Stephen."

She heard him make an odd noise before he cleared his throat. "Forget me, France."

The line went dead.

STEPHEN THREW HIMSELF BACKWARD across the width of his bed and covered his eyes with one forearm. This was his fault, not hers. Beneath his body the quilt had become cold and damp from his wet skin. He shivered but didn't have the energy to move.

Paul Richards. He'd met the guy once in the newsroom at the *Review*. Must have been about a week before Christmas. Richards had hesitated too long before shaking his hand, and his eyes had slid away the second they touched his.

Good Lord. Stephen sat up and pulled the icy towel from his waist. Why hadn't he realized then what was familiar? After the younger man had turned back to his computer terminal, Stephen had puzzled over the sensation he'd gotten. Paul Richards' eyes had that same changeable quality as France's—greenish-brown that could become brittle emerald and piercing.

The moisture had evaporated from everywhere but his hair. In the bathroom he took a fresh towel and rubbed his head hard, as if the energy spent could erase all memory. He lifted his face and his own naked reflection shot back from the mirror-tiled walls. The mirrors had been used to make the room seem larger—now it closed him in. He grabbed a rust terry-cloth robe from a hook by the shower before escaping to the living room.

Bypassing the deep-cushioned gold couches that edged the room, he went to stand by the windows. The sixteenth floor had always seemed high, but somehow it wasn't high enough tonight. He wanted to feel completely removed from everything down there. The lights of Tulsa stretched like a multi-colored laser carpet. Soon they would fade in a blue-gray dawn. The stars has disappeared. It was going to be another oppressive day—winter, yet without winter's special sparkle.

New Year's Day. Stephen laughed mirthlessly. New beginnings. Resolutions. All for nothing. The past never let go and his was gripping him more tightly by the throat with every breath he took.

He tried to shut out the hours spent with France before her brother showed up. The scene in the hall with Paul merged with similar episodes from his childhood. Different surroundings, different cast members, but one element that was always the same—violence.

The dining nook, with its low, circular glass table, filled the area where two huge windows angled together at the corner of the building. Stephen slid into an upholstered wicker couch he'd had designed to follow the lines of the windows. The couch made ideal seating for intimate meals for two. The woman he wanted to share it with was a few miles away—minutes by car—but he couldn't have her. She'd end up hating him soon, like everyone else he'd ever cared about.

When he realized he was crying, he opened his mouth and breathed slowly. He hadn't cried since he was fifteen. That was a joyless day, too: the day he'd finally found the courage to try to stop his father beating up his mother, and the day he had left home for good.

Stephen took a cigarette from the box he kept on the table, for visitors. He lit up and pulled, concentrating on the brief red flare, then sucked smoke deep into his lungs—something else he hadn't done for a long time.

His father had been violent. The man was long gone but he'd left an indelible mark on Stephen's life, maybe as deep as he'd always feared. In prison there'd been plenty of time to think, and slowly he'd started to hope he wasn't made in the same mold as Mick Foley, or Grant. Stephen was convinced his brother, Grant, abused his wife.

He didn't have to be like his father and brother, did he? But several times he'd responded to violence with violence. Would he do it again? Would he hit France if she made him angry enough?

"Oh, God, why?" Stephen rammed the cigarette into a crystal ashtray and covered his face with both hands. *I love her.*

Shocked hopelessness rushed through every nerve. He picked up the ashtray and barely stopped himself from hurling it at an exquisite Oriental screen.

"I love you, France. That's why I can't have you."

Chapter Eight

France stared at the receiver for several minutes before hanging up. Within a few short hours, her feelings had run the gamut from ecstasy to defeat. Now her thoughts seemed muddled and hazy. How much more turmoil would she be able to endure?

A shiver rippled through her and she pulled the robe tighter around her knees. Stillness and cold. She could almost hear her heart beating in the silence of the kitchen, and she fought the overwhelming desire to call Stephen back.

No. He had hung up on her. Something no man did anymore.

A flash of hot pride darted through her. She got up and dashed the scotch into the sink, knowing it would take more than liquor to dissolve the knot she felt forming in her stomach. A volley of feelings swarmed inside her—desire, concern and frustrated anger. She wanted Stephen Foley, needed him, longed to feel his strong arms around her.

But she had called him, reached out for him, offered to begin again, and he had rejected her. He couldn't even make a small effort to understand her doubts. It scared her to think that she yearned so desperately for a man she still barely knew.

France sensed that somewhere, deep inside, she possessed the strength to stay away from him. She would have to find it. He held the cards now, and only he knew what they were and how he intended to play them. If he wanted to see her again, he would have to make the next play.

Carefully, she bent to pick up the dustpan, piled with dirt, pottery and bruised leaves, the remainders of the broken schefflera. She tossed every shard, every leaf slowly and deliberately into the garbage. Damn it all. Even the sight of the garbage reminded her of him.

All her bones and muscles seemed to ache. When she'd cleaned away all traces of the damaged plant, she scuffed across the living room to the sofa and stretched out, dismally aware of the dim light of morning. She was totally and painfully exhausted.

The next few days dragged by. After New Year's Day, business slacked off at the nursery. The holidays were over, and it was too early for the residents of Tulsa to plan for spring gardening. France had always looked forward to this natural break. It gave her time to order vegetable and flower seeds and to inventory the young stock in the greenhouses.

Almost a week had passed since she'd spoken with Stephen. She'd done what she'd promised herself; stifled her desire to see him, to hear his voice. But her unsatisfied longing for the man had taken its toll. Dark circles beneath her eyes advertised night after night of insomnia.

Friday dawned with a sun that was weak and spiritless. From her bedroom window, France watched it rise into a streaked, gray sky. She didn't want to go to work and was grateful that Rachel could open the nursery for her.

Finally, around eleven o'clock, France pushed in the nursery office door. It squeaked mournfully, reminding her that it needed oil.

"Morning, boss." Rachel handed France a cup of coffee before she could even take off her parka.

"Morning. If you can still call it that." France raised an eyebrow at the dusty electric clock on the corner of the desk. She sipped the coffee, then placed the mug on the counter. "Thanks for taking care of things this morning. My head hurts—must be my sinuses. We're probably going to have a change in the weather." She shrugged out of her coat and hung it on a peg behind the door.

"No problem. It hasn't been very busy." Rachel returned to her seat behind the desk. "I've been going through seed catalogs and placing orders, like you asked me to. Bill is in the greenhouse getting lots of 'help' from Toby. I never saw a dog take a more instant dislike to anyone. But everything else is running smoothly."

"Good girl." The prison had sent Bill as Stephen's replacement. France reached for a pile of invoices in the basket, trying hard to bury the image of Stephen that fluttered across her brain.

"Before I forget, the other man came back this morning looking for you." Rachel peered up at France, her eyes wide.

"Who?"

"*He* did. That other man from the prison, the gorgeous one. Stephen Foley."

"Oh? When?" France tried to relax, to concentrate on forming each word she uttered. But her mouth suddenly felt like a sandpaper vacuum, scratchy and empty. She swallowed.

"Early. Right after I opened the front gate. He came in and looked around, then asked for you. When I told him you weren't here yet, he said to tell you he'd stopped by. Then he left."

"Did he say anything else?" France's pulse thrummed. She reached for the coffee, barely feeling the hot brew as it washed down her throat.

"No, that's all." Rachel watched her boss carefully. "Did I say the right thing to him? Perhaps I should have called you at home—I wasn't sure."

"You did exactly what you should have done." France smiled. "I can't imagine what Stephen Foley could possibly want. Why don't you see if Bill needs help in the greenhouse. I'll take over here."

France knew her order sounded like the excuse to be alone that it was, but she didn't care. She needed time to think. Stephen had been here, asking for her. He wanted to see her.

Thank God. It had taken him six days, and for France they had been six days of miserable loneliness. But he'd made the first move. At that moment, it didn't matter to France what Stephen thought. At least he was finally ready to do something, and now she could, too.

The following morning she pulled on a claret-red turtleneck sweater and tucked it into trim gray slacks. Today she must look her best, give herself an extra measure of self-assurance. She straightened her belt, then bent to swipe at an imaginary smudge on the toe of one black leather boot. She knew she'd need all the courage she could muster when she knocked on his door.

Stephen hadn't called her the night before, even though she'd thought he might. But going to his apartment was the right thing to do, and she kept reminding herself of that over and over again.

Denver Place loomed above France as she tucked her pickup into a narrow parking space at the building's base. Its penthouses jutted into the overcast sky, lost in swirls of low-hanging cloud.

She stepped down from the pickup. A chill wind whipped against her, flattening the flannel slacks against her legs. She stood briefly on the curb and tipped her face, trying to imagine which cluster of windows might be Stephen's. Was he even up there in his lofty citadel— and if he was, if he looked down, would he notice her? Would he even want to see her? A waft of uneasiness niggled at her.

France tugged the collar of her jacket against her neck. Of course he would want to see her. He'd been at the nursery asking for her the morning before. Her boots made hollow tripping sounds on the marble steps leading to the building's entrance. She had to move quickly, before she changed her mind.

A doorman, clad in forest green with a hint of gold braid, stood to one side of double plate-glass doors. His uniformed back and broad shoulders faced her.

"Excuse me, sir." France paused, feeling as if she'd just confronted an impenetrable stand of Douglas firs. "Could you tell me which apartment is Stephen Foley's?" She noticed the sparse white hair poking from beneath his doorman's cap.

"Just a second." He swiveled, and France realized the man was talking into a telephone. It's empty cradle stood in a camouflaged box behind him. He covered the mouthpiece. "Which apartment did you want, ma'am?"

"Stephen Foley's"

"Right. Sixteen-forty-one. Take the second elevator."

Before France could even say "thank you," the older man had turned away, his attention focused once more on the invisible party on the other end of the telephone line. Perhaps it was her imagination that she smelled a hint of rum on his breath. She pushed through the doors, slightly amused by the doorman's casualness. She could have walked in without his ever knowing. So much for security.

The large, elegant lobby smelled of new carpeting and growing plants. With an experienced eye, she noted the greenhouse perfection of huge potted figs and philodendron. She reached up and ran one finger down the veins of a large fiddle-leaf fig while she waited for the elevator, wondering briefly which nursery provided Denver Place with its plants. Perhaps she should expand into interior arrangements. If the lobby of Stephen's apartment house was typical, the venture would probably be lucrative.

The elevator doors closed behind her on the sixteenth floor, and the gilded numbers of Stephen's apartment leapt out at her from the beige wall. Nervously, France made an attempt to smooth her hair. Good. Despite the wind, everything seemed to be in place. Except for her courage. She had lost it somewhere between the lobby and this long, empty hallway that stretched like a tunnel on either side of her.

A wave of uncertainty broke over her. As she heard the bell chime inside his apartment, France craned around, looking for a door marked Exit. Lord, why hadn't she located the stairs before she'd rang the bell?

The door opened. Now it was too late to flee.

"France." In spite of Stephen's visit to the nursery, France could tell that he hadn't been expecting her to come. His eyes registered surprise, then brightened with pleasure.

"Did I catch you at a bad time?" Blast the fancy speeches of apology she'd rehearsed since yesterday morning. Now her memory seemed to fail her, and she clutched her purse to her breast, wanting to spill her feelings out to him, yet not knowing how. She drew in her breath.

He laughed. "No, I was just working." He stepped back. "Come in."

"But it's Saturday. You should be taking it easy, with your feet up and all that." Her small talk began to infuriate her. How handsome he looked. It made it worse that she knew intimately, and ached to touch, every square inch of him. He reached behind her to shut the door. His snug jeans clung to the solid length of his thighs, and the nubby oatmeal pullover sweater only accentuated the enticing flex of taut muscle and sinew in his arms and chest.

"Saturday, Sunday. When you work at home, it doesn't matter what day of the week it is. When there's work to do, you do it. Here, let me take your coat."

"I'm bothering you." France wanted to melt back into his chest as he pulled the coat from her arms.

"No, of course not. You could never bother me. You should know that by now." An anxious veil edged his voice. "Sit down. It's not too early for a drink, is it?" He looked tired. The fine lines about his eyes and the corners of his mouth seemed slightly deeper.

"You stopped by the nursery yesterday? I thought you wanted to see me."

Stephen stood for a second studying her, then followed when she stepped down into the sunken living room. Its walls glimmered with muted shades of champagne and gold, quietly subdued. "Yes. I wanted to talk to you—I needed to."

"You could have called." France knew that her feeble attempt at defiance failed. Stephen had to sense that all she wanted was to be swung immediately into the circle of his arms.

"I wanted to see you. If you hadn't come here today, I would have dropped by the nursery again."

"Well, ask and you shall receive, right? Here I am—in the flesh." Why was she being sarcastic? The blatant appeal in his eyes shot into her, making her legs tremble. She had wondered about his home—how he lived. Now she felt surrounded, almost oppressed by him and by the objects that were his. She lowered herself against mauve accent cushions on a tawny sofa, wanting desperately to catch her breath.

"So you are." Stephen turned away, his expression guarded. He hung her coat in a closet.

"I like your apartment. Did someone stay here when you were, ah, gone?"

"Yes. I sublet it—with an open-ended lease, since I didn't know exactly when I'd be returning."

"Oh." France concentrated on the huge floor-to-ceiling windows, feeling compelled to alter the direction of their conversation. "That's quite a view."

Stephen watched her silently for a second and finally smiled. "Yes, it is. All of Tulsa you'd care to see—and more. Come here. I'll show you the Civic Center." He went to stand beside the glass, his thumbs hooked into his jeans pockets. "If you look down, over there, you can see it."

"Really?" Damn. They were fencing the issue. France had never been good at hedging, and she had a feeling that Stephen wasn't too adept at it, either. She laid her purse on the black lacquered coffee table and moved to stand beside him, her boots sinking onto the thick carpet with each step. "Yes, I do see it."

"It's quite spectacular at night."

France could feel his nearness, sense his wonderful eyes studying her. Her own pulse quickened and she wondered about Stephen's. "Is that an invitation?" She bit her lip. That wasn't what she'd planned to say.

"Do you want one?"

She whirled to face him. "Stephen." He stood mere inches away, watching her seriously, his angular face unbearably tender, vulnerable. The smile was gone again and she longed to bring it back. "Do I need one?"

"What do you think?"

She looked up into his eyes and saw the pinpoints of fire smoldering just beyond her reach. He waited for her signal, but every gentle word, every ache she'd harbored in need of him lodged painfully in her throat. When she did speak her voice was soft, barely her own. "After our last conversation, Stephen, I really don't know."

France longed to have him touch her, tell her that his past didn't matter—that it failed to exist. But he didn't. Instead, he lifted his head and silently stared down at the frigid landscape.

Cold reached through the glass to France and almost made her shiver. She tried to ignore the discomfort by peering at the bleak gray chunks of buildings beneath her. The business district stretched out, block after block, to lose itself in silvery tendrils of distant mist.

"I'm sorry, France." She didn't look at him as he continued. "I've been a fool and I know it." The palm of his hand traveled from one of her shoulders to the other, sending a charge of excitement swirling to her toes.

Her breath wavered when she sucked it in.

"France?" His hand settled at her waist, and she could feel each blunt fingertip as it pressed into her skin through the soft woolen sweater, tugging, urging. "Look at me. Please."

"You haven't been a fool." France turned to bury her face within the comforting circle of his waiting arms. His muscles tensed beneath her cheek as he pulled her more tightly to him, and his chest raised, then lowered, with each breath he took. The subtle movement calmed yet excited her.

"But you called me that night. You offered me a chance to start over and I turned it down." His gentle breath whispered against the top of her head. "I've had a lot of time to think about that and I feel rotten about it."

"I don't want you to. We both said things we didn't mean." France nuzzled more deeply into Stephen's shoulder, remembering the New Year's Eve party, and then quickly trying to blot out the pain that followed. "You've been through so much. I should have known better than to push, especially when it doesn't matter."

"But it does matter. I've been a fool to think it doesn't. We all have a past, and mine just happens to be particularly fascinating."

"But it's behind you. And that's precisely where you should leave it." France felt him stiffen slightly, heard his heartbeat quicken. She tipped her face. "Remember that."

"You're right. Let's try to forget."

"I've already forgotten, Stephen."

"Have you?" He studied her face, his unwavering gaze stripping her, revealing her buried reservations. France knew instinctively that he wasn't fooled. A shadow of pain darkened his eyes, but it was gone so quickly that she wondered if she'd really seen it.

"You're beautiful, so very beautiful." He raised his hands to cup the back of her head. He laced his fingers through her hair and made tantalizing swirls on her temples with his thumbs. "How I've missed you. This past week has been pure hell."

"I want to begin again, Stephen."

His intense gaze was soft and slow, like a lingering caress. He lowered his head, feathering kisses along both cheekbones and the bridge of her nose. Then he nipped temptingly at the corners of her mouth, his breath warm and intoxicating. His mouth brushed against hers as he spoke. "So do I, darling, so do I."

Parting her own lips, she raised herself to meet his kiss, quivering at his sweet tenderness. His mouth covered hers hungrily, demanded and received. France melted into him. The pulsing pressure of his tongue became a tantalizing massage, a balm for her tired soul.

His warmth radiated through each of her veins, and she leaned against him, her body tingling, begging for more. A low moan escaped Stephen's throat as he reluctantly raised his head and looked down at her.

"You make me crazy, France. Every decent intention I have seems to vanish when we're in the same room." His breath was ragged, each word deliberate. His hands ran languorously from her wrists to her shoulders, then back again. "Can you stay for a while?"

"It depends on what you have in mind." France knew her voice shook. She wound her arms around his waist, beneath the rough knit of the sweater. His skin felt firm and warm. She felt at home in his arms and enjoyed her ability to tempt him.

"Let's start with that drink I promised you; then I'll show you around the place. It ain't much, but it's a place to throw my hat." Stephen whispered a stroking kiss on the smoothness of her forehead. "I've wised up, though, since I first laid eyes on you. I'm going to save the bedroom for last."

France pulled her hands from under his sweater and trailed them from his waist to his chest, the wool scratchy beneath her palms. "Too bad. But I guess I can wait for you to ravage me, can't I?" She felt excited and light-headed. She didn't want to let him go.

Stephen stiffened against her. "No one should force anyone to do what they don't want." His words were soft, and France barely heard them. "No one."

Suddenly she realized what she'd said, and her heart thudded. "I'm sorry." She pushed back anxiously. He looked the same, still gentle and understanding, but the tiny muscles on either side of his jaw twitched. "I'm sorry," she repeated. "I didn't mean that the way it sounded. Stephen, why do I always say the wrong thing?"

"Never mind. I've got to learn not to be so sensitive. My fault, okay?" He raised one of her hands to his lips. He kissed the palm and folded her fingers closed over it. Then he frowned. "Great. Why didn't you tell me that I have ink on my hands? I was going over a strip, but I could have washed them."

"Show me."

"All right, but it won't be very interesting." He stretched open the center of one hand and examined it. "There's a blob here, and an awful smear there. Don't worry, though, ink dries fast. I know I didn't get any smudges on you."

"Stop teasing. That's not what I meant. Show me where you work."

He raised a brow. "Do you really care? My studio's a bit disorganized at the moment." He hedged slightly, but France noticed that he appeared pleased.

"I don't care. Disorganization is an artist's prerogative, isn't it? I'm dying to find out how you do what you do."

"Okay. But promise that I won't plummet in your estimation when you see the slum I call a studio. I've been told by several colleagues that the place is a disaster."

"I'll bet it is. Geniuses are supposed to thrive on clutter. That's probably why you're considered one of the best cartoonists around. Let me be the judge. It couldn't be any worse than our old potting shed at the back of the nursery. That's a real dump."

Stephen chuckled, placed a hand on the small of France's back and directed her to a dim cubicle at the end of the hall. He flicked on the light and led her inside, clearing away a pile of yellowed newspapers so they would both have a place to stand.

The light made France blink. She peered around her, realizing that Stephen was right. It had been a long time since she'd seen so much junk accumulated in one place. It made a marked contrast to the ordered serenity of the rest of his apartment.

"This is my drafting board—where I actually sketch." He motioned toward a tilted desktop plastered with drawings in various stages of completion. "And this is Beardsley, the fellow who's given me what little fame I have." He pointed to a smiling, balding caricature cavorting across nearly every cartoon frame.

"He looks familiar." France warmed to the tiny character. "A little like the man in the drawing you left in my bathroom. Remember?"

"I remember, but that wasn't Beardsley. Beardsley's bald."

"Was the drawing you left for me that afternoon supposed to be you?"

"Mmmm. Think what you will. I'll never tell." He reached for a pad of softly textured paper. "Here. Feel the ridges. This is called Grafix. All I have to do is smooth my pencil over the lines like this—" he demonstrated with a few deft marks "—and they stand out. Lots of cartoonists use this stuff. Makes our work a little bit easier."

France nodded. She knew the tiny sketch resting securely in her jewelry box was Stephen's self-portrait. At least portions of it were. He'd refused to admit it, but it delighted her just the same. She picked up a squat black bottle. "What's this?"

"India ink. The lines need to be dark. It makes them photograph and print better. I make larger sketches of all my cartoons first in pencil before I recreate them in ink." He withdrew a large pad from the top of a dusty file cabinet. "See?" Stephen thumbed through page after page of elaborate pencil drawings.

"Those are good, really good."

"They could be better. But I try."

"No, I'm serious—you're really talented. Now I understand why the *Review* was so anxious to get you back on the staff." France immediately frowned and pressed her lips together. The air in the tiny room stilled, and her heart lurched when she saw him swallow.

"Yeah, they got me back all right. Right where they want me." A hint of sarcasm clouded his voice. "It's

kind of funny how my little prison stint seems to have
fine-tuned my career.'' Stephen flipped the pad shut and
tossed it a bit too hard into a corner, sending up a flurry
of dust. ''Enough, okay? This conversation's getting too
heavy.''

He flicked off the light and reached for France's hand,
pulling her back into the hall. ''There I go again, being
touchy. It's ridiculous. I've dreamed all week of holding
you, being able to kiss you.''

''Then why don't you.''

''Yeah, why not?'' Time slowed for the brief second he
looked at her before his lips came coaxingly, lightly
down. They grazed her mouth's soft fullness, tantalizing
and persuading.

''Oh, Stephen.'' France pressed against him, reveling
in the feel of him.

He looped several wayward strands of hair behind her
ear, then trailed tiny kisses where his fingers had been.
''I'm going to wash up first, then I'll get us some Irish
coffee, all right?''

France's cheek burned under the moisture of his touch.
She nodded.

''Good.'' He gave her shoulders a quick squeeze, then
turned to disappear into what France assumed to be the
kitchen.

She returned to the living room and settled quietly into
an oversized wicker chair. Its cushions, streaked with
subtle shades of mauve and beige, felt comforting against
her back and neck. In fact, the entire room, with its soft
colors and smooth, modern furniture seemed peaceful
and utterly relaxing.

France raised her head. The only sounds she heard
were an occasional clang and slam from Stephen in the
kitchen. An Oriental-style end table stood beside her

chair. Several magazines had been neatly arranged on top of it, and France absently lifted their corners to inspect the titles. *American Cartooning* and *Publishers Weekly* didn't surprise her, but a Burpee's seed catalog?

She didn't have time to wonder.

"France, come in the kitchen." Stephen's distant voice broke into her thoughts. "I'm going to throw together some sandwiches, too, since it's getting close to lunch. You can help."

Good grief, what did he expect her to do? France reminded herself all the way to the kitchen that even kids could make sandwiches. With a small amount of luck, surely she could produce something edible.

Bracing herself, she entered the kitchen. It was bright and open. Wide windows comprised an entire wall, bathing birchwood cabinets in natural light. Several large asparagus ferns trailed filigreed fronds of green, eliminating the need for curtains.

Stephen stood, with his back to her, before the open refrigerator door. On a large butcher block, a loaf of bread, still in its wrapper, lay next to a head of lettuce and a jar of mayonnaise.

"I'm looking for the lunch meat. I know I've got some in here somewhere." Stephen's muffled voice echoed from inside the refrigerator. "The liquor's in that cupboard beside you, and the coffee's in the pot. Make mine a double."

"Thank goodness that's all you want. I think I can manage an Irish coffee. You had me scared for a second."

"Why?" He pulled out a package of bologna and closed the door. "What's the matter?"

"Sandwiches. I'm not very good at making them."

"What? They're easy. Don't you like dealing with food?"

"Not really. I find it exasperating. Nothing I try to cook ever turns out."

"You're kidding."

"I'm not." She busied herself preparing the drinks. "In fact, I'd assign a permanent place in history to the person who invented the restaurant. I'd have starved long ago if it weren't for those noble establishments." Her eyes sought his, trying unsuccessfully to read his expression. "Do you mind? I realize that most women my age are supposed to have their culinary skills well in hand. I'm the exception."

Stephen shook his head, the corners of his mouth tipped dangerously. "You've got other skills that interest me more. I'd say that, most things considered, we're well suited. I like to cook. What's your favorite kind of food? Next time, I'll fix it."

"That's easy. French. Fill a crepe with hot sauce and I'd probably eat it."

"I'm sure I can throw together something more palatable than that." Stephen grinned at her, then frowned as he made two sandwiches and arranged them on a plate. "There. Certainly not gourmet, but we can use our imaginations."

"Let's eat over there." He nodded in the direction of a glass-topped dining table tucked into a corner.

More windows surrounded the table, and when France dropped into one side of an angled wicker couch, she felt as if she were floating in a crystal ball, high above the world. She and Stephen were alone in it and no one could reach them, to bother them or taint their happiness. She knew the feeling was more than slightly unrealistic but it pleased her.

Stephen placed their lunch between them and sat down beside her. He offered her a sandwich, then leaned one elbow on the table and cupped his chin,. He must have noticed the satisfied smile on her face. "Like the view? It's the same one you saw from the living room."

France took a bite of the sandwich. "I do, and I like the food. My compliments."

"The food, the view. Is that all you like?"

"You know that isn't all." She caught the amused spark in his eyes. "If it were, I probably wouldn't be here."

He smiled.

She moistened her lips.

Their gazes caught and held, and the chrome wall clock above the stove ticked out the seconds like solitary raindrops falling into a lake. France trembled as a familiar pang of warmth shot through her, and she knew it wasn't caused by the food—or the elevation. Her unabashed need for him still burned, and it excited her to watch as Stephen's teasing sparkle faded into the serious ebb and flow of contained passion.

Impulsively, she entwined her fingers with his.

His thumb began to move in a circular pattern on the inside of her palm. "Let's make a toast. What shall it be to this time?" He reached for his mug.

France picked up her own and clinked it against his. "How about to trust—a quality I need to cultivate?" She studied him carefully, worried that she'd once again overstepped her bounds. But she needed to test him, discern his reaction and let him know how far she would go to make their relationship work. *If only he knew,* she thought.

"Then I'd like to add this for me—understanding." He took a sip, then put his drink on the table. "They're both great attributes, France, but not easy ones for either of us to maintain, especially after what…''

"No, Stephen. Don't say any more."

"I know, but I hate myself when I think of what I've put you through, and your family."

"Paul will come around. Give him time."

"I doubt it. I'm glad I can do the majority of my work here at home. It would be hard to face your brother at the paper every day."

"Forget what you can't undo. Please." It alarmed her to see the lines around his mouth and eyes deepen even further. "Put last weekend out of your mind. *He* hit *you*, Stephen. You were defending yourself. I know he's my brother, but you did what you had to do."

"No, I still hit him, France, after I swore to myself, that I'd never…hell!" He brought back one arm so hard it hit the glass. "I haul off and hit your brother, and there you sit, worrying about what you're going to say or *not* say to me, wondering how to treat me with kid gloves. What a fine pair we are." He leaned his elbows on his thighs and brushed his hands nervously through his hair.

"We need each other."

"Yeah? I think we're pretty mixed up about a lot of things."

The phone rang and they both jumped.

"Excuse me." Stephen walked into the living room and picked up the phone.

France ran a finger along the rim of her coffee mug and tried, unsuccessfully, not to listen.

"Yes? This is Stephen Foley. Candace? Memorial Hospital? What's wrong with Gretchen? Oh, God, no. All right. Yes. Yes, I'll catch the first plane. Right. Thanks for letting me know."

France heard the receiver drop, then his footsteps heavy on the carpet. She glanced up to see Stephen lean against the kitchen counter.

"What's the matter? You look awful."

"That was my sister-in-law. I've got to take off for Cincinnati—right away."

"Why? What happened?" France went to him. Her fingers tugged at the sleeve of his sweater. He looked drained, as if someone had slugged him, then ransacked his apartment. It dragged at her heart and threatened to pull her down as well.

"It's Gretchen. My niece." His teeth sank into his lower lip and France saw it quiver.

"Is something wrong with her?"

He wrapped his arms tightly around his stomach as if he were cold. "That was her mother calling from the hospital in Cincinnati. Gretchen had an accident—doing gymnastics or something. Injured her spine. It doesn't sound good." Suddenly his chest heaved and he raised his eyes to the ceiling. "She's only eight years old. It's not fair, France—just not fair."

"I want to come with you."

"No. Gretchen is part of my family. It's not your problem."

"Let me help you. I want to be near you."

"No." His voice sliced.

"Stephen." She shrank away from him as if he'd slapped her.

He frowned. "Darlin', I didn't mean that." He gripped her tightly to him and rocked her back and forth in his arms. "It's just that I want to protect you. You've got enough on your mind."

"I want to come with you," she repeated.

"What about the nursery? You can't just run off whenever you want to."

"The nursery will be fine. Leave that to me."

He leaned back against the wall, pulling her with him. "France, my sweet, sweet France." He ran his hand along the nape of her neck and nestled her head into the hollow of his shoulder. "You do as you want. If you insist on coming with me, I won't try to stop you."

Chapter Nine

France remembered reading that some colors were supposed to be more soothing than others, but chartreuse and pink in alternating panels didn't relax her.

She'd lost track of time. Stephen seemed to have been in Gretchen's room for hours. A clock, ringed in a darker shade of chartreuse than the wall panel behind it, showed four-thirty. Hadn't it said that when she last checked? Puffing out her cheeks, she rolled her head in a circle and heard tiny cracking sounds in her stiff neck.

Footsteps squished on rubberized tile, and she turned sharply. One more nurse bustled by, wearing thick-soled shoes intended to preserve silence rather than cause the anxiety they brought France. The woman was young and plump with a determinedly confident smile on her face and held a chart against her jutting bosom.

"Excuse me," France said. "Could you find out for me how Gretchen Foley's doing?"

The nurse stopped as if noticing her for the first time. "Please?"

The local use of "Please" to signify lack of understanding surprised her. The purse France had been clutching on her lap slid to the floor as she stood up. She knelt to gather its spilled contents, repeating, "Gretchen Foley. I wondered how she was doing."

"Are you a member of the family?"

France shook her head slowly, peering up at the other woman's florid face. "Just a friend. But—"

"I'm sorry. I know it's hard to wait. But you'll have to let one of the family give you that information." She retrieved a pen that had rolled beneath a chair and handed it to France before she walked on.

Just a friend. The soft click of a closing door stopped her from sitting again. Stephen stood a few feet away, his eyes unfocused beneath wildly tousled hair. France hung her purse on a chair back and flexed her fingers. He gave her a tired smile and glanced at the square of opaque glass in the door to his niece's room. Below it, attached with masking tape, a card read: *"Oxygen In Use. No Smoking. See Nurse Before Visiting"*, Gretchen's name had been inserted in a slot above the window. Everything was in its place. All rules must be followed.

"How're you doing?" Stephen asked.

"What? Fine, I'm fine." She went to him and rubbed his rough cheek. "How's Gretchen? You look awful. Is it worse than... ? Oh, Stephen."

He covered her hand, then shifted it to press his lips into her palm.

Fear clamored up through France's chest to fill her throat.

Slowly Stephen removed her hand from his face. He held it against his chest, massaging its cold back with his knuckles. "Her neck's broken. She's covered with a body cast, and there's a brace around her head. Got her on drugs, I'm sure. Didn't even know I was there. My God!" He sat down abruptly, his wrists hanging limp between his knees. "She's only eight years old and there's a chance she might die. Even if she makes it through, she'll probably be in pain for a long time. Why? France, why?''

"Shh. Shh." She sat beside him and pulled his head onto her shoulder. "You can't give up. Gretchen needs all our strength now. She'll know if it's not here for her."

"I'm glad you came with me," Stephen muttered against her neck. "Just knowing you're outside the room takes away some of the helplessness. I'd better go back." He kissed her lightly on the lips.

The pink door closed noiselessly behind him, but not before France glimpsed glittering chrome and a mesh of opaque tubes.

She got up and went to the ladies' room. Harsh light over the mirror hid none of the effects of a frantic plane journey, followed by hours of waiting. Mauve shadows beneath her eyes made them appear even deeper set. Every trace of lip gloss had worn off and her mouth blended with the rest of her pallor.

No wonder Stephen asked how she was doing—she was a mess. Without enthusiasm, she applied color to her lips and cheeks and brushed her hair rapidly. At least, Stephen shouldn't have to worry about her, too.

In a lounge outside the children's unit, she bought coffee from a machine, then headed back through automatic double doors toward the forlorn row of chairs.

Gretchen's door opened at the same instant as a man drew level with France from behind. Stephen walked into the hall. The man bumped her shoulder, knocking hot liquid over her hand. She hissed air backward through her teeth at the pain before she felt a tense mantle of stillness surround both men, shutting her out.

"What are you doing here?"

Stephen tugged at the collar of his shirt. "Candace called me. Gretchen's my niece. We used to be close, remember?"

France could see the side of the stranger's face. It was good-looking but hard. The corner of his mouth jerked convulsively as he stared at Stephen.

Stephen glanced over his shoulder at the closed door. "They're waiting for you, Grant. Candace needs you." Exhaustion made his features seem hollow, and France longed to hold him, to watch him sleep and kiss away the tired lines.

"Don't tell me what Candace needs." The words exploded through the quiet hallway. "She's *my* wife. Get out of here before I call the police to take you out."

France looked from one man to the other. This had to be Stephen's brother, Gretchen's father. Why was he treating Stephen this way? She became aware of the coffee still dripping from her fingers, but there was nowhere to get rid of the cup.

"This isn't the time," Stephen said quietly. "What the hell took you so long? You should have been here hours ago."

Grant loosened his tie deliberately. "You, of all people, should remember what I do for a living, big brother. After all, it was you who appointed yourself my stand-in on another occasion neither of us will forget. Lowly traveling salesmen can get from one place to another just so fast. But I'm here now and I want you out. I moved my family from Tulsa to get them away from you. Go home."

"Save it, Grant. You know how much Gretchen means to me. Go in and see them. I'll stay out of your way."

Grant marched past Stephen into Gretchen's room, and when Stephen's eyes met hers, France realized she'd been holding her breath. She sat down with a thud, slamming the back of the chair against the wall, and stared at him. "Why did he behave like that?" Blood rushed to her face. "It's because you've been in prison, isn't it? That's why he doesn't want you here. I don't believe it."

Stephen didn't answer. He strode back and forth, one hand rammed into the front of his hair, the other locked around his ribs. Each time he passed Gretchen's door he hesitated, then paced on, a deep crease between his brows.

France set her cup on the floor and started to get up, but sat on her hands instead. "Can he stop you from seeing your own niece just because you were put in prison for something you didn't do?"

His laugh was frightful, harsh and hopeless. "Sweetheart, you are an innocent. You really think people are reasonable, don't you? Thanks for the optimism, and the vote of confidence, but yes, he *can* stop me from being with Gretchen, and as I told you before, my innocence is moot in everyone else's eyes."

She remembered Stephen's comment after his confrontation with Paul. He said it must be nice to have a brother who cared so much. The remark hadn't meant much at the time, but it did now. France suddenly hated Grant Foley. He disgusted her. What kind of man turned on his own brother when he needed him most?

"Stephen, stop pacing." The curtness of her order surprised them both. "I'm sorry. It's just that I can't bear to see you punishing yourself like this because of that…"

"Because of what?" Grant had returned without her hearing him. "Who are you? And what has the brilliant, successful Stephen Foley told you about his insignificant sibling?"

France stood up feeling herself go pale. "I don't know what you mean. Stephen and I are...friends. Your daughter is injured in there and—"

"Is she awake?" Stephen cut her off. "Can I go in, just for a minute? Candace said it was all right."

"Candace said? I'm not afraid of you, Stephen, and I don't say it's all right." Grant's voice rose slightly with each syllable.

"Shh!" An orderly came from the nurses' station farther down the hall. "Keep it down, please," he said.

Grant waited until the young man had disappeared before turning on Stephen again. "Gretchen's my daughter, not yours, and I'm the one who's going to be with her. She'll be okay in time."

"This is outrageous," France interjected. "Why are you treating your brother like this when you need each other? I don't understand."

Stephen squeezed the back of her neck. "Let's go. There's no point in your being exposed to this."

"Just a minute," Grant said. "Introduce me to your friend, Stephen. A good friend, I take it, since she must have come all the way from Tulsa to hold your hand."

"That's enough."

France allowed Stephen to propel her toward the exit before Grant caught up and blocked their path. "Oh, no. Not nearly enough, you bastard. I didn't ask you to come here with your lady friend, but since you did, the least I can do is offer her a little hospitality, Foley-style."

"Drop it, Grant." Stephen sounded more tired than angry.

"I insist. We'll find a nice quiet spot for a friendly chat. Then we can clear up all these misunderstandings—what did you say your name was?"

"I'm—I'm France. France Marriotte." Nausea made her feel weak.

"If there was time, I'd have you tell me about how you got such an interesting name." Grant's tone grated. The skin seemed stretched tight over his high cheekbones. "How long have you two been friends?"

"Grant..." Stephen began.

"It's none of your business. Now please get out of our way," France retorted.

"Certainly it's my business. When my brother gets serious about a lady, of course I want to know all about her. Has he told you all about himself?"

Stephen's hand tightened against her neck. "Don't do this, Grant."

"I know what happened to Stephen," France said. "Is that what you want to hear? He was still in prison when we met. I also know he wasn't guilty."

"How? Because he told you?"

"No."

"That's good. At least Golden Boy didn't lie to you— directly. Did he tell you who it was he beat up and tried to rape?" The man's eyes blazed hatred.

"No, because he didn't do it."

"Get out of the way, Grant," Stephen breathed. He dropped his hand to France's waist. "Go back to Gretchen."

Grant's smile was only on his lips, and it twisted France's insides. "He hasn't told you, because my brother, the man who was held up to me as an example of everything worthwhile, tried to rape my wife—his own sister-in-law."

Her knees turned rubbery. France opened her mouth. Her throat closed out the breath she tried to take. She filled the fingers of one hand with the fabric of Stephen's sleeve but stared only at his brother.

"Admit it, Stephen. Tell France what you did to *my* wife."

Carefully, Stephen disentangled her grip from his jacket. He said nothing and France couldn't look at him.

"Never mind," Grant continued. "Honesty never was your strong suit. And I think she understood every word I said, but just to make sure..." He paused and gave her his complete attention. "If I hadn't gotten home early, the charge wouldn't have been attempted rape. It would have been rape."

Chapter Ten

Stephen watched France drag her suitcase onto the bed. He knew he mustn't offer to help or try to get any closer. *Close enough to touch.* The fragmentary line of a song repeated in his head. What would she do if he did touch her—scream? He felt sick.

They'd stopped briefly to drop their bags at the Westin Hotel, in the center of downtown Cincinnati, before taking a taxi to the hospital. France had opened her case for something, he didn't remember what, now she was struggling to close it again and all he could do was stand by, useless.

"Thanks." He heard his voice crack and cleared his throat.

France pressed her hands to her cheeks as he'd seen her do so often. "For what?" she muttered.

If only she'd look at him. Her eyes, soft, greenish-brown, constantly changing, could reach his soul.

"For not walking away from me at the hospital as most women would have. It meant everything to have you stay beside me." Even if he couldn't see her eyes, he knew they were troubled. Her lowered lashes made smudgy shadows on her cheekbones.

"I'm glad it helped you."

She didn't know how to be cruel. "Thanks," he repeated, groping for something else to say and finding nothing.

"Excuse me, Stephen. I have to call the airport."

Poor little scrapper. Holding on to her pride and trying to preserve his. She bent to pick up the phone and the golden-pink glow from a floor lamp set red lights afire in her hair. Her curls were longer than when they'd first met. They spilled over the collar of her white shirt as she stood with her back to him.

He slumped into an upholstered chair. The room was beautiful, rich purple accents against cerise and pale ivory. A wide bed covered with a shimmering striped quilt dominated—a bed for lovers.

"Seven-thirty? I can't make it. When's the next flight?"

Stephen bit a knuckle. What *would* she do if he touched her? Her skin showed through the thin white fabric, broken by the narrow straps of her bra. Such smooth skin. *Oh, God.*

"What do you mean...in the morning? Can't I even get as far as St. Louis tonight?" She ran one hand down the telephone cord, wound it through her fingers. "How about Kansas City? I could make the connection from there...no, Dallas? No, forget it. Put me on the seven-forty tomorrow morning.... France Marriotte, I've got an open booking."

Her "thank you" trailed away with the snap of the receiver into its cradle.

"Nothing before the morning?" He tried to sound neutral.

She didn't face him. "No. The last flight tonight leaves in ten minutes."

"I'm sorry." But he knew he wasn't and that he had to find out if he repulsed her.

Only a few feet separated them, but Stephen covered the space slowly. When he stood close behind her, he spanned her waist. He stopped breathing, waiting for her to leap away, to pour out her revulsion. Her muscles tensed but she remained motionless. "France, I can't change what happened—or what Grant said, but—"

"Don't." She cut him off and covered his hands, pressed them against her urgently. He felt shivers tremble through her flesh.

Her fresh scent made his nostrils flare. He glanced down at the top of her head, then brushed his lips slowly back and forth across her hair. At the same time his thumbs found the undersides of her breasts and she leaned against him as if she would fall.

"Do I disgust you?" Carefully, he turned her toward him.

She stared at a point on his chest. "I disgust myself."

"Why?"

"Because I still want you. It can't be, I know that. But I want you. If you weren't touching me I could still feel you. When I'm in bed tonight, every night, alone, I'll imagine us together and long for it. And I think that must make me some kind of twisted freak after today."

She was telling him what he already knew. The sexual attraction they shared was incredibly powerful. Grant's outburst had killed any other feelings she might have had. If there'd been any. But even Grant couldn't quell the chemistry.

"Let me kiss you," he said softly. What could it hurt? Neither of them had any more to lose.

The full force of her green gaze met his and for a second he thought he was dying. *She does love me. She loves me and hates my guts at the same time. What have I done to you, France?* His closed lips grazed hers. Her mouth was cold at first, then quickly warm and parting, guiding his by some involuntary reaction she couldn't control.

Their tongues caressed, reached. France raised onto the tips of her toes to wrap her arms around his neck. Through their thin shirts he felt her nipples crest. His own body responded instantly, his arousal pulsed through his veins and he hardened rapidly. She moaned and thrust her hips into him with enough force to hurt. Such sweet pain.

They were both drawing rasping breaths. "You said you didn't believe it." He held her away and tipped up her chin.

"Don't talk, Stephen."

A quiver moved the muscles in his jaw. He gritted his teeth, hoping she wouldn't notice. He saw the way her breasts rose and fell. *Once more, darlin'.* The top button of her shirt was already undone, the rest seemed to melt beneath his questing fingers. He pulled the fabric free of her waistband and laid it back, exposing pale, swelling flesh above a low-cut bra. His lips pressed repeatedly into that softness, never getting enough.

"I can't. Please." She pleaded while she massaged him through pants that were getting unbearably tight.

Stephen couldn't stop, he didn't want to.

Lace edging slid down beneath his fingers to reveal her straining nipples. He gently seized first one and then the other between his teeth before he found the front fastening that completely released the fullness of her breasts. He surrounded and lifted them, murmuring into the deep valley between. She groaned and cradled his head.

Desire rushed over him like water from a broken dam. He felt her pull his shirt free and yank the buttons undone while he kissed her mouth again and again. "You are the most beautiful thing I've ever seen." One hand drove into the soft warmth between her thighs until she arched against him.

The friction of their bare flesh tore away the last shred of his control. "I need you." He walked her backward until her knees hit the edge of the bed and she crumpled onto the mattress. His suddenly clumsy fingers fumbled with his belt buckle.

A small cry brought his attention back to her face and he recoiled. Panic was written in her eyes. "No, no." She rolled away from the pressure of his legs on hers and sat at the far side of the bed. "I'm not an animal."

Stephen's breath ripped through his throat. "Can you say you don't want me?" *Hate is stronger than love. Who said it? Was it true?* Blood hammered in his head.

"Is that what you asked her? Did Candace refuse you? Is that why you hit her? Are you going to hit me, too?" France closed her eyes and Stephen felt his insides turn into stone.

"I should have expected that. How my brother would have enjoyed hearing you say it. Don't worry, I'm not going to come one inch closer. Just talk to me, for God's sake, talk to me."

France fastened her bra and tucked her shirt into her slacks. All her movements were jerky.

He knew she wanted to escape—from herself as well as him. "Please, say something."

She picked up her purse and walked out of the room, chin up and shoulders rigid. She was gone before he realized her coat still lay on the bed. He grabbed the fur jacket and ran into the hall.

The elevator closed as the sound of his own running footsteps pounded to a stop in the corridor. Still straightening his clothes, he watched the circular indicator light above the doors. He started violently when a bell sounded and he was confronted by a jumble of laughing faces.

Sandwiched among warm bodies in the small compartment, as expensive perfume became a stench, he almost burst into the atrium on the first floor. With France's coat bunched in one hand, he strode past a jungle of plants and vivid flowers surrounding a white indoor gazebo. A jazz group was playing to an audience that sat on steps leading to the street. The music was smooth, but it did nothing to calm Stephen.

He took the steps two at a time and emerged into the cool night air. Fountain Square lay ahead, glittering in light reflected from surrounding buildings.

France had already crossed the road when she saw Stephen come out of the hotel. She hurried on to the edge of the fountain, then circled quickly and stood shivering on the far side. He'd never see her behind the gushing water.

Bronze cupids, coated powdery green, sent foaming jets across banks of submerged lights. The cherubic faces seemed to leer. She'd almost made love with Stephen— even after learning the truth from his brother. Was it the truth? It had to be, and wanting to change it wouldn't make any difference.

A statue of a stately woman, her arms held wide, crowned the fountain. At her feet a gold-lettered inscription dedicated the massive structure to the people of Cincinnati. But what caught France's eye was the smaller note that the gift was the benefactor's memorial to his brother. For some, love was simple. Why did it have to be impossible for her?

France shuddered and plunged her hand into the frigid water. She was in love with a man who was forbidden her. For the first time, she admitted the depth of her feelings for Stephen, and simultaneously she was forced to accept that they had no future.

Long, strong fingers threaded through hers in the water. "You forgot your coat."

She'd been too absorbed to sense Stephen's approach, yet his sudden presence didn't startle her. His grip tightened, and she answered with desperate pressure. For what seemed an eternity, they clung together. Thunderous streams from high above their heads bounced onto the illuminated surface, raising a cloud of mist that dampened their faces.

Keeping their fingers laced, Stephen lifted her hand until their palms were pressed together. "Will you give me a chance to talk to you? If you don't, this may be the end for us. I don't want that, France. Do you?"

She watched his face. Every line and groove was beloved, yet caused her pain. In his devastating blue eyes she saw her fulfillment—then, too quickly, her possible destruction.

"We never had anything, not really." Pulling her hand from his was like stripping the skin from her own flesh. "Lonely people get themselves into situations that shouldn't happen sometimes. It was that way with us. It's not such a big deal."

His head jerked slightly as if she'd hit him, and France felt her own insides bruise. He touched her temple, feathered a damp line to her chin. France wanted to turn her face and kiss his fingers.

The blue-fox jacket trailed from his other hand. "I knew this would happen in the end. We both did. But we wouldn't face it." He draped the coat around her shoulders.

I didn't want to accept it, Stephen. She had to break this now—for both of them. "I'll arrange for another room tonight. You must be starving. Why don't you get some dinner while I talk to the reservations clerk?"

His long, stroking motions between her shoulders and elbows made it hard to concentrate.

"Let's go somewhere together for a meal. You haven't eaten all day, either. You said once that we could shut out the rest of the world. We did it for a while. Couldn't we try again?"

France tried to pull away, but he held on. She wished she could pretend nothing had changed—that she didn't know what he'd done. But the specter of Grant's revelation would always haunt her. "I...if only I could leave tonight. Please don't make this more difficult." She was a danger to herself as long as she was with him.

"Okay, I give up." Stephen's mouth jerked but he didn't quite manage a smile. "But at least allow me to do the legwork. You go and eat; I'll get another room."

She felt numb as he stepped backward.

"I'm sorry I never got to watch a football game with you," he said. "I'd have enjoyed that."

He turned and walked swiftly down wide steps to the street. France's vision blurred. Her nose was running. *Damn*. She pushed her arms into the sleeves of her jacket and found a tissue in one pocket.

Stephen looked over his shoulder before he moved into the crosswalk. His lips formed words she couldn't hear. France didn't want to think anymore.

Look, France. You can't go on being a hermit forever." Paul followed France back and forth between dormant fruit trees. Toby followed Paul.

France checked burlap wrapping on root balls. "I'm not a hermit. Just because I can't come to dinner tonight I'm a recluse?"

"You disappear for two days, without a word, leaving Rachel in charge. ..."

"The first thing you said to me just now was that what I do is my business. Sounds as if you've changed your mind. I needed a break."

Paul sighed and hooked a hand under her arm. "Truce?"

She smiled into his troubled eyes. "Truce, brother. You worry too much. Give me a day or two and I'll be knocking your door down for one of Joanna's good meals. I'm still tired from the trip."

"You didn't say where you went."

"Paul!"

"Right. It's funny, Foley's been out of the office, too. Some sort of family problem, I hear."

An invisible fist pushed up on France's lungs. She barely stopped herself from retorting that Stephen was still away. Paul had added up the facts correctly, but she wasn't going to confirm his suspicions. Stephen was out of her life and she didn't want any reminders.

"I've got a lot to catch up on. And it's past one—you must be due back at work. Thanks for stopping by. Forgive me for being short, but I can't talk now. I promise I'll call soon." She hesitated. "Have you seen Dad?"

"Dad doesn't know a thing. I'll tell Joanna you'll be calling." Paul turned on his heel and threaded his way toward the parking lot. He waved to Rachel through the office window as he passed.

France yanked on a length of twine. "Ouch!" The coarse hemp burned her fingers, and she concentrated on the discomfort to block out the sound of Paul's engine and the thoughts she was trying to avoid.

The office door banged. "Hey, France." Rachel approached with a wooden case of daffodil bulbs. "Guess what the latest con's name is?"

France winced. Bill, the man who reported for work after Stephen, had spent most of each day smoking and staring at passing cars. She'd requested a replacement, who had yet to appear.

"Guess, France."

She crossed her arms. "Okay, I'll bite. Ferdinand?"

"George!" Rachel exploded.

Toby rubbed against France's legs and she bent down to scratch his back. "So? It's an ordinary name—perfectly good. Same as my dad's."

"*That's* what I mean. We could change the name of he nursery." The girl choked on a giggle. "How about, Captivating Creations by George?"

France didn't want to laugh but Rachel was irresistible. Her pale eyes snapped beneath a too-heavy layer of iridescent blue shadow.

"Get it? Captivating—captured, by George! He's a prisoner—and you know Englishmen on safaris always say 'By George' when they sight a tiger or something."

"You're impossible," France groaned. "Poor man. Why isn't he here, by the way?"

"Still sick. They called and said he'd be in tomorrow."

"That's good; we could use the help. You did a fantastic job while I was gone, Rachel. I don't know how you managed so well alone."

"I wasn't."

France stared at her. "What do you mean?"

"Paul came by the morning after you left. When I told him you'd been called away suddenly, he stayed until he had to go to the paper, then Joanna took over for him. They did the same yesterday. Joanna's really good with silk floral arrangements. I think you should ask her to make up some more. We sold five of them."

Guilt and gratitude vied for France's emotions. "That's great. Maybe I will ask her. Those bulbs should be somewhere obvious. Put them out front by the peat moss. I'll help you in a minute. I just want to make a call."

France jogged inside, slapping her arms against her ribs. The snow was gone but it was still cold. Paul and Joanna had already put up with too much from her. Constancy was a rare commodity, and France intended to let them know she appreciated their loving her against all odds.

"Joanna," she said brightly when she heard her sister-in-law's voice on the phone, "you're an angel. So's Paul."

"What did we do?" Joanna sounded breathless.

"You know. Looking after things here. Keeping Dad off the track. Making floral arrangements. And probably a lot more I haven't heard about yet. Paul just left. He invited me to dinner and I refused, but I'd like to renege—if I'm still welcome."

There was a tiny sniff. "Seven?"

"I'll be there."

"France, tell Paul you forgive him when you come."

"For what?"

"He thinks he butted in where you didn't want him and he's been miserable. He loves you; so do I. We only want you to be happy."

France scrubbed the back of her free hand across her eyes. "There's nothing to forgive. This has been a hard time, but everything's going to be fine now. See you later."

She hung up and sat on the desk. Was it going to be fine? Was her life going to fall back into a normal groove, or would she keep on seeing Stephen Foley whenever she closed her eyes—or even if she didn't? How was he? And Gretchen? France had never seen the child, yet she wondered constantly how she was doing.

The afternoon dragged by despite a brisk succession of customers. Several hours later France let herself into the condo and headed for the bedroom. She unwound a stretched, multicolored scarf from her neck and dumped

with her bag and parka on the overstuffed chair. It took
another minute to strip off her work clothes and put on
a robe. She needed a bath, but all she could think of was
lying down.

Under the quilt, a blanket warm beneath her body,
France tried to relax. She hadn't slept in Cincinnati, and
last night, back in her own bed, hadn't been much better. What was Stephen doing now?

After he had left her in Fountain Square, France
walked through streets she didn't know until she reached
the Ohio River. It had been dark. From a bench in an
area called Yeatman's Cove, she watched bobbing lights
on a riverboat and listened to the water smacking against
concrete bulkheads. The flow was swift. Rippling reflec-
tions from the boat's lanterns showed the deep red of
rusty silt drawn from the river's curving banks.

Finally, too confused and tired to care about anything
but sleep, she'd returned to the hotel to find all traces of
Stephen removed. Without undressing, she stretched out
on a couch, unwilling to use the bed she had almost
shared with him. She also admitted she didn't want to be
in it without him. And she stared through sheer drapes at
the city's lights until dawn.

Before checking out in the morning, she pulled down
the quilt. It seemed necessary to make it appear that the
bed had been used. On one pillow she found a piece of
hotel stationery. She didn't need to read the initials in the
corner to know who drew the sketch on it. The familiar
little man, whose halo of hearts was now scattered
around him, lay with both feet in the air and his eyes
closed. A balloon caption read, "Bye."

When France arrived home, she put the cartoon with its earlier partner in the drawer of the jewelry box on her bedside table.

Now she sat up and opened the drawer. She found the two pieces of paper and stared at them. The man needed her. He'd told her so, not once, but several times, in different ways. And she loved him. "I love you," she whispered. "You wanted to talk and I wouldn't listen. I wouldn't let you try to explain."

Had he gotten another room at the Westin or moved to a different hotel? France's bill had already been paid, "by Mr. Foley," when she turned in her key yesterday morning. Short of making a total fool of herself by insisting on paying again, there was nothing she could do but blush and walk out. She had been too embarrassed to wonder where he was.

But Stephen needed her tonight. The surety burned through her with an insistence that sent her scurrying for her clothes before she realized there was no point in getting dressed. He was in Cincinnati, and all she could do was speak to him on the phone. If she could find him.

She called the Westin Hotel first and felt her muscles go limp with relief when the man at the desk told her Stephen Foley was registered. But after a dozen rings the same voice broke in to say what she already surmised— Mr. Foley was out. Quickly France asked the clerk for the hospital number. She hung up then and dialed again, bracing herself to fight a path through the red tape that might continue to separate her from Stephen.

The hospital switchboard operator tapped her through to Gretchen's unit, where a nurse assured France that Stephen Foley wasn't there—would she like to speak to

Grant? France declined too emphatically and hung up, trying to control a heart that wanted to leap from her body.

It was after six-thirty when she tried one last time to reach him at the hotel before leaving for Paul and Joanna's. Four fruitless calls to the hospital had been met with increasingly tense irritation by the same nurse. The hotel clerk sounded politely bored this time as he agreed to ring Stephen's room again.

"Hello."

France clung to the receiver with both hands. "Stephen, is that you?"

"Yes." His voice was so soft she could hardly hear.

"I—I've been trying to reach you for hours. I shouldn't have left you when I did." She swallowed and rushed on. "They wouldn't tell me anything at the hospital. I didn't know how to find you."

"Gretchen's going to make it, thank God. At least that's what the doctors are saying now. But she's in such a lot of pain." His sigh shuddered across the miles of wire. "And it'll take her a long time to recover, if she ever completely does."

"But she's alive, Stephen."

"Yeah, you're right. That's the main thing."

"Are you all right?"

"I'm okay." He was silent a second. "No...I'm tired, France. Worn out. But what the hell? At least my neck's not broken, right?"

Pain fluttered in her throat. She loved him and wanted to comfort him, and because of her own selfish fear she was a thousand miles away. "I want you to come home. Please, Stephen. When are you leaving Cincinnati?"

"Home?" He laughed. "You want me to come home?"

"Stop it," she rasped. "Are you leaving tonight?"

"No plane after seven-thirty, remember?"

His voice was flat, but France knew he felt abandoned and that she had caused that feeling.

"Will you be on the first one in the morning?"

"Probably."

"I'll be waiting at the airport."

He was quiet for so long, France wondered if they'd been cut off. "Are you still there?"

"Forget me, will you?"

She drew a breath and held it before expelling the air slowly. "I can't. I love you."

Chapter Eleven

France wound the fashion magazine into a tube and tapped it impatiently against the wide glass window. She'd bought it twenty minutes before at one of the airport's gift shops, but she didn't feel like reading. Any second, the first morning flight from Cincinnati would land on the gray concrete in front of her. *Please let Stephen be on board.*

Gretchen's positive prognosis was a relief, but France had left Stephen when he'd needed her, and now a primitive anguish gnawed deep inside her. In addition, less than twenty-four hours ago, she'd put into words what he most surely had known for days. She'd exposed her soul by telling Stephen Foley that she loved him.

Tears threatened to escape from beneath her eyelids, and she sniffled softly. Had it been so unreasonable to hope that he might tell her he loved her, too? Darn it, he *did* love her. She'd sensed it, known it. Now perhaps she'd destroyed it.

She closed her eyes and remembered all too clearly the stillness that followed her heart-wrenching admission, and the way he'd quickly changed the subject, then hung up. That brief silence was far more eloquent than a hundred words, and the significance of it cut deeply.

Her feelings would never change, and she would be strong until he was ready to accept them and give them back himself. He was as much a part of her as the air she breathed, and nothing in God's creation could make her let him go.

Suddenly the earsplitting drone of a landing jetliner shook the crowded concourse. She glanced at the large abstract clock hanging from the ceiling. Eleven forty-five. Flight 302 from Cincinnati via Chicago was on schedule.

France twisted the magazine harshly, then realized how nervous she must look and stuffed it into her oversized shoulder bag. She pressed one cheek against the pane in time to spot the aircraft taxi out of sight beyond the terminal.

Her stomach rolled. Perhaps Stephen had changed his mind about returning to Tulsa that morning. After all, he'd told her to forget him. What if he'd really meant what he'd said and decided to catch a later flight to avoid her? What if he didn't want to see her again? No, she reminded herself. The man she loved and was prepared to carve her world around was on that jet, and she wouldn't give in to her niggling worries.

It seemed an eternity before the plane swung close to the building and the loading arm was clamped to its side. France leaned across the rope barrier to see the first passengers funnel from the narrow corridor. Groups passed, couples, bored men with flight bags arriving on business trips; then, finally, she saw him. Stephen came into view, his head jutting taller than those of the travelers surrounding him.

"Stephen," France whispered. He was still too far away to hear or see her in the crowd, but his exhausted features tugged at her heart.

Shades of anxiety etched uneven shadows on his pale face and tautly defined the skin over his cheekbones. She noted the dark circles beneath his wonderful eyes, the hunched slope of his shoulders, and longed to soothe him.

That he hadn't slept well was obvious, but then, neither had she. Even at this distance she could see the slept-in appearance of his shirt and slacks. Unaware of her, he looked straight ahead as he moved toward the concourse, his sport coat tossed carelessly over one shoulder.

"Stephen! Over here." France waved her arm.

A frown flickered across his brow. He searched the waiting crowd and spotted her.

"Here." France stood on tiptoe.

To her relief, his expression brightened. He shifted the small suitcase he carried to his other hand and quickened his pace. "You came to meet me." The rope still separated them, but he dropped his bag and jacket and gathered her into his arms in spite of it.

France pressed her cheek into his shirt. She felt his sharp intake of breath. "I said I would. You don't have your Porsche, remember? We took a cab out here, and I couldn't let you take another one home." His broad shoulder muffled the crack in her voice.

Stephen rubbed the top of her head with his chin, oblivious to the mass of people pushing past them. "You feel so good. I still didn't expect to find you here, not after our telephone conversation."

"Didn't you?" France lifted her head. "I said I would be and I keep my promises." It was impossible to steady her erratic pulse.

"All of them? No, darlin', don't answer. I know you do. Thank God. No matter what I say or don't say to you, or how I treat you." His voice was husky, meant for her ears alone. He squeezed her shoulders, then trailed his hands down her arms. He gripped her fingers. "I'm sorry about yesterday...and before. I said things I didn't mean. Must have been the stress. And Gretchen."

"Don't worry. I understand. How are Grant and Candace holding up?" She hesitated, searching for the right words, praying desperately that she hadn't already said the wrong thing.

"Okay, I think. Considering." His sigh was deep and uneven. "Gretchen's going to have a rough time in the months to come. And none of it will be easy for them."

"Stephen, I feel useless and so sorry for your family. All I want to do is help you, in any way I can."

"You amaze me. Even after my dear brother's informative revelations?"

"Stephen, don't close me out, please."

He shrugged. "There's nothing more we can do for Gretchen right now, except wait. As for me..."

She stared at him. "It's *you* I worry about. You need me, Stephen, whether you want to admit it or not." France lowered her voice. "You need me," she repeated.

He was silent for several seconds while the deafening noise of another landing jet shook the acoustic roof. "You're right, France. I do, but I shouldn't...." He smiled thinly. "Oh, hell. Let's get out of here. There's so much I need to say to you. I should have explained a long time ago, and the middle of an airport is hardly the place."

France twisted and looked around. The other passengers had dispersed, and a solitary airline employee was emptying ashtrays. She turned back. "Are you hungry? It's almost lunchtime."

"Not really. I ate on the plane. But I expect you are, or you wouldn't have mentioned it."

"I guess I am—just a little bit. The sun's shining today for a change. It's warmer, almost like spring." She tugged at her bulky pullover sweater. "See, I'm not even wearing a jacket. Maybe we could get some submarine sandwiches at a deli, then take them to a park. Do you feel like it?"

"Okay. I could use some fresh air." He sighed and rubbed a hand over his forehead.

France bit her lip. "I'm sorry. Maybe that's not such a good idea. Sometimes I'm too impulsive. You're probably tired after all that's happened. I'll get you back to your place and leave you alone so you can get some sleep."

"No. I missed you, France. God knows how much. I want to be anywhere you are." He released her hand, then bent to pick up his suitcase and jacket. "And I'm not in any hurry to get home. Let's find that deli."

France started walking slowly. "The pickup's in the parking garage. You can drive if you want to."

"All right. But your confidence surprises me. I must look a bit rough around the edges."

"I don't care."

"I'm a lucky man."

France noticed the sadness in his smile, but the unspoken affection in his eyes quieted her troubled spirits.

He skirted the barricade and draped an arm around her shoulders. Ten minutes later the pickup chugged out of the parking garage with Stephen behind the wheel.

"There's a great deli on South Main Street. They make sandwiches a mile high, with every trimming imaginable. Let's stop there." France pointed to a blinking red light. "Turn left at this intersection, then go two more blocks."

They stopped in front of the restaurant and France hopped out. She motioned for Stephen to roll down the window. "Eating outside in January *is* crazy, isn't it? You're sure you want to do this? You can still change your mind."

He flexed his fingers around the steering wheel, bracing his shoulders against the patched upholstery. "Listen, France. Driving this contraption is hard work, and now I'm famished, too. I *want* a sandwich, believe me. And I want to have a picnic with you—in January. If we freeze to death, at least we'll be together and I'll die happy."

Her muscles relaxed with relief. "Wonderful. My treat, okay? Let me surprise you."

She turned and he shouted after her, "I don't like pastrami."

France came back with sandwiches, cookies and two gigantic cups of coffee, and they drove to Woodward Park, a few blocks away. Stephen stopped the pickup in the empty parking lot, and together they clumped across the crunchy winter-brown lawn in search of the perfect spot for their meal.

"There, in the rock garden." France clutched the food to her breast and ran in the direction of a sun-drenched expanse of grass at the base of a sheltering stone and plant formation. Huge oak trees surrounded the clearing, their massive bare branches stretching to the sky. Shards of sunlight streamed through them, painting the ground and rocks with inviting warmth.

Stephen placed Styrofoam coffee cups on top of a flat boulder. He drew in a breath, filling his lungs. "Smell that air. Quite a change from the inside of a plane."

Or a hospital, France thought.

"This is perfect, protected," he continued. "The plants are dormant but, other than that, you'd never know it's winter." Although he smiled, his voice sounded strained.

They sat on the ground to eat and leaned against the heated stones. France sensed Stephen's disquiet. Although the sun's rays soothed, they didn't melt the cold uneasiness within her.

She sipped her coffee and regarded him with searching gravity, knowing that she loved him completely, with all his attributes and failings. Whatever he'd done wrong in the past, she was ready to accept. She ached to calm him, to ease away his uncertainties.

After they'd eaten, France slid toward him and nestled her head into the hollow of his shoulder. His arm encircled her immediately.

"I want to know about Gretchen, Stephen." She reached for his other hand and pulled it to her lips. She whispered across the tops of his knuckles. "Tell me what she's been through, what *you've* been through."

He squeezed her fingers, then let them go. "The past few days have been hell, France. Absolute hell. You have no idea. Everyone thought she was going to die." He covered his mouth with the back of his hand. "Thank God, she's not. But she's in a body cast and can't move a muscle. Poor kid. The next few months are going to be so hard on her...on everyone."

"I can imagine."

"It's just not fair to Gretchen." Moisture glistened in his eyes. "I know I probably shouldn't, but I blame Grant for this. He's pushed her into so many things in the past when she wasn't ready. He's a fool. And sometimes I wonder if he even really cares for his own daughter. It's all been a nightmare." A shudder coursed through him, and he opened his arms. "Hold me, France. You're so real, so good. Bring me back the world."

"Oh, Stephen. I *do* love you." She knelt between his legs and wound her arms around him. She felt him stiffen, then melt against her, and every part of her yearned to console him.

Bone and muscle flexed beneath the palms of her hands as he pulled her almost roughly to him and buried his face in the soft swell of her breasts.

"I can hear your heartbeat." He rubbed his head slowly against her and ran his hands beneath the thick folds of her sweater. "And your skin's warm, soft." His voice was husky and muffled. "This is reality, isn't it, sweetheart? All that I could want...or dream of having."

Blood pounded in her brain. *Tell me you love me, Stephen.* She closed her eyes, then opened them. *Tell me.*

He raised his head and looked at her, his eyes still glazed with emotion. When he spoke his voice trembled. "I want to tell you what happened that night—the night they said I tried to rape Candace."

"No, Stephen," she said. "You don't have to talk about that. It will only stir up more bad memories for you. I know you didn't do anything wrong. You don't have to convince me."

He pulled back from her, and the rush of air that filled his place felt cold.

Leaning against hard basalt, he plucked at blades of brown grass and continued as if he hadn't heard her protest. "Grant travels a lot. He's a salesman, and he was gone that night."

"Please, stop" France pleaded. "I don't need to know this."

"You do...if you want to really understand me."

France hunched over and stilled, as if her breath had been suddenly cut off.

"They lived in Tulsa then, not too far from where we are right now. I used to do odd jobs for Candace, sometimes, when Grant was gone. You know, fix things, change the oil in their car. Nothing big, right?"

France stared up at him silently.

"That night Candace called and asked if I'd mind coming over. Grant had taken a trip to California, and their television had gone on the blink. She wanted me to see if I could fix it."

Sarcasm edged his laugh. "I should have been suspicious when I realized that Gretchen had been sent to spend the night with Grandma. But I wasn't...because I trusted Candace. After all, she was my brother's wife.

"What a fool I was. I couldn't have been more off base." He reached down to grab a fistful of dirt and watched as it trickled through his fingers. "That woman wanted me in her bed, and she was prepared to do anything to get me there. Can you believe it?"

France shrugged. She did believe it, knowing as she did how devastatingly sexy Stephen could be. He watched her for a second, and she felt, almost certainly, that her expression had betrayed her thoughts.

"I didn't want her, France. Not Candace. Good Lord, she's family. I refused to touch her. That's when I should have left. But she couldn't handle the rejection. She came after me.

"I tried to hold her off, but she clawed at me, scratched a bit...and her scream, God, that scream. I was confused. I took her abuse, tried to calm her down, but she'd taken some skin off my cheek and it was bleeding all over. I pushed her away, and she went for my throat." He pulled up his knees and pressed his forehead against them. His sigh seemed dredged from his core. "God forgive me, I accidentally hit her in the face."

"It wasn't your fault. She asked for it."

"It *was* my fault, damn it. I shouldn't have hit Candace. I gave her a black eye."

"I'm sorry, Stephen." France's heart pounded. She didn't know what to say.

He laughed disdainfully. "Yeah, so was I. In fact, I didn't know how sorry I was going to be until later." He looked at France and bitterness flashed in his eyes. "I have an uncanny knack for bad timing, you know. Because that's when little brother decided to come back home. Candace and I made quite a welcoming committee.''

''But he was supposed to be in California.''

''I'm sure that's what Candace thought. But Grant had been suspicious for several months that she was seeing another man and deliberately planned the trip to trap her and the unlucky lover. From the way she set me up, I'd say Grant had reason to be leery. Who knows how many other men she's tried to seduce during his absences?''

''But Grant is your *brother*. It's ridiculous to think that he'd suspect you.'' France's thighs hurt where her fingers pressed into them.

''Ha! You underestimate him. We've never gotten along, never been close. And that was a pretty damning scene he walked in on.'' Stephen's voice was low but dangerously clear. ''He hates me, France, and he was ready to believe whatever his wife told him—even if it put me behind bars. He'd always felt he had to compete with me and that I came off best. He was convinced our mother preferred me, although it wasn't true. The idea of me wanting his wife, as well, was too much. I think he cracked up.''

''Oh, no.'' France shivered and crossed her arms. The awful scene in the hospital was beginning to make terrible, understandable sense.

Stephen found a small stick on the ground beside him. He smiled cynically and picked it up, pretending to examine it. ''Candace thought fast. She started crying and screaming rape as soon as Grant opened the living-room door.'' He gave the stick a twist and it broke. ''The cops came. Then there was the trial, in which Grant proved to be the star witness. They sent me up. I think the sweetest moment in my brother's life was when the judge passed sentence." He looked at her levelly. "The rest is history."

"That's appalling." Tears brimmed in her eyes. She envisioned the sterile prison cell he'd lived in, felt his agony at his own family's betrayal. She'd seen his home, his studio, and knew how much he'd been forced to sacrifice.

"You were framed." Her voice wavered.

Stephen shrugged. "Candace was afraid. She saved herself like any threatened animal. Afterward, she didn't have the guts to admit the truth. I tried, but I couldn't fight the system." Casually he tossed the sticks onto the ground. "That's life, and I just haven't been very lucky in it." He looked at her. "At least I wasn't until I met you."

"I'm glad you told me all this, Stephen. I wanted to understand you—really know what kind of hell you've lived." France reached for his hand and felt it shake beneath her fingers. "You've been through more than most men could handle. But don't you think it's time you made another attempt to clear you name?"

"I've thought about it—being in prison gives a man plenty of time to think." He bent to lightly kiss the moisture welling in the corners of her eyes. "But Grant and Candace will be suffering so much now...with Gretchen. And I can't put that poor child through any more misery. She didn't ask for any of this, and those two fools are still her parents. No, I'm going to try to forget. No tears, France. I'm not worth it."

"You are worth it. I love you, Stephen. Nothing else matters to me—nothing."

A muscle twitched on one side of his mouth. He ran a finger along her jaw, then tipped her face to his. "Shh.

You're not being rational. Sure, I'm out of prison, but this conviction will follow me for the rest of my life. That's okay for me. I expect it. I can handle it—alone." He shook his head. "France, I've told you before, and now you should realize it, too. I'm no good for you."

"I want to be with you. Open your eyes, Stephen. We have something beautiful, precious. Something many people spend their whole lives searching for and never find. I won't give you up." France stiffened and gripped his waist. Her heartbeat jolted against her ribs.

"Relax, France. Relax." His features softened. "Don't make hasty statements. Think about what I've said."

"I have, and nothing's changed." France dropped her hands and stood up. "You don't really want me to forget you. I know you don't." Defiance ripped through her. She brushed dirt from her knees and stared down at him.

Stephen scrambled to his feet. "You're being stubborn." He studied her for several seconds, then opened his arms. "But you're so beautiful—a lovely, outspoken, impulsive idiot."

France went to him and buried herself in the firm strength of his embrace. "Oh, Stephen, I want you. Don't ask me to stay away."

"Sweetheart, you tempt me beyond reason." He rubbed his fingers slowly, tenderly, along her spine. "This is a mistake. God knows it is. But I can barely stand to be apart from you."

"When can I see you again?" Soft fabric muffled her voice. His fingers stopped caressing, and France held her breath.

"For your sake, I should say never. But I can't. How about my place on Saturday—for dinner?"

Chapter Twelve

Giant raindrops slanted across the shop windows, and France hesitated inside the florist's door. A short dash across the street would take her into the foyer of Stephen's building. But by then she'd be soaked.

Lightning split the early-evening sky. Brilliant, white streaks burst jagged paths earthward and almost immediately a dull boom shuddered in the air. Good grief, it wasn't supposed to do this in January.

Why had she given in to the impulse to buy Stephen flowers? Flowers, of all things. She looked at the tissue-wrapped apricot roses in her hand, then at her angora sweater-coat and the delicate dress visible beneath. The turquoise silk would be a clinging mess after ten seconds in the pounding rain. Another burst of light preceded a searing crackle that seemed to bounce and echo between buildings.

France glowered at her pickup, parked in front of the florist's. It should have been in the basement garage of Stephen's apartment block while she made the elegant entrance she had planned for his benefit. There was no point in moving the vehicle now. She wrapped her coat around her, clutched to her chest the flowers and the brown sack she had been carrying, and pushed her way outside.

Instantly sodden, she dodged across the road and didn't see the puddle until it was too late. One foot after the other sank, ankle-deep, in the gutter. She howled with surprise and squelched into the entrance of Denver Place.

The doorman extended an umbrella only far enough from the overhang to ensure that his own arm remained dry. He touched the shiny peak of his gold-braided cap and regarded her with a deceptively straight face.

"Evening, miss." He swept the plate-glass door open. "Nice weather for ducks."

France felt like asking him if he had any other original pleasantries to share. Instead, she wiped at her face and smiled grimly. "It certainly is." Her mascara was probably drizzling toward her chin.

The elevator seemed to arrive at the sixteenth floor almost before she pressed the button. Not that it mattered—her appearance was irreparable. Stephen had better not laugh.

Drops from her clothes made dark marks on the amber rug outside his door. France punched the buzzer. The roses smelled and looked wonderful. Tiny beads of moisture clung to their fragile petals. Why hadn't she had the sense to go home and change? Stephen would have understood.

Another longer chime from the doorbell, followed by a third, faded away into silence. Disbelief mingled with irritation. He couldn't have forgotten their date—she'd been unable to think of anything else since they were last together.

France's dress felt like a cold second skin, and she tried to pluck it free of her midriff. The invitation for dinner must have been Stephen's way of avoiding further discussion. He'd probably planned to be out when she arrived. *Fine*. At least she wouldn't have to sit around in a wet dress.

A hand on her shoulder interrupted her furious thoughts.

"Sorry I'm late." Stephen had arrived noiselessly behind her. He peered into her upturned face, then took in the rest of her. "You look like a drowned rat."

"Thanks. Between you and the doorman, I think that about covers rainy day clichés. Are you going to let me in so I can drip on some more rugs?"

He grinned and produced a bunch of keys from the pocket of his gray flannel slacks. "Touchy, touchy." His hair glistened and specks of water clung to the shoulders of a blue tweed jacket and a charcoal, rag-wool sweater underneath. The fronts of his pant legs were slightly damp.

Inside the apartment, France stalked into the kitchen. She set the flowers and paper sack on the butcher block work island and shook her head vigorously.

Stephen had followed her. "Been taking lessons from Toby?"

"What's that supposed to mean?" Gingerly holding a front edge of her collarless coat between each finger and thumb, she pulled it away from her body. The wool felt like an icy sponge.

"Nothing. Give me that." He helped her take off the coat.

France grabbed his sleeve as he headed out of the room. "Yes, you did. What did you mean about Toby?"

"It'll only make you madder. Okay. Seeing you shake yourself like that reminded me of the way he does it. Satisfied?"

She tried to frown but couldn't. "Great." She laughed. "I already knew I looked like a dog."

Stephen opened his mouth, then closed it again as if he'd changed his mind about saying something. The muscles in his jaw flicked into knots. He left abruptly, and France wondered if she'd managed to offend him. She shrugged. The way her dress stuck to her skin concerned her more at the moment—so did the unpleasant sensation of soggy leather encasing her feet.

France's purse was in the bag with the bottle of wine she'd brought from home. With the aid of a tissue and her compact-mirror, she managed to remove most of the smudged mascara, but the rest of her appearance was beyond help.

A few minutes later, when Stephen returned, she was filling a black ceramic swan with water and trying to appear nonchalant.

"You're the first woman who ever brought me wine and flowers. Thank you."

The sliver of jealousy that assaulted her at his casual mention of other women caught France off balance. She took a cleaver from the knife block. "You're the first man who offered to cook my dinner." The blade came down across the rose stems with enough force to jolt her wrist.

"Easy. You'll lose a finger. There are some shears in one of these drawers." He rummaged until he found a large pair of scissors but didn't hand them to her. Instead, he set them on the counter and stroked the edge of a dewy rose petal. "These remind me of you. Like fine velvet. Soft."

France could hear their breathing, and a thread of longing coiled in her belly. She picked up a flower and worked it carefully into wire mesh inside the swan. They had made so many mistakes; to allow themselves to move quickly now could prove disastrous.

"Put this on. It'll keep you warm while your dress dries."

As France lifted her head, Stephen thrust a shapeless gray wad at her. He had changed his own clothes. A light denim shirt, open at the throat, was tucked into jeans that hugged his slender hips and muscular thighs. His feet were bare. She assessed his handsome frame in a swift glance, but when her gaze swept from his toes back to his blue, blue eyes, she saw an answering spark of awareness.

"Thanks. I'll go change," she muttered, but stayed rooted to the spot.

Stephen took a step toward her and France turned her back. She closed her eyes when he held her gently against his long, hard body.

His breath moved her hair. "You're lovely—so very lovely." He hesitated, his grip tightening. "Maybe I should help you."

France twisted away, turning her gasp into a chuckle. She pointed an admonishing forefinger at him. "No way. This woman was promised food and she expects satisfaction—for her stomach." She finished with a rush.

"I mean to please. I guess it's back to the ovens." He stepped aside, his smile teasing.

What he had given her to keep warm proved to be an oversized sweatshirt, imprinted with "University of Oklahoma" in red letters. France put her dress on a hanger she took from the valet in Stephen's bedroom and, together with her half-slip and panty hose, hung it in the shower.

She stood in the center of the mirror-tiled bathroom and pulled the sweatshirt on over skimpy blue lace bikinis. The lettering ruffled across the tops of her thighs and the hem of the shirt ended an inch above her knees. Rolling the sleeves up four times freed her hands.

France decided that the amount of air that circulated under the fleece-lined fabric, and the seductive way the soft lining skimmed her breasts, made her feel anything but warm. The thought of facing Stephen, knowing how he would appreciate the provocative picture she made, started its own heat that quickly colored her cheeks.

The purse containing her comb and makeup was still on the kitchen counter. France ran her fingers through partially dried curls and dashed cold water over her face. Her clear skin and natural glow gave her some satisfaction. Even the light sprinkling of freckles across her nose pleased her. She felt young, excited—and deliciously apprehensive.

The soft bedroom rug squished between her toes. France paused and took a deep breath. The trembling she felt was inside, but so intense she was afraid Stephen would see it.

Almost reluctantly, she admired the bold geometric designs that dominated his room. A fitted quilt in shades of mahogany, tan and deep blue, curved to join the matching cover on the base of a king-size bed. Huge pillows emblazoned with Aztec suns lay against a padded headboard. The same colors were echoed in a tall arrangement of dried grasses and contemporary silk-screened wall hangings.

Stephen had obviously done well in his career, despite a year's enforced absence. But he explained that to her before. France compared his home to hers and felt a little intimidated. A successful man, alone, could lead a very comfortable life. Perhaps he preferred to continue as he was.

He'd been painfully open with her when he returned from Cincinnati, but even after she confessed her feelings for him several times he hadn't reciprocated.

"France, are you all right?" The soft voice on the other side of the door startled her.

"Yes. I'll be right there."

She waited for her heart to return to its normal rate before she turned the handle. But Stephen wasn't outside.

Her bare feet slapped against the tiled floor as she entered the kitchen and hurried to the far side of the work island. "Better get these flowers into water before they wilt." She concentrated intently, pretending to ignore sharp thorns that poked her fingers—and the sensation Stephen's interested gaze caused.

He leaned far over the counter and peered down the length of her, ending at her curled-up toes. "Fetching, m'dear. You'll have all the girls asking for the name of your couturier."

France batted the end of his nose with a piece of fern. "Have you looked in the mirror lately? I don't know what you're making, but from the amount of it on your face, I doubt if there'll be enough left for dinner."

His face, and the navy-and-white-striped apron he
wore, were smeared with a yellowish mixture. He raised
his eyebrows wickedly. "Want to take over?"

"Not in a million years. What are you cooking,
anyway?"

He wiped the back of one hand over his temple.
"Chicken-stuffed crepes and stir-fried vegetables."

"Wonderful. The way to a woman's heart. You remembered what I like."

"Of course I did." Stephen was serious. "Why
wouldn't I?"

France shrugged. "Don't mind me." She sat on a high
stool and stretched the shirt over her knees. "Is that one
of you mother's recipes?" He'd never mentioned his
parents.

The hand whisk beat giant bubbles into already well-
mixed batter. "No." His reply was toneless. He turned on
a burner under a small skillet and spooned in enough of
the creamy mixture to cover the bottom of the pan.

France bit the inside of her cheek. She'd accidentally
found another subject he wasn't ready to discuss. "Aren't
you supposed to put in oil or something first?"

"The oil's already in the batter. I made it last night.
You really can't cook, can you?" His vivid stare was
amused. "This is the filling." Chopped chicken and
cheese sauce bubbled gently in a saucepan.

"Smells marvelous." She decided to ignore his crack
about her lack of kitchen skills.

While France watched, a stack of crepes grew steadily
on a plate by the stove. Occasionally, Stephen flipped
vegetables in a stainless-steel wok. He worked quickly
and seemed to have forgotten her. She was leaning on her

elbows, her nose buried in the roses, when she sensed his eyes on her again. Her heartbeat accelerated, but she avoided meeting his gaze.

"I set an elegant table in the dining room to impress you." He turned off the burner. "We aren't dressed for it, but we can have a grandstand view of the storm while we eat."

France climbed from the stool and went to set the roses on the table. Two places had been arranged, side by side, in front of the upholstered wicker couch. The china was Oriental, deep umber with a single sweeping gladiolus blossom in black on each place. Silver flatware and smoky, angular crystal glistened.

"Ready," Stephen called.

She stopped him in the entrance to the kitchen. "Just a minute. Let me wipe that stuff off your face."

He held still while she rubbed at smears with the moistened end of a dish towel. Whe she trailed the fringe across his upper lip he laughed and jerked his head away.

"Are you ticklish, Stephen?" France undid the chef's apron, playing her fingertips up his ribs. He almost dropped the plate. "You are. Now I've found my ultimate weapon."

Stephen lowered his head so that she could slip the strap from his neck. "France." His voice was deep, soft velvet. "We both found the ultimate weapon a long time ago."

Skittishly, France leapt away, dropped the apron on a chair and headed for the dining table. An electric dart shot through her at the thought of sitting so close to him, of inevitable touches, accidental—and deliberate. Each look, every word that passed between them, spun golden filaments of desire along her nerves. *Go slow—keep it slow,* the weak voice in her head warned.

They ate in preoccupied silence for several minutes. A blustery wind added its stroke of drama to the scene beyond the walls of glass. Violent gusts splattered raindrops by the millions in giant chattering handfuls that hung, glittered, then sped to join each other in slithering ribbons.

"It's beautiful up here." France swiveled away from Stephen and stared into the wild night beyond her own reflection in the window.

Gentle caresses on the side of her neck brought her attention back to her mirrored image and to Stephen's outline behind her. He pushed the sweatshirt aside and she watched his dark silhouette as he kissed her shoulder, lightly, repeatedly. He smelled like the rain-laced wind, tangy and fresh.

"Stephen." France couldn't make herself pull away. "Dinner was good, but if you keep this up we aren't going to get to dessert."

He blew the hair at her nape, then wrapped his arms around her, supporting a swelling breast in each hand. "There isn't any," he whispered.

"Let's not rush this time. You said…" Her voice failed as he shifted and pulled her across his lap. His eyes shone darkly as he brought his mouth within an inch of hers.

When he didn't kiss her parted lips, she raised her head, unable to wait any longer. Tentatively, she moved the tip of her tongue from one corner of his sensuous mouth to the other, feeling his body tense. "You make me different, Stephen. When I'm with you, it's as if I turn into someone else."

"Whoever it is, I'm crazy about her. In fact, both of you are driving me mad." Purposefully, he swung her to sit beside him and grabbed their dishes. "I forgot the wine."

France lay her face against his back and encircled his waist. "Don't go."

China met glass with a brittle crack. "Darlin'." He loosened her grip and twisted to face her. "You were right when you reminded me not to rush. There's nothing casual about any of this. I want us both to be sure how we feel—really feel." With a thumb and index finger he held her chin and played his lips over hers in a searingly soft kiss.

"Do that again and neither of us is going to be able to think." But she stood up and took the dishes to the kitchen herself. She started to rinse them.

"Leave it," Stephen called from the living room. "Come here."

He was kneeling in front of a video recorder when she joined him. Raucous cheers burst from the television set. "Stephen," France squealed. "Where did you get that?"

"Sit there," he ordered, pointing to a low couch. "What do you drink when you watch this stuff?"

"Whatever you've got...beer? It's the Texas-Oklahoma game from October. I missed it. How did you find it? You can't rent these, can you?"

Stephen had already gone into the kitchen. "Borrowed it from a guy at work," he shouted. "I thought you would already have seen it."

"This is great." France patted the couch beside her when Stephen set down two tall glasses of beer. "You thought I'd already seen it but you borrowed it anyway?"

"Foiled again," he said, laughing. "I only wanted a chance to see you watching one of your beloved games. Everyone's heard of football widows but I don't recall mention of football widowers."

France looked at him sharply. Was he trying to decide if they were compatible outside the bedroom, or just making fun of her? She took a deep swallow of beer and leaned back into plump cushions. "You're not interested in sports?"

"Depends on the sport."

"I enjoy everything—but luge."

Stephen crossed his ankles on the coffee table. "I hate having to ask, but what's luge?"

"One- or two-man sled race. Mostly European—you see it in the Olympics. Look at that," she yelled. "That jerk. I don't believe it. Ever heard of a screen pass, coach?"

"Did they lose yardage?" Stephen inquired mildly.

France cut him a glance. She was on her feet. "Lose yardage? *Only* sixteen yards. Offside, you turkey. Get the guy a new pair of glasses. Gee." She plopped down, Indian-style, and leaned forward.

An odd sensation prickled over her skin, and she glanced at Stephen. He was staring at her, his jaw braced on one hand. A lopsided grin answered her questioning expression.

"Aren't you getting into this game?" she asked.

He shook his head slowly. "I'd rather watch you. You're something. I'm surprised you don't already know who won."

France realized she was showing a lot of leg, all the way up to a hint of blue lace. She hitched at the sweatshirt. "I do know who won. It doesn't make any difference. Sometimes I watch highlights of the same game on three different channels.''

"Amazing." One long finger followed the sensitive skin where her panty elastic met her thigh. "I guess there are some things—or people—we never get tired of."

A delicious shudder heated her body. As he ran his hand over the inside of her leg, she jumped. "Why, France. Are you ticklish, too?" His smile was wide.

"No, of course not." She tucked both feet beneath her. "We're an odd pair, aren't we? Sort of back to front. You cook, I watch football." Her breath caught in her throat.

"Oh, I think there's a lot to be said for that. We complement each other. I don't do much of a job on flower arrangements and you're obviously very good at that. And we definitely have things in common—including being ticklish."

Stephen quickly held her waist and pushed her back against the arm of the couch. France tried to wiggle free as his fingers made swift tracks up and down her sides.

"Stop," she begged. "We'll turn off the football and talk. Please." His grip lessened and she shot away.

"Sneaky." Stephen caught her ankle and France slid to the rug, laughing helplessly. He hit the remote control, blacking out the film.

France pulled herself slowly from the space in front of the couch with Stephen still gripping her foot. "Mercy, Stephen. Don't tickle my foot. I can't stand it."

He grinned devilishly. "What's it worth?" They had reached an open expanse, France on her back, Stephen kneeling at her feet.

A tiny kiss on her sole sent her writhing onto her side. "Anything, you sadist. Wait till I get my chance."

"Anything—good. Lie still." He kissed her leg slowly, from ankle to groin, where he breathed moist, warm air on tingling skin.

His lips found her belly above the low-cut bikinis and he spanned the flare of her hips. Everywhere he touched a flame started and grew until France throbbed with her need to have him fill her.

"Take off your clothes, Stephen. I want to feel you."

He groaned. Inch by inch he pushed the sweatshirt up, following exposed skin with his tongue, until her breasts were bared. "Your body is beautiful, lady. You're beautiful. I want to show you how much I love you."

She filled her fingers with his hair. Emotions sped along her veins, mingling with the erotic sensations he evoked in her, until she felt her mind would explode. He had told her he loved her.

"I love you, too, Stephen," she whispered. She pushed him away reluctantly and sat to pull the sweatshirt over her head. "Come to me, now."

"Wait a few seconds, my sweet. Just a little while longer." He stood up and stripped off his clothes.

Fire flashed deep into France's womb. "Stephen..."

He lay beside her, stroked her, first with fleeting fingers, then with lips and tongue. Between every exploration he returned to kiss her mouth, sucking at its silken hollow as if to devour her. France answered each touch with one of her own. She found the dip at the base of his spine, smoothed hard muscle over his buttocks. The way his flat nipples responded to her tongue tightened something low in her abdomen and she buried her face in the soft hair on his chest.

With each contact the pitch of their movements increased. Stephen slid off the wispy lace panties and lifted her hips. He kissed and probed the wire-taut flesh below her navel, moving lower until France took a long, calming breath and forced him onto his back. She sat on his thighs for several seconds, staring into his eyes, which had become black. While she stared, she touched him and gloried in what she felt.

France rose over him to wrap her arms around his neck, then lowered herself over him, slowly, deliberately. Their cries were one as they joined. She opened her heart and soul as well as her body to the high-pitched melody that repeated and repeated in her mind. It was a melody that sang out their total love.

At their climax, Stephen pushed up on his elbows, reached for all they wanted, and the music burst into tinkling fragments. He kissed her breasts, sighed against her distended nipples, and pulled her down on his sweat-damp chest without separating their union. France trembled.

Stephen smoothed a tendril of moist hair from the corner of her mouth. He cupped the side of her face, holding her other cheek against the steady beat of his heart. "Did you hear what I said to you a little while ago?"

"Yes," she said quietly. "But you can say it again whenever you feel like it."

"I love you, France. I love you, I love you. I want to hear my own voice saying it and feel inside what I feel right now over and over again. If my constitution can

ake it.'' A small rumble sounded in his throat. ''Tell me
you love me.''

France slid her arms around his neck and started to cry.
'I love you.'' She felt tears slide across her temple. ''I
hink I have loved you since I first saw you.''

''And it makes you cry?''

''Yes. Stupid, right?''

He held her close, completely wrapping her body until
he rubbed the sides of her breasts. ''No, darlin'. I feel like
crying myself. There was a long time when I didn't dare
hope we had a chance, but now I'm never going to give
you up.''

Chapter Thirteen

Stephen awoke gradually and lifted heavy eyelids to stare at the shadowy ceiling. Air entered his lungs in deep, easy breaths. Every muscle felt relaxed and warm, and the warmth seemed to fill his body with sweet, satisfied peace. He turned on his side and propped himself up on one elbow. The storm must have blown itself out. Pale silvery moonlight cast a long shaft from the window across the bedroom and the woman who slept beside him.

Fear still clung to the edges of his mind, but it was fading to a thin rim and in the space left behind lay his dream, embodied in France. She mumbled and threw her arms over her head. The sheet was tugged from her breasts and he studied her vulnerable nakedness possessively. He would not let her go, no matter what or who tried to separate them.

Logic insisted that his father's traits had not been perpetuated in him. He felt no trace of the violence and envy Grant had inherited. Uncontrolled hate and selfishness had eventually destroyed their father and, in a way, their mother, just as it was now chipping away at Grant and Candace. Stephen thought of Gretchen, lying immobile in that sterile hospital room, and tears stung his eyes. Maybe he and France would have a little girl of their own one day.

France rolled over and nestled her face into the hollow of his shoulder. His hand hovered over her hair and followed an imaginary caress an inch above her neck and back, to the dip at her waist. Carefully he surrounded her slender hips and drew her more tightly against him.

A while ago, an hour or two, he didn't know how long, they'd made love for the first time in his bed. Their bed. *My wife.* He tried the words in his head and smiled. Soon he would ask her. This was what he had prayed for and thought would never materialize. Now the woman he loved, and who loved him as unreservedly, was going to be his—for the rest of their lives.

Stephen kissed the top of France's head. He felt her smile against his shoulder and the brush of her fingers on his thigh. He tried to hold still, but she moved and he looked into her open eyes. "France—sweetheart. You're awake."

France gave an indistinct moan and stretched toward the window slightly. Her long legs were alabaster from narrow ankles to the shadowy place between her thighs. "Mmm, I don't know." Her chin nuzzled into his chest. "You feel so good, Stephen, so right. Maybe I'm dreaming."

"This is real, darlin'. Believe me." How beautiful she was. How much he needed her. Moonlight polished the peaks of her breasts, a hipbone, the arch of her ribs, and contrasting darkness filled the hollows between. "I love you so much."

"I could get used to hearing you say that." She wriggled sleepily against him.

"I've waited for you so long. My whole life."

"I want to be your life." Her voice was soft.

"You are." An overwhelming tenderness filled him. A few hours before, she had taken his love and given back her own with a mixture of wildness and gentle adoration that had left him panting and slaked. Apart they were lonely statues; together they were whole.

France lay still for several minutes, then began to sit up. "I'm going to have to prowl. Come look at the city with me."

His hand on her shoulder stilled her movement. "Stay here," he whispered. "It must be after two. Let's get some sleep."

"I already slept." She kissed the corner of his mouth and felt it twitch. "Now I'm a little bit hungry. Let's fix a snack—a moonlight munchie. Do you mind?"

Stephen groaned and turned on his stomach. "You can't be hungry," he mumbled into the pillow. "How can you think of food at a time like this?"

"I'm a woman of few appetites. Two major ones, to be exact. Stephen Foley and food. At the moment it's food that preoccupies me. But don't worry. You can snore while I make a disaster out of your kitchen."

He plucked at a corner of sheet. "Do your worst. Just hurry back to me. I miss you already."

France kissed the back of his neck and left the room quietly. In the living room she put on Stephen's denim shirt and piled the rest of their discarded clothing on the couch.

The rosé wine intended for dinner was still cooling in the refrigerator. She set it on a tray with two glasses and found a wedge of cheddar cheese and a box of crackers.

One shoulder was braced against the bedroom door when she noticed the side of a piano behind a folding Oriental screen to the left of the dining area.

Sliding the tray onto the coffee table, France went to push the screen aside. Deep scratches marred the walnut surface of the nondescript upright instrument, but its uncovered keys had obviously been replaced and she made a light, experimental run. The tone was good. Stephen must keep it tuned. She recalled the time in her condo when she'd heard him play so beautifully. Instinctively she knew this must have been the piano he learned on. A picture of a gangly, curly-headed boy, his knobby fingers banging out scales, made her grin.

Without thinking, she sat and started to play a blues version of "Amazing Grace." Automatically she hummed, filling in the spaces when her fingers failed to connect the right notes, then backing up and starting again. Some lines she knew and sang haltingly, slowing the music to the pace of her voice.

A door creaked and she heard a loud exaggerated yawn. Footfalls shuffled across the rug. France grinned but didn't turn around. Instead, she pounded out several showy chords.

Stephen came to stand beside her. "Move over," he ordered in a gravelly voice. He edged her along the bench until he could sit down. "Some people will stop at nothing to get attention. I thought you said you were hungry." He wore a rust terry-cloth robe tied loosely at the waist, and his hair lay in a dozen different directions.

"I was," France said. "Still am. Sorry I woke you. Play while I pour us some wine." She went to fill the glasses and put them on top of the piano before sitting beside Stephen again.

He lifted his wine and waited until she did the same. "To the rest of our lives. Will that do?"

"Oh, Stephen." She sniffed as she watched him drink, then took a small sip of the rosé.

"Tears mean you're happy. Will you always let me know when you're sad, too?"

She nodded and swallowed around the lump in her throat.

With his left hand he picked out a popular song until France joined him. Together they produced a discordant rendition to accompany Stephen's rumbling baritone and France's off-key alto.

Stephen chuckled and his mirth increased when she turned an offended glare on him. "Maybe we should go back to bed," he suggested. "You've probably strained your vocal cords. Rest will fix them up."

France's expression became arch. She ignored him and rubbed a scratch in the piano's finish. "Did your parents buy you this?"

"No." Stephen straddled the bench. "I went into a group foster home when I was fifteen. This belonged to the housemother, and she gave it to me when I left. No one else ever played the thing, and she said she was glad to get rid of it. I think she just wanted to give me something but was afraid I'd refuse. She was some lady."

He'd decided to let her into more of his life. France laced her fingers through his. "What happened to your mother and father? Was Grant in the same home?"

Stephen's grip ground the bones in their hands together. "My father was scum. Disappointed, vitriolic. He married my mother because she was pregnant with me and then he never forgave either of us. We ruined his life—he said that over and over again. Then he'd hit my mother. She never stood up to him and she wouldn't hear a bad word said about the man. The day I left, I'd tried to stop him beating up on her. He kicked me out. Grant stayed. He was younger, and in some ways he may have suffered more, because it got worse after I left. God!''

A surge of energy seemed to shoot through him and he stood up. He drained the rest of his wine and went to the window.

"Don't say any more now. There's plenty of time," France said. His pain became her own. Indecisiveness stopped her from going to him.

"I kept track of Grant—like the fool I was. I thought we could be friends, that we'd help each other. But he hated me as much as the old man did. 'Bastard.' That's what he called me on the phone when I told him I'd gone syndicated. And I'd expected him to be glad for me. What a laugh!''

"You don't see your parents?"

Stephen's elbows made sharp angles as he locked his hands behind his neck. "Dad was killed about five years ago. Drowned when his car went off a bridge. I think my mother remarried, but we lost touch. She wanted it that way.''

Suppressing the desire to rail against his family, France went to Stephen and hugged him tightly. "It's all in the past now. You're a survivor. We both are.''

"All those months in prison I prayed I wasn't like my father. I was afraid that the violence might be inbred. If I hadn't hit Candace I think I'd have fought harder to prove my innocence, but somehow it was as if that one rotten act had to be paid for anyway.''

"You only did what you had to.''

"There should have been another way to stop someone half my size.''

"With her hanging on your neck, yelling and scratching?'' "It's clear enough when you say it, but it wasn't then, or for a long time afterward.''

The lead ball in her stomach softened. "Sit with me, hold me.'' She pulled him down beside her on the couch.

Stephen rubbed the side of one knuckle up and down France's cheek. "Sometimes I used to wonder if there was someone, somewhere, who'd accept my bad traits as well as the good ones and still love me.''

"You don't have any bad traits.''

"I don't like football.''

"And I can't cook.''

He kissed her nose. "Who cares?''

"You will if I starve our children.'' She held her breath when she realized what she'd said.

Stephen lifted her onto his lap and kissed her neck. He unbuttoned the shirt and stroked a breast gently. "I want to watch you nurse our baby. The thought of holding you both and knowing you're mine seems incredible.''

Happiness threatened to suffocate France. "Whoa! You're getting ahead just a little bit.''

"Can't a man make plans? Wait a minute, I almost forgot. Here.''

A small package wrapped in Christmas paper materialized from the depths of Stephen's pocket, and he thrust it into her hands.

France turned it over several times. "A Christmas present? Sometimes you are a very odd man, Stephen Foley. Is this for last Christmas or the next one?"

"Open it," he growled.

Inside shiny green and red wrappings lay a flat box. France's pulse skittered as she opened it and found a delicate gold chain and pendant on a bed of white velvet. The circular pendant was formed of delicate hearts, each with a tiny emerald in its center.

"These are the hearts around my little cartoon man's head, aren't they?" She held the necklace in the palm of her hand. "Where did you find it? You must have searched everywhere."

He took it from her and opened the clasp. "I had it made." Deftly the chain was slipped around her neck. "After I was released from Minimum Security I went straight to a jeweler. I intended to come to you. You have to believe that. But it took more guts than I had to face the possibility of your rejection. And I was certain you'd detest me when you found out what I'd been convicted of."

France pushed her fingers beneath the gaping bathrobe to tangle in the hair on Stephen's chest. The circle of hearts was cool on the skin between her breasts. She met his eyes and told him wordlessly how much she loved him.

"I chose the emeralds because they reminded me of your eyes. What—?" He frowned. The doorbell had given its subtle chime. "Say that isn't what I think it is."

"What's the time?" France asked, stiffening. "Maybe there's an emergency."

"And maybe there's something wrong with our timing. This happened once before and I got your brother's fist in my belly." He stood up, taking her with him. "Paul's a good man. If he's your brother, he has to be. And I know we'll become friends. But not if he turns up in the early hours of the morning very often. Go in the bedroom."

France didn't argue. She hurried across the living room, pausing long enough to grab the pile of clothing from the couch before she entered the bedroom and shut the door.

"Sir" was the first word that carried clearly enough for her to hear. France stood still and listened. The front door closed and heavy footsteps clacked on the entry tile before whoever had arrived moved onto the rug.

Goose bumps rose on her skin. Something was wrong. Not understanding why she sensed danger, France pulled on her panties and went into the bathroom for the rest of her clothes. The silk dress was rumpled but dry. She dressed quickly and pushed her feet into shoes that were still wet.

Cautiously she opened the door only wide enough to allow her to step sideways into the living room. She froze.

"Mr. Foley. We aren't charging you with anything. I already told you that. But it would be helpful to us, and easier on you, if you agreed to come down to the station and answer a few questions."

Two raincoated men stood with their backs to her, addressing Stephen, who also faced the other way. His shoulders were hunched.

The man who had been speaking tried again. "Make it easier on all of us. There's probably a good explanation and you'll be back here in a couple of hours. We can get a warrant if we need it.''

Stephen still didn't turn around. "What are you charging me with?"

"Nothing," the other, thinner man said. "*Yet*. We just want to talk."

"So do it here."

France's heart raced. "What's the matter?"

At first she thought they hadn't heard her small voice. Then all three men were staring at her. The two, who must have been police officers, assessed her stolidly. Stephen's face was white, his eyes dark with an emotion she recognized as panic.

"Evening, miss." The heavier officer nodded. "I'm Sergeant Turner and this is Officer Cranborne. Didn't realize Mr. Foley had company. How long have you been here?"

She tried to answer him but couldn't form the words. Little lights spun in her mind. "Stephen, what do they want?"

"You'd better go home, France. This has nothing to do with you." He took a step toward her but the policemen blocked his path.

"We'll decide that, Foley," Turner said. "There was some trouble in the building earlier this evening, miss, and we want to take Mr. Foley in for questioning. It might be a good idea if you came along, too."

She wiped the palms of her hands on her skirt. "But we've been together...all evening."

The man smiled tiredly. "Then you won't mind saying that at the station, will you?"

"I don't want her brought into this," Stephen ground out.

France looked from one face to the other, trying to find the clue that would explain what was going on. She took a deep breath and straightened her shoulders. "You go on to the station, officers. Stephen and I will follow as soon as he's dressed." She tried not to blush.

"Thank you, ma'am." Cranborne spoke for the first time. "But we'll wait for Mr. Foley. You take your own car, since you'll be needing it to get home later."

Nausea engulfed her. What did he mean? Wasn't Stephen coming home?

Chapter Fourteen

Papers shuffled and a file cabinet drawer slammed. France clutched the arms of the black vinyl chair and strained to hear what the officers were saying to Stephen. Their forms made cloudy images on the sides of the plastic panels they sat behind.

Terrified, she pressed her knees together, her lips moving in silent prayer. The rest of the office seemed deserted, wrapped in predawn lethargy. She sighed. The pungent combination of stale cigarette smoke and pine-scented cleaner turned her stomach.

The policemen's words droned in a dismal monotone, punctuated by Stephen's succinct replies. The words she could discern—suspect...detain...fingerprints on file—cut through her like icicles.

The men stood up, and so did she. They came around the edge of the partition.

Officer Cranborne held Stephen's arm. When he turned to her, France cringed at the stark fear that glazed his eyes.

"Stephen." She took a step toward him, but he stiffened and shook his head to silence her.

"Sorry, ma'am." Officer Turner blocked her way. "This is as far as we can let you go."

She ignored the big policeman and tried to push around him. "Where are they taking you, Stephen? What's happening?"

He attempted a smile. "Hey, chin up. I'll be okay." He reached for her, but Cranborne nudged him and nodded in the direction of the double doors behind them.

France flinched. Glass panels in the doors were lined with discreet but visible bars. An armed officer in a uniform opened them from the other side. A long, barren corridor stretched beyond.

"Through there, Foley. Don't worry about the lady."

Stephen began to move but twisted his head to toss France a final look. His cheeks seemed sunken, his expression haunted. Blue eyes drilled into hers, as if thirsting for the sight of her. Then the door swung shut, cutting him off.

"No, wait." She tried to follow, but the pressure of the burly older man's fingers on her arm stopped her. She whirled to face him. "This is insane. He didn't do anything."

Turner nodded calmly, as if soothing a disturbed child. "Have a seat in there, ma'am." He gestured toward the now-empty cubicle. "We've got a few questions we'd like to ask you. I'll be with you in a minute. And don't decide to leave."

France tipped her chin defiantly and walked into the tiny office. She sat down in an orange plastic chair facing the cluttered desk. It was where Stephen had just been, and the seat was still warm. She could make out

Turner's rumbly voice as he spoke to someone down the hall.

Stephen stared at the thin patch of fluorescent light at the end of the corridor. *Oh, God.* Each step took him closer to hell. He was about to lose it all—his freedom, his career, the woman he loved. *France, my dear, sweet lady. What have I done to you?*

"Move it, Foley. We haven't got all night."

"Yeah, yeah." Maybe they didn't, but he would have. He'd have plenty of time from now on if these morons had their way. Months, years who could guess? Voices filtered out to him, a telephone shrilled. He knew what waited beneath the white lights. Weren't all receiving jails the same? More cops like the ones who prodded him on now and a computer that could spit out his entire life story. They were going to book him.

"I didn't do anything." Desperation, cold and sharp, surged through him. He jerked his arm out of Cranborne's fingers. "You can't keep me here. I'm a free man."

The other officer immediately closed in behind Stephen and locked his arms back harshly. Cranborne blocked out the light. "Maybe, maybe not. Right now, you'd better cooperate."

Stephen glared first at Cranborne, then over his shoulder at the man who held him. His back was beginning to ache. "Let go of me."

Cranborne eyed him silently, then nodded. "Then don't make any more fancy moves, Foley. The fastest way out of this building is our way—by the rules."

Stephen felt himself being released, then pushed forward. Soon the light bathed him. Like an empty wax figure, he went through the motions that had already been scorched into his memory little more than a year ago: fingerprints, photographs, questions. He sat, then stood, then walked. It was odd, he thought. Tragically hilarious. The policeman labored to record every inch of his physical being while his own identity was slowly, painfully being sucked out of him. It made him want to cry, but instead he laughed.

"This is no joke." Cranborne leaned against the opposite wall and watched as an officer led Stephen into a cell. "Why don't you guys ever learn?"

Stephen's heart pumped. He swiveled to face the two men just in time to see the beige bars slam into place. "I didn't do anything," he repeated. *Save it, you fool. They don't hear the words.*

The men smiled, then walked away.

Stephen slumped onto a bottom bunk in the empty cell and buried his face in his palms. *Not again, not now. Please.* His head felt like a giant wad of cotton, his thoughts seemed almost incoherent. Moisture welled from beneath his eyelids, then mingled with the sweat at his temples. Where was France, he wondered. What must she think of him now? He loved the woman so much. Yearning briefly filled him, then receded into self-derision. *Sure, what must she think of me now? Back in jail. Probably the story of the rest of my life.*

Heavily he let out his breath, and the sound echoed back to him along the silent, concrete corridor. Somewhere another inmate coughed.

"No." Stephen couldn't tell if he'd thought the word or said it aloud. Rape. How could he escape this new accusation? He'd gone for a walk in the rain before France arrived. He'd talked to no one, touched no one. But a woman in his apartment building had been raped last night. And now they thought that he...

I'm innocent. Damn it, I'm innocent. He lifted his head and every muscle seemed to cramp. He'd fight it, he vowed with a vehemence that dried the tears. No way would he be charged with another crime he didn't commit. He had too much to live for now. He had France Marriotte—if they didn't manage to ruin that, too.

The bright overhead lights had begun to burn France's eyes. Turner came to face her; then he pressed into the narrow space behind the desk. He dug out a form from a file, found a pen and prepared to write. "Full name?"

"France Genevieve Marriotte." She spelled it out for him, and her thin voice reflected her nervousness.

"Mrs.?"

"Yes. I've already told you that."

The man nodded. "Yeah, you did." He jotted down the information, then eyed her. "You a friend of Mr. Foley?"

"I am." A chill coursed down her spine, and she tugged the hem of her sweater-coat around her knees. The officer continued to write.

"And you said earlier, at Mr. Foley's home, that you and he were together last night?"

"No, tonight...we were together tonight."

Turner examined his watch. "It's 4:00 A.M., ma'am. You must mean last night and this morning."

France felt flustered, and she stammered, "Yes, that's what I mean."

"You and he didn't go anywhere?"

"No, we didn't." France frowned.

"Did he go anywhere without you?"

"No, of course not. We had dinner, watched TV...together."

"All right." The officer raised his head. "I noticed that you have your own vehicle. You drove it to Mr. Foley's last night?"

"I did, but that shouldn't matter...."

"Was he at his home when you arrived"

France hesitated. Her heart pounded unsteadily "No, he wasn't. He came up behind me in the hall."

"And what time was that, ma'am?"

"I'm not sure."

"I see." Turner resumed his note taking.

"But I didn't wait very long." She hurried on. "Only a matter of seconds, really,"

"Did Mr. Foley tell you where he'd been?"

"I didn't ask. He was expecting me for dinner at six, and he wasn't very late." France shifted forward. "Officer, what's going on? Why are you detaining Stephen?"

Turner stuck the pen in his shirt pocket and leaned back in his swivel chair. He crossed his legs. "Mrs. Marriotte, a woman was raped early last night in Foley's apartment building. Your friend matches the description given by the victim."

"Then she's wrong—everyone's wrong." A suffocating blanket of apprehension enveloped France. Her heart skidded and she felt like running away.

He continued. "I don't know how well you know Foley, ma'am, but he's got a prison record. The court found him guilty of trying to rape a woman not too long ago, here in Tulsa. In fact, he's still on parole." The officer tapped the arms of his chair with his fingers. "That, combined with the other evidence, makes him a suspect."

Another policeman, young and eager-looking, stuck his head around the partition. "Here's the info you wanted, sergeant."

"Thanks, Drake." Turner stood up, then dropped back into his chair with a computer printout. He gave it a cursory glance, then raised his brows and looked at her. "You manage a landscape nursery that participates in the work-release program, Mrs. Marriotte?"

They'd obviously run a check on her. She nodded. "Yes. That's how I got to know Stephen...Mr. Foley. He did a good job."

"Mmm. Yes, I can see that you gave him a satisfactory reference."

"Sergeant Turner, I know Stephen—Mr. Foley—quite well. He couldn't have done what you say he has."

The big man sighed wearily. "Ma'am. We haven't said he's done anything. Foley's a suspect, that's all. Look. Go home and get some rest. Visiting hours start at ten 10:00 A.M. Okay? You can come see him then if you want."

France nodded numbly. Her mind went blank, and for a second, she didn't realize that she had been dismissed. "Where can I find a telephone?" She needed to talk to Paul. He would know what to do.

"There's one in the lobby—pay variety. Go down that corridor." Turner gestured to the right.

France rose and started to turn.

"Ma'am?" Turner had lifted a coffee mug to his mouth. He inspected her calmly over its rim. "I'm sorry, real sorry about all this."

The adrenaline that had been pumping along her veins seemed, suddenly, too thin. Fatigue tingled through her as she looked at the officer and realized that he had meant what he'd said. Somehow his feelings didn't cheer her. She managed a grim smile before she headed toward the lobby.

France wrapped her arms around herself as she walked, as if trying to pull together the giant tear in her heart. The man she loved, her very essence, had been ripped from her and locked away. She visualized him, tormented and alone, probably wondering what the dawn would bring. Fear of the unknown wound inside her.

She rounded the corner to the lobby and found the phone in the dim shadow of a column. To her right, a brightly lit area, bustling with activity, drew her attention. Several huge maps of Tulsa covered the walls, and lighted buttons on a bank of telephones blinked for attention. This was the nerve center of the police station. She tried not to notice, but several policemen looked up when she passed.

The change jingled into the telephone's slot. France's hand shook and she sank into the dark shadow of the column, out of sight of the information center. She gripped the receiver tightly so she wouldn't drop it. The telephone rang once, twice...five times.

"Paul?"

"Huh? Who is it?" His voice was scratchy with sleep.

"It's me. France. Sorry I woke you up."

"France?" Her brother was suddenly alert. "Are you okay? It's the middle of the night. Where are you?"

"I'm at the police station—but I'm all right." She pressed her head against the concrete wall, realizing that she could barely talk.

"The police station?" Paul's vice crackled along the line. "What's happened? Have you been hurt?"

"No. It's Stephen...."

"Foley? I knew it! What's that creep done to you now? Why I could just—"

France felt unable to cope with his anger. She interrupted him. "Can you come down? I'll wait for you in the lobby. The pickup's here, but I'm so upset I don't think I can drive it home." Her voice wavered, then broke into a sob. "Stephen's been arrested, Paul. Please." She choked. "Please come and get me."

"Stay there. I'm on my way."

The line clicked to silence, and France sniffled as she hung up the receiver. She rubbed at her nose and glanced around, desperate for a place to sit down. Several rows of chairs sat back to back in the center of the open lobby. Every person in the information centre would see her there.

She moved to the plate-glass doors, exhaustion weighing her limbs. A solitary vapor light bathed the street in a shower of silver. Her pickup might be a refuge. It was parked in the lot, but it was cold outside, and her coat was still damp with rain. And it would be at least thirty minutes before Paul arrived. Grimly, she concluded that she had no choice but to collapse into a seat in the lobby and wait.

She must have dozed off. A hand on her shoulder startled her, and she straightened.

"France, you fell asleep." Paul eased into the adjoining chair. "Are you okay?"

Gratefully, she leaned against him and pressed her head into his smooth ski jacket. Her eyes felt gritty. "I'll be all right now. You're here."

She'd expected him to put his arm around her, to comfort her the way he always did. But he didn't move, and she raised her head. "Paul?" She saw his jaw clench.

His eyes flashed at her in the subdued light. When he spoke, he formed his words slowly. "What's Foley done?"

The tone of Paul's voice alarmed her. "He hasn't done anything. It's all so awful...."

Her brother emitted a hard laugh. "Sure. You don't get thrown in the slammer for doing nothing. Tell me the truth, France. And don't bother to defend him."

France could sense her brother's simmering anger, and her pulse raced. She *had* to make him understand.

"A woman was raped last night in Stephen's building. The description matched his. But he's innocent. They think that because he was convicted for trying to do it once, that he..." She couldn't finish. "It's all so crazy, like a nightmare."

Paul didn't look at her but focused on a point in space beyond her head. "Rape. Again. Why that filthy son-of-a..."

"Don't judge him, Paul, please," she cried.

He looked down and gripped her arm. "Then answer this, France. Were you with him all night? Can you vouch for his whereabouts every second of the last twenty-four hours?"

Shock silenced her and he shook her. "Can you? I want to know."

She tried to swallow, but the muscles in her throat refused to work. "No," she whispered feebly. Every part of her quivered. She wanted strength and support from Paul—not interrogation.

"I thought not. Did the police question you, too?"

Her head ached with anxiety. She nodded, afraid of his reaction.

"Asinine. This whole mess is absolute madness." He gave her arm another hard squeeze. "France, for Pete's sake, open your eyes. Haven't I had Foley's number from the beginning? Hell, didn't I drag my feet at the newspaper when they wanted to hire him back?"

France tried to pull away from him but couldn't. "Stephen isn't a rapist, Paul. He's loving and tender. He was innocent before, just as he is now. Please try to understand him."

Nerves twitched beside his mouth. He let go of her arm and bent to lean his elbows on his thighs. "I *can't* understand him. I refuse to try. That man will always be a criminal. The tendency's in his blood." He twisted to face her. "What, in God's name, is the matter with you? The incredible part is that you've stuck by him every inch of the way." The muscles in his face relaxed slightly. "Look where this misplaced loyalty's landed both of you. Foley's back behind bars and you're sitting in the police station in the infernal wee hours of the morning."

"I need him, Paul." France's expression welled with silent entreaty. "And I don't regret it. I never will."

Paul hunched his shoulders in resignation. "Joanna and I were afraid of this. I suppose the next thing you're going to say is that you love him and that you're going to get married, too. Is that what you want—to spend the rest of your life with a sex maniac?''

Anger flashed through her. She'd had enough. She stood up and fumbled in her pocket for her keys. "This is getting us nowhere, Paul. I'm going home.''

Paul leapt to his feet. "France, you've been through a lot tonight. You shouldn't be alone." He hesitated and his arms dropped loosely to his sides. "Look, we're both tired and upset. Neither of us is talking rationally. You need family right now. Come back to our place and get some sleep. There's nothing more you can do for Foley at the moment, anyway.''

Sleep. France thought of Stephen, undoubtedly awake in a cell somewhere in the bowels of this concrete building. Her body trembled, and she felt the burning rise of fresh tears. Paul touched her arm gently.

"Hey. I bet Joanna's already put fresh linen on the bed in the spare room.''

"But my clothes..." She forced back the tears, knowing her protest sounded weak.

"No problem. Get the truck and I'll follow you back to your place. Then I'll wait while you throw a few things together. We'll try to sort all this out later, when we're rested. Nothing makes much sense at this hour of the day.''

France wanted to argue but didn't have the strength. When Paul wrapped his arm protectively around her shoulders, she clutched his waist and decided to go along with his plan.

A FEW HOURS LATER, pale sunlight streamed through dainty flowered curtains, hitting France square in the face. She rubbed her scratchy eyes and, for several seconds, didn't know where she was. She pushed herself up by the elbows and blinked. Everything about the tiny bedroom seemed alien—the oak bureau, the light fixture, two small ink etchings on one wall.

Suddenly she remembered. She'd spent the night, or what little had been left of it, at Paul and Joanna's. And just as quickly, she recalled why she was there. Stephen. The jail. Her fingers kneaded the bedclothes. Familiar waves of apprehension and helplessness shot through her, but she felt rested and alert. Thank God for that.

The irresistible aroma of fresh coffee wafted up the stairs. France tossed away the quilt and grabbed her wristwatch from the nightstand. Nine o'clock. Joanna must be in the kitchen.

Mustering the courage she felt she needed to face her sister-in-law, she pulled on her robe and headed downstairs.

"'Morning, Joanna." She scuffed into the kitchen, knowing her pleasantness sounded false.

The other woman turned from the stove, her face screwed into a concerned frown. "How'd you sleep?"

An eating area filled one corner of the kitchen, and France slid into a chair and shrugged. "Okay, I guess, considering…"

"Sorry. You had quite a night. Here, have some coffee." Joanna placed a mug on the table in front of France and sat down opposite her.

France fidgeted with the cup's handle, not wanting to look at Joanna. "You sound like a mother."

"Maybe you need one—or at least someone you can talk to." Joanna's voice lowered. "You know what I mean—woman to woman."

France sipped her coffee and eyed Joanna over the mug's rim. She wondered how much Paul had told her.

As if reading her mind, Joanna continued. "Paul's still sleeping. He doesn't go to work until three this afternoon." She ran a fingernail along the edge of the wooden tabletop. "He told me what happened last night. I feel so bad—for both Stephen and you."

France saw the empathy in her sister-in-law's eyes and wanted to cry. "Thank you."

Joanna stared at the wall behind France. Neither woman spoke, and the room became so quiet that France could hear the coffee maker drip.

Finally Joanna broke the silence. "Do you love him?"

France studied her carefully before deciding to tell her the truth. "Yes, and he loves me."

"What a mess."

"I know, Joanna, I know." France leaned an elbow on the table and rubbed her fingers across her brow.

"Call Rachel."

"Huh?" She raised her head.

"Tell her to open the shop without you. Better still, I'll call her. You've got enough on your mind. If she needs any help I can always pitch in."

Disjointed thoughts rattled through France's brain. "I don't understand. I realize how disheveled I must look, but I'm fully capable of working at the nursery."

"Not this morning. You're going in to see Stephen. You'd planned on it, hadn't you?" Joanna's brows lifted.

France nodded.

"Good. Is there a special time when he can have visitors?"

France picked through her memory. Hadn't Officer Turner said something about ten o'clock? Yes. She looked at the clock on the stove. If she hurried, she could still make it.

Chapter Fifteen

"Wait here please, Ms. Marriotte."

France jumped when the jail attendant closed the door behind her. The smell of disinfectant made her eyes smart. A row of chairs faced a mesh panel at the far end of the room.

She plucked at the sleeve of her coat and paced slowly toward windows that were too high for her to see out. Her sneakers squeaked on worn linoleum. They'd made her leave her purse at the front desk, and her hands felt too large, yet strangely light.

Joanna had been right to suggest this visit. France's insides twisted. She should have insisted on staying here in the first place instead of listening to Paul. Stephen had no one but her, and she'd left him alone. She beat back the sliver of common sense that reminded her she couldn't have been with him last night anyway—that he would have had no way of knowing where she was after he'd been taken away.

The sound of another door opening brought her attention back to her surroundings. A burly policeman ushered Stephen to the other side of the wire divider, then stood by the pea-green wall with his arms crossed, staring straight ahead.

France was almost surprised to see that Stephen wore the same clothes he'd had on the night before. Driving to the police station, she'd invented images of him in prison garb, perhaps even handcuffed. The haggard man who faced her now looked as if he'd slept in his jeans and sweater. But he was clean-shaven and his hair had obviously been combed before he'd started raking at it with his fingers.

She opened her mouth but found she couldn't form any words.

Stephen sat down and covered his face with both hands. "What did they tell you?" he asked indistinctly. "I'm sorry you had to go through this. It's all so ugly."

In a rush, France crossed to sit opposite him. "Stephen. Look at me. This is a great big, ghastly mistake. They brought you in because...we both know why. And it's not fair, but you can't go to pieces." She stopped when Stephen lifted his head. The exhaustion imprinted in his features, the flat sheen in his eyes, terrified her.

"Explain why I'm here. I want to hear you say the words."

He was asking her to tell him he'd been right when he said they had no future, that his conviction would always follow him and eventually taint her, too. Saliva clicked in her throat, and France jabbed wordlessly at the air with the side of her hand. Why couldn't she get enough oxygen?

"I love you, France. But it's no good. For a while last night I thought I might be able to fight this thing and win, but now I'm not so sure. You can't pretend this hasn't happened or that even if they let me go it won't happen again. Say it. 'Stephen, you were convicted of attempted rape and now they say you raped another woman. You're on parole for one crime, and any time a similar atrocity is perpetrated on a helpless female within a hundred miles, the police are going to drag you from your home and throw you in jail.'' His eyes filled with tears. "Say what you came to say—good-bye. Then I'll tell you I'm sorry and that I would have done anything, including giving my life, to save you from this disgusting exhibition."

Her hand came to rest on the wire. "Do you think I'm going to let you give up? I love you. You love me. We're going to fight this together. Help me do something. Give me a hint where to start."

Stephen pressed his palm and fingertips against hers and closed his eyes. Slowly he shook his head. "I didn't do it."

"I know that."

"But they locked me up before. And I was innocent then. They're going to do it again, and I don't think I can take it. This time there'll be no early parole. Who knows how long it'll be? I'll die in there, France—I know I will."

France curled her fingers until her nails drove beneath his. "You have to remember where you were before we met in the hall. Tell me who you saw, if you spoke to anyone...."

The guard scraped his feet. He took out a bunch of keys attached to his belt by a length of chain and looked at a wall clock. They didn't have long.

"You'll probably be out before tomorrow. But if things move slowly I'll come back. They can only hold you forty-eight hours without making a charge." France hurried on, trying not to see the hopelessness in Stephen's eyes.

"That'll have to be it, folks. Sorry," the officer said.

The man didn't look sorry, France thought. Then she realized his face was expressionless, and her lower lip quivered. "You said you loved me, Stephen. You gave me this." She pulled the pendant of hearts from the neck of her blouse. "Do you remember putting this on me?"

"I'll never forget."

The guard stood behind Stephen. "Let's go, Foley."

France felt the blood drain from her face. "Then say you love me now. Tell me we'll get out of this somehow. I need you."

His chair slid smoothly backward as he stood up and stared down at her. "I love you, darlin'. But please stop needing me. You're the only alibi I have for last night. Why the hell didn't I stay home?"

"Don't worry. We'll figure..." The words trailed into silence as the door closed hollowly on the two men.

GEORGE RICHARDS SHUFFLED LANDSCAPE plans on the oak table he used for work. A thin wintry sun made patterns on polished floorboards and across bookshelves on one wall. The room had been a den while the Richards children lived at home, and it was still France's favorite place to spend a quiet hour.

"Dad," France said softly, "tell me what to do. Paul's convinced I'm in love with a sexual pervert and won't even talk about the subject. Joanna's trying to be understanding, but she's bound to side with Paul."

Gnarled hands smoothed a roll of paper flat. "Your brother cares about you. Maybe too much. So does Joanna. What are we all supposed to believe? I want to see justice done, and if this man's guilty he's where he belongs."

"He isn't," France shouted, leaping from a worn leather couch to march back and forth in front of the table.

"Then he'll be set free."

She faced her father and stopped his fidgeting hands with her own. "Do you really believe that? If you do, and you can convince me, then I'll go to work and wait for Stephen to show up. Should I do that? What if I stay there till he does? Will I die at that nursery?"

Her father eased himself carefully back into his swivel chair, pulling his hands from his daughter's. "Have you been...did you sleep with Stephen Foley?"

France straightened so abruptly a pain shot up the muscles in her neck. "I'm not a child. How can you ask me something like that?"

"Because I think that if you have, it would give you the best perspective on what kind of man he is—sexually. France, this isn't easy. I'm from a different generation. We didn't talk openly about such personal things. But I'm trying to be logical.

"Paul called just before you arrived, and I told him you'd phoned from the prison to say you were coming. He'll be here soon, and if I'm going to have to mediate a war between my two favorite people, I'd like to be better informed. You've both been trying to spare my feelings, but it's too late for that now. And it's too late to spare yours, either, young lady."

The floor beneath her feet seemed insubstantial. France looked down at the faded rose tones of a worn Aubusson rug and felt them rise to meet her. "Just what I need, Dad. Another run-in with Paul." She sat on the couch again and curled her feet beneath her without remembering to take off her shoes.

"You came to me for help." George Richards sounded weary. "I want to give it to you, but you won't even be honest with me. If you can give me some idea what you expect, I'll do what I can. France, this is a mess. You know the statistics. Rape's an emotional issue for more than the victim. You may find yourself in the middle of a trial and in a very unsympathetic position. How many times have you read that women don't always seem to get treated fairly in these cases? If this goes to court, Foley may not be the only one who won't be welcome in Tulsa. You could end up wanting to live elsewhere out of self-preservation."

France wished she could cry; it would have been a relief. But all her tears seemed to have dried up. "Stephen and I are lovers." The words sounded disembodied, but she gained strength from them. "We want to be married and have children. We were talking about our future when the police barged in last night. Dad, he's gentle. He has a wonderful sense of humor and a tenderness that I've felt in so few men. This is killing him. He wants me to bow out of the picture because he's afraid of hurting me. Paul doesn't understand. He won't listen to me. And I don't want to be alienated from anyone I love. Oh, Dad."

"Sweetheart, sweetheart." Her father moved surprisingly quickly from his chair to the couch and gathered her in his arms. "You are so much like your mother. She made her decisions with her heart—and she was almost always right. Believe, for once. Try expecting the best of people and maybe you'll find it. I think I hear Paul's car. He's like you and your mother, too. Tell him what you told me. In the end, we'll probably have to stop him trying to take on the entire judicial system."

They sat in silence until Paul walked through the house, calling his father as he passed each room on the way to the den. He peered around the half-open door and frowned slightly.

"Has something happened? What's the matter with you two?"

France straightened but stayed in the circle of her father's arm. "I just came from seeing Stephen. Dad and I were talking about it."

"You went down there to see that—"

"Paul," their father interrupted quietly.

France started to rise but George's gentle pressure held her still. "Okay, Paul. I'm going through this just once, because Dad wants me to. Then what you decide is up to you. Only don't make another negative comment to me about Stephen, ever."

Paul hesitated as if he were going to argue, then closed his mouth tightly and sat on the edge of the worktable. "Shoot." He crossed his arms.

His mind's made up—he doesn't want to hear what I have to say. France stood and walked to the window. She explained about Grant Foley's stormy relationship with his brother and Stephen's terrible night with Candace. A sick hammering pulsed at her throat. How many times did she have to relive the horror? "Stephen was innocent then and he is now. We love each other, and when this nightmare's over we'll be married. I'd like my husband and my family to be friends. If they aren't, it won't be Stephen's fault. And I'm sure you'll understand where my first loyalty will have to lie."

Paul's hand, massaging the tight cords in the back of her neck, made France flinch, then relax. "France, I'm sorry—I guess I made up my mind about Stephen from what I was told at work, and I haven't given the guy a chance. Would you tell me one more thing?"

"Ask."

"Why hasn't he made any attempt to reopen the case? Couldn't he have found some hotshot lawyer to break down this Candace at the time? If he's not guilty, why is he so passive?"

"He hated himself for reacting violently to Candace. He even convinced himself he deserved to be locked away. Now he doesn't want to try to clear his name because he thinks Grant and Candace have suffered enough from their daughter's recent injury. She broke her neck in a gymnastics accident and faces months of rehabilitation. And maybe I agree with him. As long as the law leaves Stephen alone and the people who matter to him in the future believe in him, what does it matter?"

"What are you going to do now?" Paul asked, stroking her arm a little. "If you trust the guy—and you obviously do—I'll back you up. But I feel so darn useless. Do you know what happens next? Have they, uh, run any tests, or—good God, this is awful."

"Hey, you two." George Richards stirred on the couch, and they faced him. "I have an idea. Not very innovative, but it'll do for now. Let's make a pact to support each other through the next day or two, or however long it takes the police to perform their routine investigation. We may have nothing to worry about. If we do, then we'll regroup. How's that?"

France smiled hesitantly at Paul and received a lopsided grin in return. His eyes were still troubled, but she could see he'd made a decision to try to be open, and she hugged him.

Brother and sister left the house side by side, turning simultaneously to wave to their father, who stood propped in the doorway. Paul backed his station wagon out first while France watched. She climbed into the pickup and headed for the nursery.

Toby disrupted the afternoon by managing to tear a pad on the bottom of one paw, requiring France to take him to the vet for stitches. By the time she'd returned him to his bed in the office, where he'd promptly fallen asleep, it was time to close up and go home. She considered taking the dog to the condo with her, but he seemed so comfortable she decided against it.

During the evening, two offers for rug shampoo, at prices "never to be repeated" brought her rushing expectantly to the phone, only to leave her more depressed than before. A third call, this time from her father, gave a smidgen of the human support she needed, and Paul's call from the newsroom made her feel that some of their old rapport had returned. But she heard nothing from the man who filled every crevice of her consciousness.

Soft, misty drizzle blurred the edges of the world when France awoke the next morning. Rachel already knew France intended to keep an appointment before going in to work. The girl would carry on, with the help of their latest recruit from the prison, until France could get there. Rachel was proving more and more competent and seemed to thrive on extra responsibility.

France bathed in water scented with essence of the perfume Stephen had always said he liked. She dressed in a cinnamon-and-ivory-striped shantung blouse, tucked into a softly swirling fine wool skirt of a dark beige tone. A twisted cord belt, the same color as the cinnamon in her blouse, drew attention to her small waist and the flare of her breasts and hips. It had never seemed so important to look good.

Disguising the effects of a restless night on her face took time. The result wasn't entirely successful, but the light in the visiting room was poor and she hoped Stephen wouldn't notice.

At the front desk in the police station, she encountered the same middle-aged officer she'd spoken with the day before. He gave her an appraising look that sent an unpleasant stricture through France's stomach. It was as if he was trying to sum her up and not liking his conclusions. *I'm beginning to imagine things.*

"I'll take your purse, Mrs. Marriotte."

Had he accentuated the "Mrs."? She decided he had and that it meant more inquiries had been made about her background. "Thank you. How is Mr. Foley?" Her voice sounded steadier than it felt.

"Keeping track of prisoners' health isn't part of my duties." He came from behind the desk and his expression softened slightly. "But he'll be able to tell you himself. This way."

The same room where she and Stephen had talked the last time swallowed her into its desolate emptiness. The door banged behind her with its familiar hollow ring, followed by the swell of disinfectant odor that didn't quite cover another, more muted stench. France sat by the wire panel and waited, willing herself not to allow what she felt to show in her eyes.

"Stephen. Good morning!" she said when he entered and sat facing her. "How did you sleep?"

"Fine. You look so lovely." He swallowed as he studied her. "But you seem tired." Gray smudges in the hollows beneath his own eyes had taken on a yellowish tinge.

"I'm okay," she lied.

They watched each other in silence for several minutes. France could hear their breathing and also see the folded hands of the guard at the corner of her vision.

"I..." Stephen began.

France cut through his second of hesitation. "What?"

"Nothing."

"You were going to say something. They won't give us long. Yesterday I asked you to think about anyone you might have spoken to before I saw you on Saturday night. Where were you, anyway?"

A nerve flicked beside his right eye. "Raping som
woman in another apartment."

"Damn it all, Stephen." *He was giving up.* "I tell yo
we don't have long and you get flippant. Where did yo
go? Who did you see?"

He lifted his chin until he stared down at her, his eye
agonized. "The lawyer will take care of everything.
don't want you involved. They didn't make you—yo
didn't have to see a doctor—"

"Oh, no. No." She pushed her forefinger through on
of the bottom holes in the wire and he squeezed it be
tween finger and thumb. "Please humor me, Stephe
Reconstruct the missing space."

The pressure on her finger increased as seconds ticke
by. Then Stephen stirred. "Walking. I told them." H
jerked his head in the direction of the lard-faced guar
"I told the lawyer, too."

She flushed. "It was raining. You weren't very wet."

"See? Even you have doubts."

"No, I don't. But you must have answers ready."

Stephen ran his thumbnail over her cuticle. His smi
was wistful. "Darlin', you're a babe in the woods. Don
you think they've already asked every question you'
likely to think of—and a lot more? The truth is I went fo
a walk—nothing more. I wasn't very wet because I wa
on the same side of the street as Denver Place, and
stayed under the awnings after the rain started. And n
I didn't go into a shop, or buy a newspaper, or give
quarter to a bum. I didn't even say 'hi' to anyone."

"What about the doorman?"

"I let myself in through the back entrance with my ke
Evidently, the poor guy tried to say he thought he'd se
me, but he didn't and he only made things worse. I sa

him. He was out front, holding a taxi door for some lady.
Did you mention my not being very wet to the police?''

France glanced at the guard, then met Stephen's eyes.
He smiled wryly. "Right. Doesn't matter whether you did
or not, does it?"

"I didn't. Did you tell the police about seeing the
doorman by the taxi?"

He tilted his head, drawing his lips back from white
teeth. "Yup. But I guess Graves didn't remember *that*. Or
at least not quite quickly enough. They want me for this,
France—it'll make their lives simpler."

"You're only reacting, not thinking."

She meant to go on, to try some other tack to draw him
out, but he interrupted her thoughts with oddly penetrating determination. "Don't pursue this. Leave everything to my lawyer. He knows what he's doing. Either I'll
get out of here or I won't."

"Stephen."

"No. It's enough. I should have known I was being an
empty-headed optimist when I thought we could tran-
scend the past. The knowledge was there, really, but I
chose to ignore it. Let's break this up before they start
ordering us around." He stood. "Don't come back here,
please. They'll probably move me after today, anyway."

France felt as if all the marrow had been sucked from
her bones. "And I'm supposed to forget you, and us, and
everything we planned? I can't, Stephen. And if I don't
hear from you soon, I'll find out why. You're never going
to get rid of me."

She still swallowed, like a fish trying to cope out of
water, minutes after she'd been left alone in the bare
room.

Leaving the police station and driving to the nursery
was an indistinct blur, colored by bursts of frustration.

Noises of passing vehicles came and went, rattling her
nerves. Each intrusion into her concentration on Stephen infuriated her, and several times she blasted her
horn at bewildered motorists.

When she arrived at George's, Rachel was with a cus-
tomer. France stormed into the office and rummaged for
her old blue mug. She filled it with coffee and cleared a
pile of invoices from a chair. A soft scratching outside the
door stopped her from sitting down.

Toby slithered awkwardly through his dog-flap and
lolloped toward her on three legs, the fourth held protectively beneath him.

"Poor old boy," France grimaced, feeling guilty. "I
forgot all about you. Come and sit by me. We'll help keep
each other miserable." She dropped onto the chair and
took Toby's head in her lap.

"Boss lady!" Rachel came into the office with a swirl,
part wind, part her own effervescence. "Paul called three
times in the last hour, your dad and Joanna once each.
All would appreciate hearing from Your Eminence."

France laughed. "What would I do without you,
Rachel?"

"Go bankrupt in a hurry." Rachel assumed a haughty
lift of the chin. "As it is, between toothless inmate
George—who works like a slave and watches me just as
slavishly—and yours truly, business continues to boom.
France?"

At the sudden marked change in Rachel's bantering
tone, France studied the girl's face, hoping she wasn't
about to hand in her notice. "You deserve a raise. I was
going to give you one anyway, but I've been
preoccupied."

"Don't worry about that," Rachel replied. "You're
very good to me. And I love it here. But I know some-

thing of what's been going on. Joanna let a few bits and pieces slip. It's that hunk, Stephen Foley, isn't it? What happened between you two?"

A bubbly shaking started in France's throat at the same time as her stomach flipped over. "We fell in love." She swallowed too much hot coffee and covered her mouth, not believing what she'd said.

"I gathered that," Rachel's matter-of-fact response would have been funny at any other time.

"That's all. The end for now. You'll get further bulletins when they're available." France suppressed a wave of sickness. She'd almost said "released."

"I looove weddings—"

"Rachel." France interrupted the start of what promised to be a lyrical and, for her, a painful speech. "There are two more customers wandering around. I'll settle Toby down and be out to help. The phone calls can wait awhile."

Mondays were never very busy. During lulls, France spoke to her father, Paul and Joanna. Each carefully avoided probing questions, but long gaps in the conversations said as much as any words could have.

France was the last to leave the nursery. She locked up and hesitated before heading for Maple Ridge. Part of her dreaded being alone with her thoughts. But she couldn't face the kind of awkward sympathy she knew she'd get from her family.

The pickup heater had gone out weeks before, so she kept on the tattered work gloves that she hadn't found time to replace. They were thin as well as torn and her hands felt numb on the steering wheel. The same iciness tingled over her cheeks and around her neck.

On very cold days when Paul and France were children, their mother had occasionally given them hot milk with a little brandy. It had made them feel warm and cared for. France decided she would make some and drink it by the fire when she got home.

The pickup rattled into the driveway. "I'm going to have to fix you or replace you, old friend," France said aloud, patting the dash.

When she opened the front door of the condo, a wave of frigid air greeted her. "This place feels like a refrigerator." She stomped into the hallway and squinted at the thermostat. "Good grief!" It was nearly as cold in the house as it must be outside. She gave the switch a nudge. Nothing happened.

"Don't tell me," she muttered. "Of all the miserable luck." She pushed the switch again with the same result. The furnace refused to kick in. The thing would have to be fixed. It was bad enough that she had to freeze in the pickup, but inside her own home?

France turned on more lights and slammed the door shut. The furnace was inside a closet at the back of the house. She turned off the gas line, found a flashlight, then dug through a kitchen drawer for a screwdriver and pliers. It didn't matter that she'd never really given the contraption more than a cursory glance before now. There couldn't be much to fixing one. Probably a slipped wire or loose screw, she decided.

Leaving her coat on for warmth, she dropped to her knees in front of the furnace. Within seconds, she'd taken off the metal panel on its front. A confusing jumble of parts faced her and she felt her hopes shrivel. She hadn't the slightest idea how to begin.

"Darlin'." A familiar deep voice came from behind her and made every joint stiffen. "How many times do I have to tell you to lock your front door."

Chapter Sixteen

"Stephen." France scrambled to her feet and flung her arms around his neck. "It's you. It's *really* you. I'm not dreaming. You're free."

"Yeah. They decided I wasn't a keeper. Hard to believe, isn't it?" He hesitated, then slowly his arms encircled her and pressed tightly against her ribs. "But you should have locked the front door."

"And kept you out?"

"I would have rung the bell. France, it's not safe unless you do. Anyone could have walked in."

"You're not just anyone. I don't care about doors or bells right now. Only you." France heard him sigh, felt his chin nuzzle into her hair. "Stephen, tell me now...who?" The reality of his presence filled her, and tears of happiness blurred her eyes. She tried vainly to catch her breath, but it escaped in tiny puffs of silvery vapor against his chest.

He noticed. "Good Lord, it's cold in here. And you've got the furnace open. Is something wrong with it?"

"The infernal thing's on the blink. But I think I can fix it. If not, I'll call the repairman in the morning. Don't worry about it. When were you released, Stephen? No, it doesn't matter. Just hold me." The words came out in a

jumble. She snuggled her face more deeply into the folds
of his suede jacket, desperate for his touch and the security of his embrace. Only hours before, she hadn't
known if she would ever enjoy the comfort of his strong
arms again. "You feel so good."

"Do I, France?" His fingers spread wide, then stilled
against her back. "Do I really?"

She pushed her hands inside the jacket, savoring the
scratchy texture of his sweater and the firm muscle beneath it. She barely noticed the remoteness tingeing his
question. His solid bulk and the warmth emanating from
his body soothed her and temporarily dulled her awareness. "I've been so afraid, but you're all right now. I can
see that. Everything's all right. We're together and that's
all that matters."

She lifted her head and planted tiny kisses along the
rough skin of his neck, feeling almost giddy with happiness. "I've missed you so much—prayed for this
moment."

"France, don't."

The hard cords in his neck flexed under the light pressure of her lips, alerting her. "Don't?" She stopped, and
her mouth dried. "What's wrong now? They let you go,
didn't they? We won't ever be parted again." Apprehension made her afraid to look at him, and she pressed her
eyelids so tightly together they hurt.

"Quit it, France," he pleaded. "You'll only make it
tougher on both of us." He covered her hands and gently
pulled them away from his chest. He frowned and pretended to concentrate on her gloves. "These are really
terrible. You need new ones." He gave her fingers a
squeeze before releasing them.

"To hell with my gloves." Her eyes flipped wide open.
She stepped back and stared at him. "What on earth'

the matter with you?'' Her brow furrowed. ''Did I over-
react just now? Is there some code of behavior for a time
like this? I realize I haven't had a lot of experience with
men I love being released from jail, but am I the only one
who's delirious with happiness?''

''Slow down. Of course I'm happy. I'd be crazy if I
weren't. Look at me, France.'' He forced up the corners
of his mouth. ''Don't I look happy?''

''Sure. Like you're about to be shot.''

His face relaxed. ''Can we talk? I can't stay long. I just
wanted to let you know I was okay.''

''Can't stay? Why not?'' Her mind fumbled with what
he'd just said. ''When did you get out of jail?''

''A few hours ago. I took a cab home to get cleaned up,
then decided I'd better see you in person to tell you the
good news.''

''Thanks for thinking of me.'' His attitude so amazed
her she couldn't keep the sarcasm from her voice. She
swiveled to check the driveway beyond the hall window.
''How did you get here? Where's you car?''

''Blasted thing wouldn't start. Guess the battery went
dead while it sat in the parking garage. I had to catch
another cab just now.''

''Your transportation's getting expensive, isn't it? I'm
surprised you think I'm worth it.'' The remote look
coating his eyes angered her and, for a second, she felt
like shaking him. ''Maybe you shouldn't have bothered
to come at all.''

''France, please. I don't mean for you to feel this way.
The last thing I want to do is make you unhappy.''

''Really? Well, you're doing a fantastic job of it anyway. And you're also making me very nervous.'' She
watched him closely and her insides shook. Something
was terribly wrong, and a premonition made her want to

delay whatever was coming. "Look, the stove still works. I'll fix you a hot drink. Milk and brandy, okay?"

"I don't know." He frowned; then his face softened. "Oh, I guess so. But make it a short one. It would be a mistake for me to stay too long."

"No one's asking you to." She entered the kitchen and rummaged in the refrigerator for the carton of milk. What did he mean, a mistake to stay? How could everything have changed between them in less than two days? Her thoughts crowded against each other as she checked the milk carton. Yes, she decided. There was enough for their drinks. If not, she's merely dump in a little more brandy. They'd both need it if Stephen kept up this craziness.

She heard Stephen reposition the panel on the furnace, then his footsteps on the tile behind her.

"France, I'm sorry for all this. God, it seems all I ever do is apologize to you."

Her back was to him, but she felt him, heard the cabinets creak as he must have leaned against them. Her shoulders lifted in a sigh. Silently, she poured the milk into a pan and flicked a burner on low.

"France, don't ignore me." His feet made hollow sounds as he moved across the hard floor. "We need to get all this settled between us, once and for all."

She reeled to face him and wanted to cry. His lean hips pressed into the counter across from her. How handsome he looked, how tired. Her anger faded, only to be replaced by the familiar burn of longing.

Her palms felt damp, and she rubbed them along her thighs. "Get what settled, Stephen? I don't understand."

"You and me—our relationship." He swallowed and studied the ceiling. "I've had a lot of time to think about it the past couple of days, and I've finally come to my senses. It may never work out for us—as much as we want it to." A wet sheen edged his eyes when he looked at her. "Do you understand that?"

France fought to subdue her own tears. "No. And you're beginning to sound like a broken record. All I need is the man I love—the man I want to share the rest of my life with."

"The man you love. How did I look facing you behind bars, talking to you through a cold mesh of wire? What a fine picture that must have made."

"Stop doing this to yourself. Forget what's happened. It's over. You're free and all that...that...it's all behind you."

"Free?" Stephen closed his eyes briefly and flattened his lips across his teeth. When he spoke again his voice cracked. "Oh, hell. I don't deserve you, France. I never really will." He ran a shaky hand over his brow. "How can I make you realize... Sure, I'm loose *now*. But only because the test the cops took didn't match up and because that woman in my building picked another poor sucker from the lineup."

Dismay welled within her. She bit her lip and watched him, wanting but not knowing how to curb his self-torment.

"I'm an ex-con. I always *will* be. Sure, I can marry you. But who knows when we might get interrupted by another doorbell. I may not be behind bars at the moment, but I'll always be a suspect. Always. Free...ha! I'll never be free, and you won't be, either, if you stay with me. How does a man reconcile himself to dragging down someone else—someone he loves?"

Helplessness filled her, and she went to him. If only there could be some way to erase his anxiety, to absorb it herself. She had to make him understand that she didn't care what his past had been—that neither of them would have a future without the other.

"My darling." Their eyes locked and she reached for him, brushing her knuckles gently across his cheekbones. The cold air around her suddenly seemed to fade. "For better or worse...isn't that what they say?" Her hands came to rest on his shoulders. "I'm willing to take the chance."

Without lifting his gaze from hers, he reached for her fingers and pressed them to his mouth. Slowly with infinite tenderness, he kissed each one, then held them against his chest. "I won't allow myself to be selfish. Yes...yes, I want you, but I can't allow myself to have you until I'm sure it's right. It's for your own good. Please try to understand."

"My own good? I don't want to hear that." She shook her head. Why was Stephen being so closed-minded? Hazy visions of another man filtered into her brain—images of someone she'd tried to relegate to her subconscious because he'd hurt her so terribly.

"You have to listen to me," Stephen said.

"No." France tugged her hands from beneath his and moved away, glaring at him. "*You* listen to *me*. My life is beginning to feel like an instant replay, and I won't let it. You sound just like Larry, my former husband." She rubbed at her temples. "Let me think...yes, when he asked for the divorce, he sounded very similar to you. What did he say? 'I want you, but I can't let my own desires influence me. You're a wonderful woman, France, but we need to lead our own separate lives. Don't cry, dear wife. I'm only thinking of you. You'd be so much better off without me. Believe me, it's for your own good.'" She peered up at him. "Does the sentiment sound familiar?"

"France, this is not the same thing at all." Stephen took a step toward her. "Don't—"

"No." Quickly, she bent to a cupboard and found the bottle of brandy. In one swift motion, she twisted off the cap and dashed a healthy measure into the pan on the stove.

"That's not too much liquor, is it? Think of it this way, it'll warm you up."

"I'm leaving." Suddenly Stephen reached behind him to the telephone on the wall.

"Why?" France knew her voice sounded too high. "The drinks are almost ready." Her knuckles had turned white from gripping the counter. Why had she carried on about Larry? None of that mattered now.

"It's something I should have done five minutes ago." He watched her as he punched in the numbers of the cab company and quietly made his request. Then he hung up the receiver.

"It's all so simple for you, isn't it, Stephen?" France said. "You barge into my home, tell me you want to call it quits, then take a taxi and zip out of my life forever." Her eyes stung. "I've got to be the luckiest woman in Tulsa, the way the men in my life come and go."

Stephen turned to a cupboard and brought out two mugs. Silently, he went to the stove, turned it off and poured a cup of steaming liquid for each of them. Finally he spoke. "See how upset you are? All this just proves my point. Your life would run a hell of a lot smoother without me."

"And you've got rocks in your head." She flexed her fingers to ease their stiffness and reached for the drink he offered. "I didn't mean to drag up all that ancient history about Larry. I don't know why I mentioned it."

"I do. You think I'm doing the same thing to you that he did. He hurt you, darlin'. Something I never want to do. I don't know if he loved you, but I do. I thought about you constantly, every waking minute in that stinking jail cell."

France set her untouched mug on the table. "Then why don't you let me love you back—the way I want to? Let me touch your soul, the way you've touched mine." She reached for him and brushed her fingers along his arm. "Please, Stephen. Don't shut me out, not now, when you need me more than ever. I can help you. Let me share your life. Let me."

He watched the movement of her fingers, then lifted his eyes to hers. He opened his mouth, held his bottom lip between his teeth an instant. "I'm not sure, France...."

The chime of the doorbell brought them to attention.

He looked at her for a long second. "That's my cab."

"Send it away." Her gaze burned into his as if trying to dredge from him the answer she longed to hear—that he would stay with her forever. *I can't let you go, my love. I can't.* Then a bold idea flashed through her mind. *Do I dare?*

"I have to leave now." He didn't move.

"Wait, Stephen. I'm going with you."

"What? To my place? It's warm there, but I don't think..."

"Don't worry. Denver Place isn't what I have in mind. But it's obviously too cold for me to stay here tonight, and I don't feel like troubling my family. Let me catch a ride with you to a hotel. The Excelsior's not too far. All I want you to do is drop me off." She held her breath. *Please don't let me ruin this, she prayed silently.*

Before Stephen could answer, the bell rang a second time, followed immediately by a thump on the door.

"Tell the cabbie to wait while I throw a few things together." She couldn't let him leave without her.

He hunched together his shoulders. "Okay, but hurry."

France almost ran to the bedroom and was back in minutes with a small overnight bag. She made straight for the hall and Stephen fell in behind her.

"Give me the keys, France. I'll lock your door myself. Then I'll know it's done."

She scrabbled in her pocket and tossed them to him. "How touching. I'm surprised you even care." Her voice was low.

His jaw jerked. "Cut it. You know I do."

Chapter Seventeen

France slid across the worn cab seat. The car was stuffy inside, but she leaned back gratefully against the upholstery. At least it was warm. Stephen climbed in next to her.

"Where to?" The young driver craned around.

"The Excelsior, then Denver Place." Stephen settled beside France. He glanced at her before he cleared a circle on the steamy window with the side of his fist and stared out.

The taxi backed from the driveway and headed for town, houses and trees sliding rapidly by in an opaque blur. France huddled in the corner of the seat and prayed that her plan would work. Every move now would have to be carefully choreographed. If it wasn't, this could be the last time she would be with Stephen.

Before long, the driver pulled in at a curb and jerked to a halt. "The Excelsior, folks."

The man leaped out and opened France's door. "One more request." She touched Stephen's arm. Come in with me while I make sure there's a vacancy. It won't take more than a second. The driver will stay. Please."

"We should have called from your place to make a reservation."

"Probably, but we didn't. Guess we had too many other things to think about." She handed him her overnight bag. "Here. I just want to be sure there's a room for me before you leave."

He shrugged and unfolded his long legs from the car. "Of course." He hitched the bag over his shoulder and said to the driver, "Wait for me. I won't be long."

"Go on ahead, Stephen," France said. "I think I dropped a glove on the seat." When France was sure he wasn't looking, she handed the man a bill and whispered, "Leave."

The driver looked from France to the money, stuffed it in his coat pocket and grinned. "Thanks, ma'am." He climbed behind the wheel. In a second, he gunned the engine and swerved the car back into traffic.

France smiled and turned to Stephen. *So far, so good.*

He stood under the striped hotel awning. His jaw had dropped. "What the...?" Amazed, he watched the cab disappear. "The guy left.... I hadn't even paid him."

Good, he was too preoccupied to notice. France lifted her shoulders. "Probably had an emergency call. I'm surprised he went without being paid, though. Oh, well, there are plenty more cabs in town." There could be little harm in a so small a deception, she decided—especially since the stakes were so high. Smiling, she tucked her arm through his and half dragged him into the hotel.

France headed immediately toward the check-in desk, but Stephen twisted to catch her waist as soon as they'd cleared the double doors. "Not so fast. Something funny is going on here, and I want to be let in on the joke."

It isn't going to work. "I'm going to get a room for the night, that's all." France tried to pull away, but his long fingers pressed into her ribs. "Or would you rather have me freeze to death at home?"

"Don't be ridiculous." Suspicion glittered in his eyes when he released her.

Stephen stood at the end of the counter while France arranged a reservation, signed the register and picked up her key.

"This is crazy. Why didn't you call Paul or your father? You could get one of them to come over and fetch you." Stephen stiffened his back, causing soft suede fabric to stretch across his broad shoulders.

She stepped away from the counter. "If you'd been listening you might have heard me say I didn't want to bother them. I don't want my father or Paul to rescue me yet again. But I don't feel like being alone right now, either. These past few days have been hard on me, too. I wasn't locked up in the physical sense, but I might as well have been. Picasso's is right over there. We could have a drink...and talk."

"Sounds to me like the plot's thickening."

"Plot? Oh, so what if it is.... Stephen, I need you with me for a little while longer." She didn't care that she was pleading.

"I should have known that you wouldn't let things cool off—even for a little while. France, listen. I know that none of this has been easy for you." Hopelessness crossed his features. "But I want to spare you any more ugliness. Haven't we done enough talking for tonight, darlin'? We'll both be better off if I walk right out of here this second."

"How can you be so sure we'd both be better off?" France bit back what she really wanted to say—that she loved him more than life itself and that the possibility of losing him was slowly sapping away every ounce of her vitality. "Come into the lounge with me. There's music." She threaded both arms beneath Stephen's. "Take me dancing before you go, for old time's sake." She pressed her cheek against his chest and the erratic beat of his heart made her smile.

"This is impossible." He slid his hands down her arms and caught her fingers in his.

Frustrated tears welled beneath her eyelids. "Lord, I'm tired of arguing with you. Go home, then. You haven't had much rest yourself lately. I'll just sit in Picasso's and watch the merriment."

"I'm not leaving you in any club...alone." His thumbs made widening, maddening circles on her palms.

"I can take care of myself. You couldn't wait to get out of here a minute ago."

"That's when I thought you were going to your room to spend the evening quietly."

France's heart speeded as she looked up at him. Every inch of the man was dear and embedded so deep in her soul. She knew her idea had been rash and that it was failing.

"Why don't you let me take you to one of the restaurants here? You haven't eaten. The Parisien serves crepes. After a good meal you might feel differently, and I'd feel better about leaving you alone. You may even decide it's not such a bad idea to contact your family."

"No." She would have her way. The evening had barely begun, and she vowed to give her original plan one last try.

Impatience and frustration crept into his expression at her tart rejoinder. "Okay, I give in. Lead me to Picasso's—or wherever will make you happy. But I'm not going to play games. I couldn't take any right now."

Let me bring this off. The temptation to say she'd like him to take her to her room was unbearable, but France took his cool hand meekly and led him into the dimly lit lounge. A hostess seated them in a plush booth. France slid in first, moving only halfway around, so that Stephen was forced to sit close.

She smiled up at him serenely. "I'll have a double martini with a twist. Straight up and very dry. We'll run a tab."

A hovering waitress took the order and looked questioningly at Stephen, who was still staring, open-mouthed, at France. France nudged him. "What are you going to have?"

"I...the same."

France studiously watched two couples circling a dance floor half the size of her own tiny kitchen. Taped music, soft and romantic, played while the band took a break. "I could stay here forever," she breathed.

"You may have to after you drink a double martini. I didn't know you drank gin. I'm not sure I've ever seen you finish as much as a glass of wine."

She leaned against him and rubbed his arm. "There are times in all our lives when we need to break out of the mold."

His hand covered hers. "I like you the way you are."

But you said we couldn't be together, sweetheart. When she spoke, her tone was softly demure. "This is a hard world. If I'm going to live in it, I'm going to have to get tougher."

"Double martinis don't change a woman's entire personality. Thank God!"

She looked at him for a long time. Stephen Foley did love her. Every word from his lips, including the harsh ones, said so. His eyes, black in the subdued light, stared back at her.

The drinks came and France took a sip, controlling a grimace with difficulty.

Stephen made no attempt to touch his own glass. "We'll dance to this." He sprang from the booth, pulling her with him.

On the tiny dance floor, Stephen wrapped her close. His touch was gentle, slightly trembling, as if he were afraid he might hurt her. She closed her eyes and began to hum unconsciously.

"You always do that." His breath moved her hair as he rested his chin atop her head. "When I first saw you, you were humming."

She nestled closer, letting his muscular thighs guide their slow progress. If she could choose a moment to stay in forever, this might be one to consider.

When she didn't answer, Stephen's hands moved to cup her chin. He kept the gentle rhythm of the dance with his body while his thumbs massaged her cheekbones. Before France realized what happened, he'd danced her into a secluded corner, where they stood, gently swaying.

"My lovely, lovely lady. You truly amaze me."

Even in the shadows, she noticed a slight frown crease his brow. "What do you mean, Stephen?"

"France, I know what you've been trying to do all evening—the cabdriver didn't have an emergency call or a mental aberration, did he? You sent him away, paid the fee. And the room upstairs, Picasso's—they were all part of the plan." He stood motionless, holding France slightly away, while other couples passed them, staring curiously.

"Well…" She fought to ignore the hard pounding in her chest. "My furnace *did* go on the fritz. And I needed a warm place to spend the night. Coming here was only common sense."

"Common sense?" He shook his head. "No, I understand you far better than that. What we have is too strong, too special. You couldn't bear to let it go."

A thin layer of tears misted her vision as she gazed up at him. The hard lines of his face had softened. "We found some happiness, Stephen. Was that so wrong? Is it wrong for me to want it back? Many people spend their entire lives searching for just a taste of what we've already had."

"My smart lady." A faint smile played about his lips. "You've always known what I needed long before I realized it myself."

"And now, my darling?" France knew instinctively that she had to take a chance. She stretched to brush his lips, felt their instant response beneath her own. "What do you need now?"

He looked down at her for a long second, oblivious to the music's lilting rhythm. "As if you didn't know." His voice was a whisper. "I need you, I always will. I can't shove aside my feelings any longer. God, I don't want to. Every fascinating inch of you is precious to me. I need your warmth, your understanding...your love."

"Stephen, I've prayed for this." The music radiated around them, encasing them in its softness. She leaned against the wall, aware of Stephen's hands spanning her waist.

He dropped his face to her neck, lingered with kisses on the soft skin, then explored her ear with his tongue until she clung to him, her legs suddenly weak. "I want you more than I've ever wanted anything. I've been a fool to try and hold out—there's no way I'd have made it. Thank God for one level head between us. You wouldn't know how to give up." His cheek rested on hers. "Can you forgive me for all the pain... ?"

Her arms went around his neck. On tiptoe, she kissed is angular jaw, the groove beside his mouth, the tiny ollow beneath his lower lip. "Oh, Stephen," she said oftly, "I love you. I'll never stop loving you."

He swallowed convulsively. "I want to give you so uch, sweetheart. Make you so happy."

The music changed to a stronger beat, its bass chords ensuously insistent. Stephen smiled, then picked up the ace, enfolding France, faultlessly guiding her back onto ie dance floor. His power and tenderness transmitted gnals that heightened her need.

"I can't stand it any longer, France." His movements owed; his chin nuzzled her temple.

She pulled away dreamily. "Mmm?"

His hands slid to massage her shoulders, the heat of his esh radiating through the thin fabric of France's blouse.

"What you do to me. I want to touch you, really hold ou." He drew in his breath. "I want to get out of here."

"You do?" She grinned.

"Darn it, France. You know what you've been doing me. And if we wait any longer before leaving, the rea- on's going to be obvious to everyone."

She watched his lips move then looked into his eyes. Where are we going?"

"You do have a room reserved upstairs." Even in the imness France saw Stephen's pupils dilate. "How about iaring it with me?" he whispered.

"That's a possibility," She laughed softly and pressed ven closer to his tensing body.

"Witch." He chuckled deeply and stopped dancing. You and your diabolical ruses. I should have known ours ago I wouldn't be able to resist you. Now it's too ite—I'm under your spell. Stand there while I pay for ie drinks."

He took out his wallet and threw some bills on the table before ushering France from the lounge to the elevators. They rode in silence to the tenth floor, carefully avoiding eye contact until a bump announced their arrival.

"Give me the key," Stephen said, glancing at room numbers as they entered the hallway. "Go left. Must be all the way at the end."

The room had a corner exposure.

Stephen pushed open the door and strode through a small sitting room to the bedroom. He returned and dumped France's overnight bag on a white velvet couch. "Some layout. I like it. You're quite a schemer." His blue eyes were first amused, then darkened by desire.

"Only when the cause is worthy." France laid her coat and purse on a chair. Their eyes locked.

Stephen pushed his jacket aside and rested his hands on his hips. "Come here."

She dodged around him and went to the window. "Look at this view. There must be a million lights down there."

He joined her. "Similar exposure to my apartment. Didn't they have anything on the sixteenth floor?"

"I probably should have tried, but..." She stopped, one hand over her mouth, and pressed her forehead against the cool glass. "I don't know what I'd have done if you'd left me tonight."

"I'm not going anywhere, France. Let me hold you." His arms circled her back and he nipped at her ear. "We're together—alone—in a beautiful room. What more could we need?"

"All *I* need is you."

The steady trailing of his fingertips up and down her spine stilled. "We've still got something to get settled," he murmured.

"'Ask and you shall receive.' Isn't that how the saying goes?" France didn't like the threat of hesitation she detected in his voice. She grazed her lips across his cheek.

"All this is wonderful, and I'm having trouble not pulling our clothes off and tossing you into that marvelous bed." He kissed her forehead lightly, then looked briefly at her mouth. "I love you, France. I want you. But there's always an afterward. What about tomorrow? I've got things to straighten out and the going could get tough—for you as well as me."

"I can take it. As long as we're where we should be— with each other. That's all we'll ever need." She laid her cheek on his chest.

"I doubt that it'll be that clear-cut. Nothing worth having ever is." Stephen lifted her as if she weighed nothing and carried her to the bed. He leaned over her while France's heart skittered. So swiftly that he had no time to react, she pushed her fingers into his hair. She parted his lips with her own, driving her tongue past his teeth before his arms surrounded her and she was crushed to his solid chest. Desperately, the pressure of their kiss intensified until Stephen drew back to search France's face.

"Don't you see?" she said. "You and I can't live in this world at the same time in different places. If you moved to Outer Mongolia I'd last about a week before I mailed myself to you. Not that I'd want to be accused of chasing a man."

"Thank God if you did—this one, anyway." Firm lips covered hers again in a brief, hard kiss. "But I want you to realize what you're facing by sticking with me." Stephen straightened resolutely. He stood up and took off his sport coat, then his sweater, before sitting beside her again.

France swung her legs around Stephen until she sat with one thigh pressed to his.

He stopped her as she started to unbutton her blouse. "You were prepared to do all the giving if necessary, weren't you? I continued to throw up roadblocks and wail about injustice, and you just offered me more chances. What did I ever do to deserve you?"

"What else could I do until you came to your senses?" The attempt at humor sounded flat in her own ears.

He brought her hand to his lips and kissed each finger slowly, deliberately. "I wanted you with me from the beginning, France, but I convinced myself you were a sweet dream I could never allow myself to have. This last jail stint seemed to prove it. I was sure all I could bring you was misery."

"I suppose I sensed the way you felt. That's why I went through so much elaborate nonsense to get you here. I couldn't come up with another way to break down your resistance. I thought if I could keep you with me, you'd see again how perfect we are together. But if I'd stayed home tonight, even with the furnace out, we wouldn't have been able to avoid each other—not for long. We'll make it work. There's too much at stake not to."

"I'm going to reopen the case and clear my name," Stephen announced resolutely. I hadn't wanted to before because of Gretchen—but I realize now it's the only way. It'll work. It has to."

"I *know* it will," Frand said with conviction. "You're innocent, Stephen. You always were. And you deserve to have the whole world accept it. Gretchen loves you. One day she'll understand and be glad. Anyone who really cares about you will. This should have been done a long time ago.'' She leaned her face against his chest.

Stephen stroked her forearm. ''France, you've helped me do the impossible.''

''What's that?''

''Made me believe in myself again.''

Emotion caused her jaw to tremble. ''I always had faith in you.''

''Yeah...even when I had very little faith in myself. For years I waited for some sign of my father's violence to show up in me. Then—with Candace—I thought it had. I despised the streak and decided only self-denial and punishment would stamp it out. France, I guess trying to give you up was the ultimate sacrifice. I must have been mad. You've given me hope, shown me what it is to be alive again. The crazy thing is that I've known all this for a long time underneath, but I was afraid to admit it in case it slipped away again.''

''And you've shown me how to love again, Stephen, something I'd given up on in the past few years. I never dreamed there could be so much happiness.''

''I'm only a man. Nothing's perfect. We'll have so much to face, so many pieces to fit together.''

''Doing it side by side will make all the difference.'' She leaned back to study his face, unashamed of the tears running down her cheeks.

''How beautiful you are.'' With his thumbs, he smoothed the moisture. ''There'll be a lot of legal stuff to go through, too. It won't be any fun for you, darlin'.''

''Being without you would be a whole lot worse. In fact, I refuse to put up with that.''

Stephen pushed her back on the bed. ''I love you, sweetheart.'' He undid the top button on her blouse and slid a hand across satiny skin to her shoulder. ''Hey, I just had a fantastic idea.'' His fingers brushed under her bra to surround one full breast.

France shuddered and lifted her chin. "What?"

"Ms. Marriotte?"

"Mr. Foley?"

His thumb worked her nipple to a tense peak. "Would you marry me, please?"

"You already know the answer to that. When?"

He stretched beside her, rolling her against his length. His arms threatened to crush the air from her lungs. For sweet, searing moments only the feel, the scent of each other surrounded them, and the gentle sound of their breathing.

"How about as soon as we can get a license—and a minister? I think I'd like to let God in on this. Someone else is having a hand in pulling us out of disaster and He's the only one I can think of. Will that stiff-necked brother of yours come?"

"He wouldn't stay away. Neither would Joanna or my Dad. We could have the ceremony at Dad's house. He'd like that."

"We may not have a smooth road, France. Some of the fears I've told you about could become very real. Are you sure you want to risk it?"

"Try and stop me. Think 'wedding.' Maybe Toby can be our ring-bearer."

Stephen tickled her ribs. "Whatever makes you happy." He slid a hand beneath her skirt to stroke her thigh. "Do you know when I fell in love with you?"

"Tell me." She pushed him onto his back and kissed the crease between his brows.

"You won't believe it. I was sitting at your piano the day I took your Christmas tree to the condo. That's when it happened. I jumped as if I'd been hit, and you looked

like a scared kid. For a year I'd been nothing but a number. But then you touched me and whispered,
'Stephen...'"

You're invited to accept 4 books and a surprise gift Free!

Acceptance Card

Mail to: **Harlequin Reader Service®**

In the U.S.
2504 West Southern Ave.
Tempe, AZ 85282

In Canada
P.O. Box 2800, Postal Station A
5170 Yonge Street
Willowdale, Ontario M2N 6J3

YES! Please send me 4 free Harlequin American Romance®
novels and my free surprise gift. Then send me 4 brand new novels
as they come off the presses. Bill me at the low price of $2.25 each
—an 11% saving off the retail price. There are no shipping, handling
or other hidden costs. There is no minimum number of books I
must purchase. I can always return a shipment and cancel at any
time. Even if I never buy another book from Harlequin, the 4 free
novels and the surprise gift are mine to keep forever.

154 BPA-BPGE

Name	(PLEASE PRINT)

Address	Apt. No.

City	State/Prov.	Zip/Postal Code

This offer is limited to one order per household and not valid to present
subscribers. Price is subject to change.

ACAR-SUB-1

Readers rave about
Harlequin American Romance!

"...the best series of modern romances
I have read...great, exciting, stupendous,
wonderful."
>   —S.E.*, Coweta, Oklahoma

"...they are absolutely fantastic...going to be
a smash hit and hard to keep on the
bookshelves."
>   —P.D., Easton, Pennsylvania

"The American line is great. I've enjoyed
every one I've read so far."
>   —W.M.K., Lansing, Illinois

"...the best stories I have read in a long
time."
>   —R.H., Northport, New York

*Names available on request.

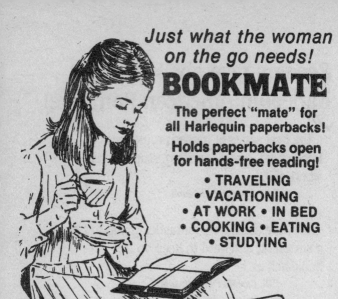